He was racing to kill the woman he loved.

Dec's heart beat heavily with anxiety and fear. He heard the mournful howl from the back of the house. He realized as he rounded the corner of the house that she was no longer the woman he loved.

She had been taken over by evil.

He pulled the vials out of his pocket and drew a cc of tetradotoxin into the syringe. He watched her, standing in the middle of the yard, arms thrown wide in celebration and triumph.

She was a stranger looking back at him with Markie's eyes.

"Hi, honey," he said, smiling as he had always smiled when they met.

Markie felt the darkness inside her try to force her to reach out and hurt…. "Dec…"

He leaped at her, knocking her to the ground. He dropped to his knees beside Markie, beside the love of his life, whispering, "God help me…I'm sorry…." He plunged the needle into her arm and rammed down the plunger.

Markie grew still. Dec felt for her pulse.

It was gone.

Also by RACHEL LEE

WITH MALICE
JULY THUNDER
A JANUARY CHILL
SNOW IN SEPTEMBER
CAUGHT
A FATEFUL CHOICE

*And watch for the newest novel
of romantic suspense from
RACHEL LEE
Coming January 2005*

RACHEL LEE

SOMETHING DEADLY

MIRA

ISBN 0-7783-2004-9

SOMETHING DEADLY

Visit us at www.mirabooks.com

Printed in U.S.A.

SOMETHING
DEADLY

Prologue

Shadow smelled it first. He lay on the living-room floor at his owner's feet, sprawled on his left side with a rawhide chew bone a whisker's length from his nose. He'd worked the knot for a while earlier, massaging his gums, as close as he was likely to get to the satisfaction of gnawing fresh, warm meat from the bones of a kill. Now the comforting scents—the half-chewed bone; the master's feet wrapped in old leather slippers; the rug still rich with the aroma of pipe tobacco, though the master had long since stopped smoking; beef and potatoes and carrots and red wine in the pot on the stove; the barest remnant of the master's wife's perfume, even though she'd gone out the door; the salt air that was ever-present; loam on the master's slippers from the garden; the varied and precious scents of Shadow's world—were displaced by something else.

He drew in the air in quick, rapid sniffs, emptying his lungs when he could hold no more, repeating the process again and again, focusing, letting his agile mind filter out the familiar to pinpoint the new odor. Cold. Earth. Must. Decay. Chill. Death. Evil.

Woof.

One quick noise, as much to chase the horrid scent from his nostrils as to alert the master. But the smell would not leave. The growl grew low in his chest as he rolled onto his haunches, not yet standing, still sampling the air.

Go away!

"What's wrong, buddy?"

The master's voice, so soothing with its deep rumble, barely reached his mind. In a smooth, graceful motion, he rose and trotted to the front window, his nose still foul with the air. Couldn't the master smell it? Probably not. The master and his wife missed so much of the world.

His pupils widened as he approached the glass, beyond which lay the dark world, full of the rising scents of nighttime. But they held no interest. It was there. It was right out there.

Arrf-arr-arr-arr-arr-arrf!

Begone! This is my master's home! You may not enter!

If it heard him, or understood, it paid him no heed. But his friends in the other houses heard, and understood, taking up the cry.

"What, Shadow?" the master said, now at his side.

Shadow looked up at him, then out the window again, growling an angry warning as it approached.

"There's nothing there, boy! Stop that racket."

The master couldn't see it? Of course he couldn't smell it, but couldn't he *see?*

ARR-ARR-ARR-ARR-ARRUFF-ARR-ARR-ARRUFF-ARRUFF!

No! You can't have him! I will die before I let you near him! Begone! Evil! Danger!

Shadow looked up, his teeth bared, as it came through the glass—how could that be?—and leapt up at it, snarling and snapping, clawing at it and finding nothing.

"Calm down, boy!" the master said, though his scent now held the tiniest inkling of fear.

Be afraid, Master! Run!

Shadow grabbed the cuff of his master's pants and pulled.

Run! Please!

The master reached down to push him away. Noooooo! Shadow made one last lunge, then turned to the foul horror that seemed to stab at his nostrils like the quills of a porcupine and let out a savage growl, leaping between it and the master.

But it passed right through and into the master's body, now curling and ripping inside him. The master crumpled to the floor. Shadow pushed at him with his firm nose.

Fight it!

He pawed the master's arm, then his face, carefully, so that only the soft hairs between the pads of his paw touched the skin.

Don't go!

But the awful evil would not be deterred. With a

horrible, joyful cry, it tore something deep inside. Shadow heard the ripping sound and saw the light go from his master's eyes.

Noooooo!

But the master's spirit wouldn't listen. It floated up and off, leaving nothing but the limp husk on the floor. Sated, the evil left, though Shadow was only dimly aware of its leaving.

The master's spirit was gone.

No more morning walks to talk to Shadow's neighbors.

No more of his rough hands behind Shadow's ears, working fur and skin and flesh as joy danced in Shadow's heart.

No more easing his feet into the slippers to settle in for dinner with his wife.

Shadow turned his nose to the heavens and howled at the master's soul.

Please don't leave me!

Please don't leave!

Please don't!

Please!

1

Kato wanted to take a walk. The barking of the neighborhood dogs a while back had seemed to unsettle him. Kato, more wolf than Siberian husky by nature, temperament and appearance, often paced for hours, mimicking the forebears who traveled thirty or forty miles a day through the woods.

Thanks to his husky sire, Kato was smaller than the ordinary wolf, only about eighty pounds. But he had inherited the long legs and huge paws of his wolf mother, as well as coal-black coloring and tawny eyes. There was no mistaking his maternal heritage.

Markie Cross, his owner, kept him only by virtue of the fact that she was a veterinarian and there was no local law against wolf hybrids.

But a half hour ago, the neighborhood dogs had burst into a frenzy of barking. Kato hadn't joined them, but Kato rarely barked. He sat at the sliding glass doors that opened onto the back lanai and stared out into the darkness, listening to the cacophony of yaps and woofs that seemed to come from every direction.

Markie hardly paid it any mind at first. As always, it had begun with a lone dog in the distance and steadily spread, until all the dogs outside their homes were engaged in the chorus.

But as the sound built, she realized she was feeling a shiver of unease. It didn't sound like the usual howl-fest that dogs would start and stop for no reason other than sociability.

Finally she looked up from her book and paid full attention. These were definitely barks of warning.

She glanced at Kato, her closest connection to the canine world, but he was sitting with his back to her, staring out the glass doors. He didn't join the chorus, nor even move as if he were impatient to be out there howling along.

He simply sat, his ears pricked. Staring at something she couldn't see.

Shortly, the dogs fell quiet again. Kato stayed at the window for a while, as if awaiting a reprise, then finally yawned one of those big yawns that said he wasn't quite certain about something.

And then the pacing had begun.

Markie ordinarily ignored his pacing. He did it a lot, and she was inclined to let him and all other animals be themselves.

But tonight his pacing disturbed her. There was something about the way he was doing it, the way he was pausing at each window and sniffing, that wouldn't let her go on reading.

Finally she put her book down and asked, "Walk, Kato?"

With a huge leap and a skitter of claws on the wood floor, he headed for the leash. No mistaking that message.

Smiling, she clipped the leash to his collar, grabbed her keys and stepped out into the balmy tropical night.

The nightly breeze was blowing, a gentle, moist kiss filled with the scents and sounds of the Caribbean Sea that surrounded the island of Santz Martina. It was a tropical paradise, where the wealthy could hide away from the rest of the world in geographic privacy, with all the advantages of being a U.S. territory.

At this end of the island lay Martina Town, home to over half the island's population. All but the very old and the young had jobs. The schools were excellent, the shopping ample. The best *of* everything provided by the best *at* everything.

The houses here in old town, and the businesses, retained the flavor of the old Caribbean, with doors that were open all day, Bahamian storm shutters and courtyards rich with tropical blooms. The narrow streets created breezeways that kept the town surprisingly cool even on hot days. Life was slow. Life was good.

At the north end of the island, on the shoulder of Mount Cortez, the expansive estates of the island's elite looked out over the teal glitter of the sea, rivaling the best the Monterey Coast had to offer.

Tonight, though, Markie and Kato strolled west along Second Avenue. Normally she would have turned left at her office, at the corner of La Puerta, and ambled down to the waterfront park. Tonight, however, Kato was having none of that. He practically dragged her past the businesses and shops and on westward, past rows of houses, narrow alleys and tiny yards occupied by unnaturally quiet dogs.

When she had come here, Markie had realized that she had stepped into a sort of adult Disneyland, where everything was, and was expected to remain, perfect. On the other hand, the people were warm and friendly, the climate wonderful, and the pay too much to refuse. She was on salary, had the most modern equipment known to veterinary medicine and was able to perform everything from surgery to dental cleanings. How could she possibly complain? She didn't even have to charge her patients.

And so far, being beholden to the elite power structure had proved to be no burden whatever.

Kato tugged firmly on his leash, saying in no uncertain terms that they had not yet reached his chosen destination. Markie shrugged and decided to let him lead. It was rare that he ever did such a thing, and she was disinclined to argue with eighty pounds of stubborn wolf. She had no agenda, and she'd long since learned the wisdom of picking her battles when it came to dealing with this particular canine.

They strolled down another block, Kato's head up in the air as if he were scenting something above him. How far up it might be she had no idea. Dogs could smell faint odors in the air three hundred feet above their heads. Kato, with his heritage, might be able to do even better.

But he was definitely following something. A bird, probably. Or a person.

Her thoughts had started to drift again, and then they reached the end of Second Avenue and Kato yanked her left onto Harbor Street. Fifty years ago, before developers had added subdivisions and suburban sprawl, this street had marked the western edge of town. Beyond this point, Caribbean charm gave way to planned perfection.

But not tonight.

An ambulance and a couple of police cars stood out in front of a house, lights swirling. Something bad had happened. She meant to walk right by as quickly as she could, but Kato once again had other plans.

When they reached the edge of the yard, Kato sat. He planted himself firmly, his entire posture saying that he wasn't going another step, no matter what. Markie felt embarrassed. She didn't want to stand here like a ghoul, but even tugging sharply on Kato's collar didn't persuade him to move.

A police officer walked her way. Tom Little, she realized, owner of one of her more frequent patients, a toy poodle with digestive problems. Tom was a Jamaican who spoke with an accent at once British and lilting, and whose skin was the most beautiful shade of coffee. "Hi, Tom," she said.

He nodded. "Hello, Doctor. Is Kato giving you problems?"

"He seems determined to stay right here."

Tom chuckled. "Well, let him. You won't see anything gruesome. He probably smells it, though."

"Smells what?"

Tom jerked a thumb toward the house. "Carter Shippey passed on a little while ago. His wife came home and found him gone. Looks like a heart attack."

"I'm sorry."

"It's sad. Cart wasn't but sixty-three."

Prime age for a heart attack, Markie thought sadly. "Is someone taking care of Mrs. Shippey?"

Tom nodded. "A group of the neighbors carried her away to one of their houses. She won't be alone tonight."

"Good."

She looked down at Kato, but he still wouldn't budge. Every fiber of his being seemed to be pointing toward the house.

"Don't worry about him, Doctor," Tom said, giving Kato a quick scratch behind one ear. Kato flicked the touch away with an impatient twitch of his ear. "He'll go when the body's removed."

"I hope so. I don't want to be stuck here all night."

Just then a car pulled up, a BMW that Markie recognized. Declan Quinn, one of the island's dozen or so full-time physicians. She hadn't had cause to need any of them yet, but she knew them by sight, the way she was getting to know most everyone, little by little.

Dr. Quinn climbed out of his car, dressed in khaki chinos and a blue polo shirt that somehow emphasized his dark Irish good looks: black hair, brilliant blue eyes. But he didn't just walk past the police cordon. He flipped out a badge.

So he was here as the medical examiner. Something inside Markie twisted a little. Somebody didn't think this was an ordinary heart attack.

Declan signed in at the door, another indicator that this was being treated as a crime scene, then disappeared inside.

Maybe, she thought, this was standard procedure. Maybe all sudden deaths were treated this way initially. That would make sense.

She looked down at Kato again and realized his ears were not only at high alert, but they were twitching, twisting this way and that as if scanning the entire area for something. He sniffed at the air again.

Then he did something she'd never before seen him do: he curled back his lips, baring his teeth. Just a little. But even that little was unnerving. She shivered in the steamy, still night air.

Part of her wanted to scoop him up, right then and there, and stagger down the street with him in her arms. Another part of her was afraid to walk off down the darkened streets right now. He sensed a threat of some kind, and Tom Little's presence nearby was comforting. A block away, she and Kato would be on their own.

"Kato."

He looked up at her, his golden eyes dilated so wide they appeared nearly black. And somehow she felt a warning from him.

"Home?" she asked.

Apparently not. He returned his attention to the house, and she wound up standing there like the obedient owner she was. Under other circumstances, she would have found this funny. But not tonight.

Well, she told herself, indulging in a silent lecture in order to avoid thinking about what was really happening, *what did you expect from a mix of the two most independent breeds in the world?* Not a lapdog, certainly. Wolves were wild animals that could be tamed just so far, and Siberian huskies were only one step removed on the genetic chain, bred to think for themselves, sense dangers a musher couldn't see, and protect the sled and their teammates, even to the point of disregarding the musher's commands.

The result: Markie Cross was stuck standing on a street in the middle of the night, like a ghoul waiting to pick over the bones, because her damn dog wouldn't budge.

She tried again. "Kato. Bedtime."

He huffed at her, that unmistakable sound of disgust. *Not yet.*

A gurney appeared in the doorway, bearing its load in a black rubber bag. Instinctively Markie crossed herself and said a quick prayer for Carter Shippey. Kato watched the gurney's journey to the back of the ambulance, his gaze intent and unwavering. Then the ambulance door slammed, and the vehicle pulled away. No lights, no sirens, the silence speaking volumes.

Declan Quinn appeared at the door. He spoke to a couple of officers, his words too quiet to hear.

Then he spied Markie. For some reason, she didn't like the way he walked toward her. It wasn't the way he moved—with a supple, graceful ease—but rather the look on his face. He bore down on her as if...as if she were guilty of something.

Kato, however, chose this moment to assume his best "I'm a cute doggie" pose, lying down with his head between his paws and looking upward soulfully. She almost huffed back at him.

"Dr. Cross," Declan said, extending a hand.

"Yes. And you're Dr. Quinn."

"That's me. Not the medicine woman." His mouth twisted into a roguish smile.

"I never would have made that mistake." Impossibly, she felt herself smile back.

His smile evaporated as quickly as it had appeared. "Is there a reason you're waiting out here? Did you have something you wanted to tell someone?"

This could get embarrassing, she thought. "Uh, no. I'm here because my dog dragged me here and won't let me leave. He's stubborn."

Declan squatted and looked at Kato. "What's his name?"

"Kato."

"Hi, Kato." Declan held his hand out, palm up. Kato lifted his head, sniffing the hand at a distance. His ears flattened back against his head.

"He's part wolf," Markie said. "He doesn't make friends easily."

"I can see that," Declan said. "Should I be worried?"

"No. Putting his ears back is a submissive posture. It means he's wary of your strength."

He looked up. "Well, he has no need to be."

He reached out and brushed his fingertips over Kato's head. The dog accepted the touch, but Markie could see the tension in his haunches.

"Better to let him come to you," she said quietly. "When he's ready."

Declan stood, and Kato rose to his feet, sniffed the air again, and made a low, mournful sound. Markie felt the hair on the back of her neck rise.

Declan seemed to sense something, too, and took a half step back. "Does he do that often?"

"Only when he's trying to tell me something."

Those brilliant blue eyes fixed on her. "What's he trying to tell you?"

"I haven't a clue. Did you hear the dogs barking earlier?"

"Sort of. I wasn't really paying attention."

"It was like every dog on the island was sounding off. After that, he got nervous, so I decided to bring him for a walk."

"And you wound up here?"

"He *dragged* me here. And once we got here, he wouldn't let me leave."

Declan gave her a long look, as if measuring her truthfulness. Apparently satisfied, he squatted again. Kato sat and met the man stare for stare.

"What do you know, boy?" the doctor asked quietly. "Do you know something?"

The question chilled Markie. "It wasn't a heart attack?"

Declan looked up at her. "I won't know for sure until the autopsy." The apparently straightforward statement seemed to Markie to be withholding something. As if there were more, but he wouldn't discuss it.

Once again, he straightened. "Can I give the two of you a ride home?"

"That's up to Kato."

Declan took a step in the direction of his car. "Come on, Kato, time to go home."

To Markie's surprise, the dog followed.

"Make a liar of me," Markie said under her breath. Kato looked up at her and yawned.

Across town, a telephone rang. Tim Roth hit the pause button for the DVD player and picked up the cordless receiver at his elbow. "Yes?"

"Carter Shippey's dead," Steve Chase said.

"And?"

"There are cops all over the place."

"So?"

"If they find the hole…"

"If they find the hole, it'll mean nothing at all. It's under his house." Tim paused, his fingers drumming on the arm of his chair. "How did he die?"

"I'm told they think it's a heart attack."

"Those happen."

"What if it wasn't? What if she's back?"

Tim sighed heavily. "That's myth and local legend. Carter was aging, and not well. He'd been sedentary ever since he sold his fishing boat. Not a good recipe for longevity.''

"What about his wife?''

"Nothing's changed. She thinks we're looking for a leak in the water main.''

"All right. All right.''

"Relax,'' said Tim. "We're not doing anything illegal.''

"I know, but…''

Tim sighed again. "No buts. Send flowers to the widow Shippey, from the Senate. Express your deepest, most heartfelt condolences. Then get back to work.''

He hung up, shaking his head, and returned to his movie. Some people would panic over anything. They had no taste for life.

Or death.

2

At six the next morning, Declan stood outside the hospital morgue and waited for his assistant to show up.

Over the door was a beautifully scripted sign in black on red that said Rue Morgue. Beneath it was another sign, this one carved in natural wood: Abandon Hope All Ye Who Enter Here.

He'd put the signs there eight months ago when he had first arrived on the island. He'd left his job as chief trauma surgeon at a large inner-city hospital to take a surgical post on an island paradise. By dint of his prior experience, he had also been appointed to the post of territorial Medical Examiner. He had one-and-a-half jobs, which, together, were a million times less stressful than his previous position. And nobody had ever complained about the mordant humor of the signs.

Nor should they, he thought. Hell, in addition to his surgical-cum-general practice, he was the only qualified pathologist on the island. The latter job was something he needed to grin and bear.

His assistant, a nurse named Hal Devlin, showed up at last, carrying two takeout coffees.

"Latte for you," Hal said. "Cappuccino for me."

Even in the middle of nowhere, Santz Martina boasted not one but two Starbucks. "Thanks, Hal."

They stepped into the small anteroom together; then Declan unlocked his office. Hal followed him in.

The office was just big enough to hold a desk and bookshelves fully loaded with every imaginable up-to-date reference on pathology, autopsy and homicide investigation. Declan was the only one who ever opened most of them. The unsparing, graphic photographs were worse than Hollywood's most vivid imaginings.

"What's on the agenda today?" Hal wanted to know, flopping into the chair across from Declan's desk.

"Male in his early sixties, sudden death. No obvious signs of foul play."

"Heart attack," Hal said, with the surety of one who has seen it before.

Declan shook his head. "I don't think so."

Both of Hal's dark eyebrows rose, his eyes widening. He was a trim young man in his late twenties, his skin and broad cheekbones kissed golden by his native heritage. "You mean we have a mystery?"

"I'm not sure what we have. When I saw the body last night, it felt squishy everywhere."

Hal shrugged. "Congestive heart failure." In congestive heart failure, the body could retain thirty or forty pounds of excess water.

"Ankles weren't swollen."

Finally Hal frowned, getting the message. "What are you trying to tell me?"

"I don't exactly know, Hal. It *could* be edema, but if it is, it's the worst I've ever heard of. It was more than a spongy feeling."

"Lovely. Who was it?"

"Carter Shippey."

"Oh, Jesus."

Declan nodded. "I gave him a physical a month ago. He was fine."

He put his feet up on the desk and sipped his coffee, pretending that he hadn't been anxious since last night. Coming to the island had been his attempt to unwind, to leave behind the tension that had been nigh on to killing him. Unfortunately, the nightmares hadn't been left behind, and unpleasant events reminded him that his natural tendency was to stay wound up tighter than a drum.

It didn't help that Carter Shippey hadn't looked like any sudden-death heart attack victim he'd ever seen.

Hal was still shaking his head in disbelief.

"Of course," Declan continued, "a fatal arrhythmia could strike without warning. That's why it's called sudden death. But the way Cart looked, the way his body felt when I knelt to examine him last night…"

The dead were always flaccid until rigor began to set in, but Carter Shippey had been more than flaccid.

He'd almost felt like…dough. As if there had been nothing rigid beneath his skin at all. That degree of edema was extraordinary, and congestive heart failure didn't usually come on so rapidly.

"He should have been having other symptoms," Declan said, more to himself than Hal. "Shortness of breath, coughing, swelling of his extremities."

"Yeah." Hal took a deep swig of coffee. "Well, let's go see if we can figure it out. No point waiting."

The hell of being the M.E. on an island this size was that you were apt to know the person who had lived in the body you were cutting open. Declan still had a bit of difficulty with that. On rare occasions it even made him long for the anonymity of the big city E.R.

They suited up in scrubs, Tyvek surgical gowns, rubber gloves and, finally, plastic face shields. Declan pointed to the cooler door, and Hal opened it. Carter Shippey's body, covered by a paper sheet, slid out on its tray.

A chill crept along Declan's spine, and he found himself ardently praying that he was wrong, that he'd missed something at Carter's physical, that the doughy feeling had indeed been edema from congestive heart failure. The thought surprised him, for he would feel awful if he'd missed the diagnosis on an easily treatable condition and cost Carter Shippey his life. But the alternative frightened him more.

He pulled the sheet back and gasped.

Carter's body was still fully clothed, and that was all that made him identifiable as a human being. He looked like an inflatable mannequin that had sprung a leak. Last night he'd been flaccid. This morning he was flat, as if his body were nothing but a puddle within his skin.

"Jesus Christ," Hal said.

"Make that a prayer," Declan said. "For me, too." Even though he didn't believe. He hadn't believed in God for years now.

Their eyes met across the body.

"Don't touch him," Declan said. "Get out of here now, and strip your suit this side of the door."

Hal didn't hesitate to obey. Declan felt an equally powerful urge to get out, but he stood a moment longer, looking down at his friend's remains, astonished that someone he knew could become unrecognizable so fast. With a rubber covered finger, he pressed Carter Shippey's side and felt his finger sink in as if into jelly, meeting no resistance at all.

Then he took his own advice. He left the body on the table. The less it was handled the better. Outerwear and gloves went into the biohazard chute, and he hurried into the office where Hal was awaiting him, trying to steady his cup of coffee in an unsteady hand.

Speaking the words out loud wasn't easy. Even to Declan they sounded a little nuts. But his instincts, honed by years of experience and training, and an innate honesty that sometimes got him into trouble, wouldn't allow him to dissemble about something like this.

"It's got to be infection. I'm reluctant to say a

hemorrhagic fever…there was no hemorrhaging from the body orifices, nor apparent ulceration of the skin. But…'' Declan looked past him, reconsidering all the unhappy thoughts that had been troubling him since last night. ''Ebola and Marburg don't kill that fast, anyway. And I don't know of anything that dissolves bone.''

''Bone?'' Hal looked sickened and reluctant to believe it, though he had just seen it. ''Can I resign now?''

Declan met his gaze directly. ''Sure. You didn't sign on for Biohazard Level Four.''

Hal took a slow, deep breath. His gaze lifted slowly. ''Neither did you.''

Declan nodded. ''We follow the strictest sterile procedures. I'm calling the local Haz-Mat guys to deliver us a couple of their decon suits and masks.''

Hal sat and settled back in his chair. ''Good. Time to finish my coffee.'' The milky liquid sloshed as his hand shook.

Declan made the call, then stared through the glass window between him and the body on the tray and hoped to hell that whatever killed Carter Shippey wasn't airborne. Because if it was, a whole lot of people were in trouble.

Chet Metz, of the island's fire department, showed up twenty minutes later with two gray-blue decontamination suits. Santz Martina's Haz-Mat team had never been called out before, as far as Declan knew. The island had the usual small-town collection of hazardous materials: dry cleaning fluids, petroleum products, fertilizers, insecticides. The fire department maintained a team for the sake of preparedness.

"So what's going on?" Chet wanted to know as he helped Hal and Declan into the suits. He was a beefy man in his early thirties, with steady gray eyes and a thick head of hair.

"I just don't want to take any chances," Declan said.

"Chances, huh?" Chet looked him straight in the eye. "Must be a big chance."

"Don't say anything."

"You know I won't, Dec. Okay, let's tape you in."

Chet wound yellow duct tape around their ankles and wrists, making airtight seals for their rubber boots and gloves.

As they hefted their masks, Chet said, "You know, there's no way to decontaminate you here after you're done. Not if it's a biological hazard."

"There's a shower in there," Declan said. "And plenty of bleach. We'll wash down."

"If you think that's enough. I'll wait."

Declan nodded at him. "Thanks, Chet."

Biohazards were part of hospital life and of autopsies in particular. Ordinary care was usually enough: rubber gloves, a face shield to protect the eyes, nose and mouth from any kind of spray from the victim, Tyvek gowns over scrubs. But Declan wasn't going to be happy with ordinary precautions this morning. He was very, very nervous about what was *inside* the body.

Once the masks were in place, he and Hal were breathing the purest air in the world. The micron filters would capture even the smallest virus.

"That's as good as we can do," Chet said. "I hope to God it's not airborne."

"If it is," Dec said, "we're all already dead."

"Oh, cripes, thanks," Hal muttered.

If Carter Shippey had died from an airborne infection, the chances were high that dozens of other people had already been infected. Carter, after all, was active in the Rotary and his church, and volunteered in the high school shop classes.

Declan and Hal walked into the autopsy room and faced one another across the body. Metz was watching from the other side of the glass, and when Declan glanced up briefly, their eyes met.

Hal picked up the camera he brought to every autopsy and began shooting from every angle, even climbing on a ladder to shoot from above. No step of this process would be overlooked.

The first task, after initial photos, was to remove the victim's clothes intact. The job proved nearly impossible with a body that sagged formlessly. They managed it, though, and after examining each piece of Carter's clothing, they put all the pieces into red biohazard bags.

"Nothing," Declan remarked. Nothing other than the usual loss of bodily control at death. No blood. Not a smidgen anywhere. Nor did an examination of the body itself, now little more than a fluid-filled sack, reveal any sign of wound or blood.

"Well," Declan said, "it's not Ebola or Marburg. Or any other known hemorrhagic fever."

"Thank God for small mercies," Hal muttered.

"I'm not sure that's a mercy," Declan said. "Those take time to kill you, and with proper treatment a lot of people can survive. This was fast. His wife said he was okay when she left for her bridge club and dead when she came home."

"And it's still working," Hal said. "He didn't look like this last night, did he?"

"Hell no." Declan picked up a scalpel. He wouldn't need a bone saw. Nor did he want to make a large incision into this body until he knew what might come out.

His hand paused over what had once been a man's abdomen. He looked toward the glass.

"Chet? This island has to be quarantined immediately."

Chet didn't answer for several seconds. His gaze was fixed on the body on the tray as if he couldn't believe his eyes.

"Uh…can I do that? I don't have authority."

"I do," Declan said. "It's under my emergency powers. Call the Emergency Management Office and tell them. I want this island shut down. No one in, no one out, until we find out what the hell did this."

Chet nodded.

"Then get back here," Declan said. "Because after I open up this body and take some samples, and Hal and I hose each other off, I'm sure as hell going to need help getting out of this monkey suit."

"Right."

Looking green, Chet turned and disappeared.

Hal didn't look too much better. "Do we have to open him?" he asked. "It's obvious something's eating his insides. I mean...what if it explodes all over us?"

"We're covered," Dec said, refusing to admit that he had any qualms. "Look, Hal, we've got to do it. We've got to find out what did this before somebody else dies."

Hal nodded. He drew an audible breath. "Okay. I'm documenting."

Declan made the first cut with his scalpel.

Carter Shippey hadn't rotted. He had liquefied inside his own skin. There were no identifiable organs left to remove, and what remained of the bone had become rubbery, almost like cooked cartilage. Declan saved as many samples as he thought would be useful, telling Hal to freeze them all.

Carter Shippey's brain and spinal cord were the only parts still intact, though they showed violent hemorrhaging. More samples were frozen.

Declan sewed up his incisions as quickly as possible and put the body back in the cooler. He didn't allow himself to think much about what he'd just seen, beyond the clinical notes he'd dictated to Hal. Interpretation would come later. Right now, he was simply collecting evidence.

Inside, deep inside, some quiver of unease refused to be silent, though. It wouldn't let him completely ignore what faced him. What might face the entire island.

Dec and Hal scrubbed the entire autopsy room, then poured bleach over each other and took turns under the overhead high pressure shower. When they were done with the shower, they hosed each other and the entire room. The water and the contaminants flowed down a drain into a deep septic tank where hazardous waste was chemically treated and could decompose safely.

Out in the antechamber, Chet helped strip them out of the suits. For the first time, Declan realized that sweat had plastered his clothes and hair to him.

"What did they say?" he asked Chet, when at last he could sag into his chair. His legs felt weak, as if he'd just run ten miles. His hands were shaking, an old and familiar reaction.

"Well," Chet said, "they weren't happy about it. But I told them if they'd seen what I saw, they wouldn't hesitate. So the order's going out. The flak should begin any minute."

"Yeah." Flak. For some reason he thought of *Jaws* and the mayor who didn't want to close the beach. "I need to call the Centers for Disease Control. This is way beyond my expertise."

"You know," Chet said, "this is going to freak out the whole damn island."

"I'm sorry about that," Declan said, "but we can't be irresponsible. Anybody who's worried is better off staying at home anyway."

Hal's dark eyes reflected doom and gloom. "Remember what they tried to do to that town in *Outbreak?*"

"Oh, jeez," Chet said. "Let's not even go there, okay?"

"Right," Declan agreed. "We don't know what we have here. It might not be infectious at all."

But he could feel they were sitting on a time bomb.

Ken Wilson died today. No one knows why, or if they do, they're not saying. I asked the medic about it. I've heard all kinds of stories about Caribbean bugs. Wouldn't that be my luck. Get drafted, avoid the Nam, and end up on an infected island.

I should've left those bones alone. Bad luck to mess with bones.

3

At her clinic, Markie Cross repaired a dachshund's torn ear, quilting the two pieces of cartilage back together. It would never look quite right again, but it was better than leaving the cartilage separated. So much damage from another puppy's bite.

She twisted her head, easing the tension in her shoulders. Mornings were for surgery. She'd already done one neuter, one spay, a tumor removal and extracted an infected tooth. If all went well, the ear should be the last surgery of her day. Then she could move on to the office visits, which she generally enjoyed, because they allowed her to interact with both patients and owners.

A movement to the right caught her eye, and she glanced over to see Kato standing on his hind legs, looking through the window that separated the surgery suite from the rest of the clinic. He was looking more somber than usual this morning.

Not that she blamed him. Last night hadn't exactly been pleasant, and it must have been worse for him.

She had no doubt his nose had given him a far better picture of what had happened to Carter Shippey than the words had given her.

He had seemed to like Declan Quinn, though, which was a rarity for him. Kato's usual habit was to stand several yards away and watch new people until he'd made up his mind about them, a process that might take multiple encounters. Last night, though, it was as if Kato had known Declan was there to help someone.

She shrugged away the thoughts of last night and focused on her work. One more stitch, then done. The dachshund was already starting to wake from anesthesia.

Markie's first routine client of the morning was one of her favorites, Dawn Roth. Dawn had more money than one person could possibly spend in a lifetime, but she remained amazingly unspoiled. Apart from volunteering in every conceivable way, she raised English mastiffs.

To Markie's way of thinking, anyone who could handle two hundred pounds of slobbering dog was special. Someone who loved them enough to breed them, and love each of them as her own child, was a rare gift. To adopt one of Dawn's mastiffs required a background check that would have put the FBI to shame.

Today her patient was Brindle Castlereagh, a champion female who was into late pregnancy. Brinnie, as Dawn called her, had gone into heat out of season. The result was going to be a litter that couldn't be registered, because the sire couldn't be identified. That didn't faze Dawn; she was caring for this litter as carefully as all the rest.

"Isn't it horrible about Carter Shippey?" Dawn asked as Markie palpated Brinnie's belly, identifying two healthy and vigorous pups.

"Soon now," she told Dawn. "Any day, in fact."

"I thought so."

"And yes, it's terrible about Mr. Shippey."

"He was only sixty-three."

Markie nodded. "He wasn't all that old."

"No. To tell you the truth," Dawn said, her voice dropping, "it put me into a tailspin about Tim. He works so hard at his fishing business, and lately he's not even having time to play tennis or golf...."

Markie patted Brinnie's shoulder, then turned toward Dawn. "Tim's a lot younger and very healthy. You know that."

"So was Carter, I thought." Dawn shook her head. "Not that I really knew him all that well. I understand he was quite the character in his younger years, when he owned the boat."

"So I'm told," Markie said. She had only known Carter Shippey as a somewhat grizzled old sailor who loved his dog more than life itself. He'd sold the boat and retired just after she'd come to Santz Martina. "I didn't know him well, either."

"But I know his wife, Marilyn, from my work at the school. She teaches English, you know. A wonderful woman. She and Carter had such plans...."

Dawn's voice trailed off. "Well." She visibly gathered herself.

Markie straightened and sat in the chair next to Dawn's. Brinnie, sensing Dawn's discomfort, gave her owner a sloppy kiss. Dawn managed a chuckle.

"I'm worrying for no reason," she said. "Sometimes people die young. But most don't, right?"

"Right," Markie said. "But when it's someone near our own age, it makes us really uneasy."

"Yeah. I think I'll go home and make Tim a key lime pie. He loves my pies. When we first got married, he was always so tickled when I'd bake one. I haven't done that for him in years now."

"That sounds like a wonderful idea."

"Yeah, it does." Dawn was suddenly smiling again. "I'll call you when Brinnie decides to whelp, then."

"Yes, do. I want to be there." Mastiffs sometimes had trouble giving birth, and none of Dawn's ever whelped without a vet present. Markie loved the opportunity to be there; most dog owners didn't bother, and nearly everyone on the island had their pets neutered anyway. Seeing puppies born was becoming something of a treat for her.

After Dawn left, Markie noticed that Kato had vanished from the back rooms of the clinic, no doubt gone to his cool retreat in the farthest reaches of the kennel. The reason was soon evident, as Markie discovered that her next three patients were cats.

Kato took after his husky forebears in his dislike for cats. At least he merely disdained them and didn't look upon them as part of the food chain, as many huskies did. The cats, of course, weren't insulted. They disdained *him* as the lower order creature he clearly was.

Once the cats were gone, and the iguana and the rabbit arrived, Kato reappeared, licking the rabbit comfortingly and regarding the iguana with sympathy as Markie cleaned and patched a festering wound in its side.

The day passed as so many others before it had, with only two differences: Declan Quinn popped into her mind dozens of times, and by the end of the day she was wishing she had invited him in for coffee last night. And she couldn't shake the memory of Kato's low, mournful howl.

"I am *not* going to quarantine this island," Stan Freshik told Declan on the phone. He was the chief of the emergency management team, a good man who was used to dealing with hurricanes, not diseases. He had plenty of excellent evacuation plans, but no quarantine options. Such an eventuality had never been considered. "Do you have any idea what kind of panic that will cause?"

"It's going to cause a panic anyway," Declan told him flatly. "I can't keep this a secret. That would be criminal. And CDC is already sending a biohazard response team. If you won't shut us down, *they* will."

"Jesus, Dec. You don't even know what this is. You can't say for sure it's contagious."

"But I can't say for sure that it isn't. I can't even

tell you how long its incubation period is, if it *is* contagious. I wish I could. But my point is, there's going to be panic whether you declare a quarantine or CDC does. My advice to you is to get some planning underway and take the first steps, because you might be able to minimize the public response if you start right away. Because once CDC gets here, the shit is going to hit the fan.''

Stan's sigh was both irritated and impatient. "God damn it!"

"That's not going to help anything," Dec reminded him. He was looking through the window at the cooler where the body was once more stashed. "You know I have the authority. I'm the chief medical officer on this island. Consider this a heads-up. CDC will be here by five."

"By *five?* My God, that's not any time at all."

"Exactly." Dec glanced at the clock on the wall. "Seven hours. I suggest you shut down the airport first. If you don't call the Coast Guard, I will."

"If this isn't contagious..."

"Then you can have my head on a platter. Stan..." Declan hesitated. Finally he said, "I'm scared, too. But we have to do the responsible thing."

When he hung up, assured that Stan would do what was necessary, Declan continued to stare into the autopsy theater. Because he had already had two unprotected exposures to Shippey's body, he had canceled all his appointments for the day, not wanting to risk infecting a patient.

It was sort of like sitting on death row, he thought

sourly. Trapped here with that body, basically. He'd already sent Hal home, with strict orders to stay there. At least Hal didn't have a family.

But there were others who'd already been exposed: Carter Shippey's wife, certainly. The cops, the crime scene team and all of Carter's friends and family.

He could, he supposed, judge himself to be no more contagious than anyone else. But he was. Decon suit notwithstanding, from the instant he had cut into the body, this entire morgue had become a death zone. An airborne virus couldn't be contained by a mere door.

The morgue had its own air circulation system because of the highly contagious diseases that were sometimes autopsied here, so whatever it was shouldn't spread beyond the morgue very fast, especially since a slightly lower atmospheric pressure was maintained in here. Nothing was too good or too expensive for the wealthy.

But this wasn't a maximum security biocontainment facility. It was state of the art for the routine types of contagion that were expected, but it was not proof against the worst that Mother Nature could offer.

Declan had never had any desire to be on the cutting edge of research. Doctoring people had been his highest ambition. It gave him no pleasure at all to consider that he might have discovered a brand-new disease.

Happiness filled Kato when the day was over and he and Markie began their evening walk home. It wasn't that he didn't enjoy being at the clinic. Being so near to other animals, especially dogs, filled him with joy, even when they hurt and needed his attention. But today there had been too many cats.

He'd learned from Markie at a very early age that cats were off-limits. He couldn't begin to understand why—they clearly smelled like prey—but it seemed that many humans actually liked the creatures. So, to please Markie, he simply departed the vicinity of any feline.

Which was not to say he didn't occasionally pretend that his tug toy was a cat. But dreams were only dreams.

Traveling down the sidewalk at a brisk pace, he noted that some human had recently passed, leaving a trail of illness in the air. He tested it, drawing quick bursts of air into his nose and expelling them through his mouth. No, it was not the smell of last night.

As they passed one house, a small dark dog yapped annoyingly from behind a window. *Oh-look-oh-look-another-dog-another-dog-oh-look-oh-look!* Kato gave the dog a dismissive turn of the head. Such a waste of energy. He preferred to remain silent and watchful. One's voice was meant to sing, and singing was reserved for special occasions: play or need or union. Otherwise, silence aided the senses in being watchful.

The world was a plethora of smells: flowers, grass, trees, people, animals, insects…oh, the joy of filling his nostrils with the teeming life of the world.

But then the pungent scent of fear wafted to him.

Faint, it seemed to come from elsewhere. He sucked it in, concentrating on it, following it along the sidewalk as best he could at the end of a leash. Markie was not cooperating. But then, he'd long since realized that Markie didn't have a real nose. He sometimes pitied that little thing on her face, so useless. On the other hand, he could taste the wind for her. And her eyes and hands were far more adept than his. They worked well together.

The fear-smell went away, then returned as they rounded a corner onto his own street. He lifted his head, sucking it in, and felt his hackles stir.

Last night...last night he wasn't sure what he had smelled. He had merely felt compelled to follow it, despite Markie's objections. Sometimes she just didn't know what was truly important.

But Kato found himself remembering last night, the smell he had followed, the way all the dogs around had grown frenzied, some with anger, some with fear. Not all barks were the same, though most had been protective.

Then there had been the scent. A different scent. One he had never before known. And it had led directly to death. Terror and death, two very powerful smells.

He would have left, but somehow it had seemed important to remain, to make sure his mistress knew there was danger. He hoped she had understood.

Now the lingering scent of fear led him to a palm trunk. He sniffed around it, getting glimmers of how local dogs had been doing lately. Most were happy and healthy. One or two were angry. A female was beginning to enter heat. And one... Kato sniffed the sad scent and made a whimper of sympathy.

"Kato?"

He ignored her. Moving upward, he finally zeroed in on the aroma that had called to him from so far away. Fear. Terror. Bad thing. Fresh. Recent. Large dog, healthy, but terrified.

The hair on Kato's neck rose, and he backed away from the tree. Something was very wrong in his world. He would need Markie. And she would need him.

Declan watched the two CDC team members, fully suited, working on Carter Shippey's remains. Remains seemed the only word for that travesty of a body on the table. But as far as Declan could see, there had been no further deterioration since this morning.

Behind him, another suited member of the team spoke. "The physical deterioration occurred overnight?"

Declan turned to face Marshall Wilcox, the team leader. "Most of it, yes. At least the part that was visible."

"So let me see if I have this right. Last night you were called to a sudden death of a sixty-three-year-old male, retired fisherman."

"That's correct."

"And you'd given him a physical only a month ago and found him to be fit?"

"As fit as a much younger man, yes." It was unnerving talking to someone who was hiding behind a decon suit and hood, breathing his own air, a man whose voice was coming through a speaker.

"And upon examination of the body, the only unusual thing you noticed was a sponginess."

"That's correct. He felt doughy. But he wasn't swollen as far as I could see. At that time his face appeared locked in a rictus of terror."

"Not unusual with heart attack deaths."

"No, I've seen it before."

"Okay." Wilcox came over to stand beside him. "And the way he looked when we got here was the same way he looked this morning when you pulled him for autopsy."

"That's correct."

"And nobody else is sick?"

"Not yet. Not that I know of."

"Not even his wife."

Declan shook his head. "She called me a couple of hours ago, wanting my autopsy results."

"And you told her?"

"That I needed to run some extensive blood work and tissue tests before I could say anything. That it might be a while before we pinpointed the exact cause of death."

A slight movement of Wilcox's hood seemed to indicate a nod. "Good. Well, from what I've seen so far, I'm going to support your quarantine of the island. In the meantime, I don't see any need for you to hang around here."

It was a clear dismissal. Declan felt pinpricks of anger in his face. "He's my patient."

"He's *our* patient now," Wilcox said flatly. "You don't have the facilities or knowledge to handle this."

Declan turned to face him, forcing Wilcox to do the same. "Just what *is* 'this'?"

Wilcox hesitated. "I don't know. We've never seen anything like it."

The icy finger crept up Declan's neck again. "I was afraid you were going to say that."

"At this point, I'm not sure we even have a contagious disease," Wilcox continued. "I can't think of a single disease that dissolves everything in the body except the skin and nervous system."

"Me, neither."

"But…" Wilcox hesitated. "At this point, given the victim's social involvement, I'd say that exposure has to have been extensive. So there's no reason you can't leave here and go on with life. If you really want to help…"

"I do."

"Then you can help me with demographics. People know you and will talk to you more easily."

Declan was only too willing to help however he could. "What do you need?"

"Start with his wife. Find out if she noticed anything at all unusual in his behavior in the past week or two. Then see if you can build us a list of everyone he routinely comes in contact with, so we can start interviewing them."

"That's going to be a big list."

Wilcox nodded again. "As fast as this hit him, that gives me hope."

"Hope?"

"You haven't had a new case in nineteen hours. That you know of. Unless this has a long, silent incubation period, this may be the last of it. Or it might not be disease at all."

"That's what I'm thinking," Declan said, for the first time admitting the nagging feeling that had troubled him all day. "The longer I sat here thinking about it, the more I began to think he had a toxic exposure of some kind."

"That could well be. We'll have a better idea after we complete the tests. In the meantime, Doctor, your help with demographics will be appreciated. We're only five people."

Declan left, stepping out into fresh air for the first time since six that morning. The tropical sunset was just beginning, a gorgeous display of reds, golds and pinks that filled the entire western sky. He filled his lungs with the soft sea air, washing away the taste of antiseptics and death that had permeated him…to his very soul, he thought unhappily.

Then, squaring his shoulders, he climbed on his Harley and rode through town toward the Shippey house. He had no doubt Marilyn was there, surrounded by friends, people who were now scared half to death because the island had been quarantined.

Marilyn was at home, but she wasn't surrounded by friends. She was all alone, her face tear-streaked and swollen.

"Are you sure you want to come in here?" she asked him almost bitterly.

She was an attractive woman of sixty, with carefully tended, smooth skin and dark hair with a white streak. Right now she looked older than her years.

"What do you mean?"

"Oh, only that everyone is treating this house as if it were full of lepers. Nobody wants to even get close. They'll call me, make vague remarks about helping and dropping by soon, but not a single one has showed up."

"I'm sorry."

She shrugged. "I thought it was a heart attack."

He hesitated. "I don't think so, Marilyn."

Her face twisted; then she stepped back, inviting him in. "Want some coffee? I've been living on it."

"Sure, that would be great."

He noticed that she didn't lead him to the living room where her husband had died last night. Instead they went into the kitchen and sat at a small dinette with mugs of coffee. Under the table, at their feet, the Shippey's King Charles spaniel seemed to cower.

"Sorry," Marilyn said. "He's a mess. He misses Carter."

Declan reached down, gently scratching the dog's ears. "I'm sorry," he said. Sorry for the whole mess, though there wasn't a damn thing he could do about any of it.

"So it wasn't a heart attack. I knew you were going to say that. The minute I heard about the quarantine,

I knew it was something else. Am I going to die, too?"

She looked at him straightly, her expression seeming to say that she hoped so, because right now life was past bearing.

At this moment, he didn't have a shred of hope to offer her. She was locked too tightly in grief and shock to respond. Without thinking, he reached out and took her hand.

Something in her eyes tightened, then relaxed. "You're not afraid to touch me."

"No," he said. "I'm not."

The tears came then, a flood of them. He held her hand, letting her squeeze his fingers until her nails dug in, and wondered what the hell was going to happen to all of them.

4

"He wasn't sick at all," Marilyn told Declan when her tears abated. "Just before I left for my bridge club, we were talking about taking the catamaran to Jamaica next week. He'd been looking forward to that for ages, and with Christmas vacation starting, we decided to sail around the Caribbean a bit."

"So you didn't notice anything amiss."

She shook her head, her eyes filling with tears that this time didn't fall. "I didn't notice anything at all, Dec. Not a thing. He hasn't been sick. He's been eating normally. He even took a walk before dinner, like he's always done."

Declan nodded, gave her hand a comforting squeeze. Much as he'd been trying to hold his own feelings in abeyance since last night, they were still there, and right now his chest ached painfully for Marilyn and Cart. "Not even a sneeze or a sniffle in the last few weeks?"

She shook her head. "I'm sorry, Dec. Everything

was *normal*. He was healthy. So unless there was something he didn't tell me, nothing was wrong.''

Riding toward his house, Declan noticed for the first time that the streets were empty. At nine at night on these balmy tropical evenings, there were usually plenty of people out for a stroll, or sitting on their porches. Despite the advent of satellite TV, few people regularly spent their evenings in front of the tube. The weather was too nice, the beach too inviting, the shops too attractive. And being such a small community, where everyone knew everyone else by sight, evening was a time to socialize.

Square dancers met in the park; street entertainers dotted the waterfront; ice cream was hawked from shops that were little more than a counter with an open window. The place had a flavor all its own, carefully nurtured by the wealthy inhabitants to be both exotic and Caribbean in nature. Or at least what they thought of as Caribbean. Sometimes Dec felt he'd been caught up in a Disneyesque version of Key West.

But tonight even the marimba band wasn't playing downtown. The restaurant doors were closed, a shock in itself, since the doors of all the businesses were always wide open. Every shop was closed tighter than a drum. No music spilled from bars; no one strolled the streets; no cars were parked along the narrow side streets except near dwellings.

The word of the quarantine had scared everyone. The panic he had feared had transmuted into people hiding within their closed-up houses. He was driving through a dead zone.

Shaking his head, he turned left on La Puerta, past more closed shops, heading toward his subdivision north of town and its winding, palm-lined streets. As he passed the veterinary clinic, he realized he was only a couple of blocks from Markie Cross's home. As if the bike had a mind of its own, he found himself on the street in front of her house.

She was home. Lights were on, and as he pulled up along the curb, he saw the head of her dog silhouetted in a brightly lighted window.

Her *wolf.* That probably explained a lot about the critter, Declan thought as he sat on his bike, engine still rumbling, debating whether to drive on or get out and go to her door. Kato's silent watchfulness was a whole lot more unnerving than a dog's barking.

But the wolf had been fairly friendly to him last night, so that was certainly no reason to drive away.

Finally, not even sure why he was there, but unable to forget Markie's smile and feeling a need for something to brighten his day, he switched off the ignition, climbed off his bike and walked to her front door. As he approached, he saw Kato's tail wag in a distinctly friendly fashion.

Well, at least one of the residents here welcomed him. With that amused thought, he rang the doorbell.

Markie opened it a minute later, wiping her hands on a dish towel. "Dr. Quinn! What a nice surprise." A smile spread across her face. "What's up?"

"Not a damn thing," he admitted.

Her smiled deepened. "Well, come on in. I'm just making dinner, and I made way too much. Stuffed mahimahi. You're welcome to join me."

Fish sounded good. He forced himself to remember that this was a professional visit, coupled with ordinary island hospitality. Because for some reason he wanted to read more into it.

He stepped inside and closed the door behind himself. Immediately Kato approached him, sniffing at him as if he were full of interesting information. Declan waited a few moments, then squatted down, letting the wolf continue his exploration.

"You're good with animals," Markie said, sounding as if that surprised her.

"Well, I figure Kato is in the driver's seat. He'll let me know when it's okay to touch him."

"Yes, he will. Most people don't understand that. Listen, I'm going to put the mahimahi in the oven. Kitchen is straight back when you're ready."

"Thanks." He smiled up at her, then returned his attention to Kato. Fascinating animal, coal-black with golden eyes. His tail was down right now, as if he were a bit uncertain, but his ears were pricked with full alertness and even a bit of caution as he sniffed the man.

Declan found himself wondering what the dog was learning. Smells of the morgue. Smells of Cart's body or disease? He hoped not. The taco he'd had delivered for lunch, a decision he'd been regretting ever since? The scent of Marilyn Shippey. That would be fresh. The odors from his drive through town?

But Kato's world remained beyond his reach, and Declan could only imagine what it must be like to have your most important sensory input through your nose. Did it create visions? Or just feelings? Was it pleasurable? Or merely informative?

Sphinxlike, Kato completed his examination and sat back on his narrow haunches, looking straight at Declan with those golden eyes.

"Hi, Kato."

The tail twitched a little on the oak flooring and the ears relaxed backward a bit, not submissive, but a hint of welcome. Declan held out his hand, palm up. Kato considered it a moment, then nosed it aside.

Okay, they weren't that far along.

Then Kato rose and trotted toward the kitchen, honoring the man by being willing to turn his back to him.

Declan straightened, accepting the honor and ignoring the way his knees—battered by too much basketball and soccer—creaked at the change in position.

The kitchen was bright, a mix of stainless steel countertops and appliances, with glass-fronted oak cabinets. The backsplash was steel, too, but the soffits over the cabinets were painted a delightful Chinese-red, bringing a huge burst of color into the nearly monochrome room.

Markie stood at an island, tossing a salad. She greeted him with another one of those smiles and said, "It won't be long. Have a seat."

He perched on the stool across the island from her and realized he was salivating for that salad. Physician or not, he didn't eat nearly as well as he should, for lack of time.

"Somebody's into cooking," he said, indicating the kitchen, which did a fair job of impersonating a high-quality restaurant kitchen.

"Yeah." She gave a little glance, her eyes dancing as she looked at him. With practiced ease, she sliced the fillets open and spooned in a homemade bread-crumb stuffing packed with minced sautéed zucchini, mushrooms and onions. "It's my hobby. And my therapy. It cuts me loose after a long day at work."

"I'm surprised you're not too tired to bother."

"What else would I do? Watch television?"

"You could walk on the beach."

She laughed and put the fish in the oven, then began dicing a tomato. Her hands were nearly a blur, moving what was obviously a razor-sharp chef's knife with a confidence that made him wince.

"That comes later. Although the longer I'm on the island, the less peaceful that becomes. It's more like going to a huge party."

He grinned. "Amen. The mountain can be a pretty good bolt hole, though. In the daytime, anyway."

"I've been meaning to climb the volcano cone. I hear the view up there is breathtaking."

"So is the smell of sulfur."

She laughed again. "I still find myself wondering sometimes why I'm living at the foot of a volcano."

"Dormant volcano," he corrected. "It hasn't erupted in three hundred years."

She was a fascinating woman. He felt as if he had

her full attention, even while she monitored a pot of boiling pasta and stirred a creamy white wine sauce.

"Just yesterday, in geological terms," she retorted. Satisfied with the sauce, she turned it down to simmer, retrieved tableware and dishes, and set two places at the bar with cloth place mats and wineglasses. From the refrigerator she returned with a bottle of chardonnay and poured them each a glass.

Dec reached for his and offered a toast. "To hope."

"To hope," she agreed.

The wine was crisp on his tongue, and he rolled it around, savoring it.

"So," Markie said as she began to serve salad into bowls, "what's going on with the quarantine?"

"Maybe nothing." Which was true.

"And maybe something?" Her eyes caught and held his, drawing him to places that seemed as haunting as her wolf's gaze. "Something to do with Carter Shippey?"

"We don't know what killed him. That's all."

Her eyes narrowed slightly, letting him know she didn't believe that was the full story, but that for now she was going to let it pass.

"How was your day?" he asked her, seizing on any safe topic he could think of.

"The usual," she said, as if he would know. "The same thing you do, I expect, except I do it on animals."

A smile flickered across his face. "Dogs and cats?"

"Mostly. Today I had an iguana and a rabbit, too."

"Your job is harder than mine. You have to know about many more species."

She laughed. "You know, the basics are pretty much the same for mammals. I have a different slew of diseases to know, that's all. It gets interesting with the exotics, though. Since coming here, I've had to do some cramming. Iguanas, turtles and snakes weren't something I focused much on before. But if worse comes to worse, I can always call a specialist."

"The way I do."

Smiles again, exchanged over the wineglasses.

"I bet," he said, "you do more sterilizations than I do."

At that she laughed outright, her eyes dancing merrily. "By far."

The mahimahi was just coming out of the oven when Kato suddenly appeared in the kitchen, standing at the counter and staring out the window over the sink.

"Kato, get down."

He ignored her.

"He listens well." The remark was offered with a laugh.

Markie rolled her eyes. "It depends. When he's in the mood, he's obedient. It's just that he's rarely in the mood. Kato, get down."

The fish, on its baking pan, sat on the nearby stove, but the dog didn't spare it a glance. He was intent on something out back, something in the darkness. And his tail was down.

"I hate that," Markie sighed.

"When he doesn't listen?"

"No, when he stares out the window like that."

"Maybe you're picking up on his feelings."

"Could be."

Then, low in Kato's throat, a deep growl began.

Markie swung around quickly to look. The chef's knife had returned to her hand as if by magic, seemingly without her awareness. Declan saw Kato's hackles rise.

"There's someone out there," she said.

"I'll go look."

But her free hand shot out, gripping his forearm. "Don't, Declan. Whatever it is, it won't try to get past Kato. It's probably just somebody crossing the backyards."

The knife in her other hand belied the confidence in her eyes.

"Maybe," Declan said. "Does he do that often?"

Her gaze wavered. "No."

"Then maybe I should look anyway."

"Please. Don't bother. Whatever it is, we're safe in here."

He forced himself to relax onto his stool because it seemed her wish, but he looked at the dog again and didn't at all like what he saw. Maybe that was what Markie was reacting to, the strength of Kato's response.

The hair was raised along Kato's entire spine. His head was lowered between his shoulders as he stared out the window, a definite *don't you dare come near me* posture.

"Kato?" Markie called him again.

This time he glanced at her, his golden eyes inscrutable, a small whine coming from his throat. Then he turned back to the window.

The neighborhood erupted.

Declan had his limits, and he reached them as the barking spread like a wave through the surrounding area. Dogs did that sometimes, he knew, but rarely were so many barking at the same time, both indoors and out, and he remembered how they had done that last night, about the time that Carter Shippey had died. It made him wonder about things like poisonous gases. Surely the dogs couldn't smell a virus?

But maybe they could. Recent studies seemed to indicate that they could smell nearly undetectable enzymes in cancer cells. Why not a marauding virus?

Leaving the delicious aromas behind, he ignored Markie's protest and stepped out through the sliding glass door onto her patio. The night smelled the same to him as it always did, the soft scents of the sea, the greener scents of the growing things. The ceaseless breeze blew gently.

A sliver of moon rode above, and the light from street lamps helped illuminate the backyard areas of the nearby houses. There was nothing to be seen, except the tossing of palm fronds and shrubbery in the stiffening breeze...and a few dark, deeply shadowed places where nothing appeared to move.

But there was plenty to hear. The yapping and barking filled the night. This wasn't the idle barking of canine conversation. Something was seriously disturbing the dogs.

He glanced back over his shoulder and saw Kato firmly planted at the sink, still looking out the window. Their gazes met, and there was something in Kato's stare that made a shiver run down his own spine.

Gradually, however, the barking stopped, a wave of silence moving across the island. Then Kato dropped down out of sight. Whatever the threat had been, it was gone.

Back inside Markie's kitchen, Declan tried to brush aside the chill that insisted on creeping up his nape. Kato certainly didn't appear distressed anymore. He was sitting at Markie's edge of the island, nose lifted hopefully toward the mahimahi.

"Do you feed him from the table?" Declan asked.

"Sometimes. I'm a softie."

He managed a grin he wasn't feeling. "Somehow I expected that."

Markie scooped a serving of pasta into a glass bowl, then put a dinner plate upside down atop the bowl and flipped them over. She quickly spread a ring of diced tomato around the lip of the bowl, and lifted it away, leaving a perfect circle of pasta. Next she gently laid a slice of fish atop the pasta, drizzled the sauce over the fish, and finally added a few sprigs of fresh parsley as a garnish. When both plates were ready, she set them on the place mats with a flourish.

"I give you baked stuffed mahimahi over angel-hair pasta, with a creamy white wine sauce and diced tomato."

"Five-star cuisine," Declan said, taking in the aroma. "It's too beautiful to eat."

"Thank you, but please do," Markie said. For just a moment, her eyes sparkled. "You wouldn't want to offend the chef, after all."

But he noted that her eyes darkened, and she toyed with her food, seeming uninterested in it. He paused, realizing he hadn't said grace. Not that he believed a God existed or was interested in his prayers—he didn't—but it was a habit his mother had ingrained in him from his earliest childhood. Even in his current state of atheism, he did it for his mother, whispering the words and crossing himself before taking up his knife and fork.

Except he didn't exactly feel like eating, either.

Finally he sighed and swiveled on the stool to face her. "What's wrong?"

She looked at him, her eyes a bit hollow. "I don't like the way Kato was behaving."

"Why didn't you want me to go out there?"

She looked down at her plate again. Finally she murmured, "The dogs know."

The back of his neck prickled anew. "What do the dogs know?"

A couple of seconds ticked by; then she shook herself visibly. "I'm sorry. I'm just…a little unnerved."

"I can't blame you. After all, they were barking the other night."

"Exactly." She smiled wanly. "They have senses we don't have. Sometimes it can be...scary."

"Yeah, it can."

"Do you have a dog?"

"No, it wouldn't be fair. I'm not home enough."

"Cat?"

"I'm, uh, not at all fond of cats."

"No wonder Kato likes you." She managed a laugh. "He thinks cats should be on the menu."

Declan chuckled, but it sounded hollow. "Tell me about a dog's senses."

She poked at her fish again before looking at him.

"Well, their eyes are extremely sharp. Most people think they're color blind, but they're not. The only color they can't see is green."

"Really?"

"Yup. When you think about it, it makes sense. An awful lot of the natural world is green. For a predator, it would be a distraction."

"That's fascinating. I had no idea."

"Most people don't. Another myth is that dogs can't process two-dimensional images. Kato loves animal shows on TV. He prefers bears, horses, deer...and most especially other dogs. Sometimes I put on movies that have dogs in them just for him."

Declan smiled. "I like that."

She shrugged. "On the other hand, people generally bore him. He'll sit on the recliner through a full hour show about bears, but the commercials bore him.''

"He has good taste.'' He shook his head, still smiling.

"If you take a look at my TV screen, you can see how many times he's poked his nose at it in the last few days.''

Now Declan laughed, and his uneasiness began fading. "Trying to smell?''

"Yes.'' She was totally ignoring her dinner now, wrapped up in a favorite subject. "That's a dog's most important sense. I think they read entire novels with their noses. When I'm out walking him and he stops to sniff a tree…well, I call it pee-mail.''

He laughed again. "I like that.''

"We know dogs can discern sex in each other's urine, and whether a female is in heat. Some studies suggest they can also sense the dog's emotional state—fear, pain, joy—although we've really no idea how much they can read. It might be far more than we can imagine.''

"Our noses certainly don't come close.''

"No, they don't. But there are some things we do know. A dog can follow a scent that's weeks old, despite overlaying scents. We're talking about a nose that's sensitive to a few parts per billion.''

"I'll be the first to admit I can't imagine that.''

"None of us can. It's a whole different world. And we can't begin to guess how they process that information. We know they react to it, but we don't know how they piece it together into their view of the world."

Declan looked at Kato with new respect. "I wish I could find out."

"Me, too." Finally she forked a piece of fish and put it in her mouth. After she swallowed, she added, "Pascal justified vivisection by claiming that dogs were nothing but a bundle of hard-wired responses without any real consciousness, that everything a dog does is instinct, that they're not self-aware, that they have no ability to reason. That view was widely held for a long time."

Markie shook her head. "I defy anyone to truly pay attention to a canine and believe that. They feel guilt and shame, they feel jealous, and they make decisions. And they love." She trailed off and suddenly blushed, a very charming blush. "Sorry. I'm on my soapbox again."

"That's okay. I'm enjoying it. Unfortunately, I've never owned a dog, so I don't know any of this."

He looked at Kato, who was still waiting patiently for a tidbit from Markie, and all of a sudden felt the acute intelligence in the animal's gaze, sensed that he was being weighed, measured and judged.

"So," he said, still looking at Kato, "when he gets upset about something, it's natural for it to unnerve you."

"That's the whole point, isn't it? We allied with dogs a hundred thousand years ago because they have better senses than we do. Because we can rely on them to alert us and protect us."

"True. He alerted. I was going out to check on it."

She looked at him again, and her eyes held something almost as unnerving as what was in Kato's. "But don't you see, Dec? That wasn't just an alert."

"But…"

"No, wait. Kato doesn't bark like other dogs. His way of alerting me is to stare out a window in silence. A trespasser wouldn't raise his hackles. This was something a hell of a lot more threatening."

At that instant, for some utterly unknown reason, Declan felt his own hackles rise and a chill pour down his spine.

His gaze drifted from Markie back to Kato. Golden wolf eyes were heavy-lidded now, as if to convey that the threat had passed, that it was okay to relax.

Declan flaked off a bit of fish, twirled some pasta with it, and finally ate. "It's delicious."

The flavors melded perfectly, each bite a bright taste explosion that very nearly drew an ecstatic moan from him. Markie smiled at his obvious enjoyment and joined in the feast. For a few minutes they ate silently.

"Wow," Declan said, looking at the empty plate. "Just…wow."

"Thank you," Markie said, a wide smile creasing her delicate features. "I'm honored."

"The pleasure was entirely mine, I assure you."

Markie put the plates on the floor, allowing Kato to satisfy his palate. But the dog gave them barely a sniff. His golden eyes were still fixed on the window.

Declan stayed to help with the cleanup and was just

about to leave when his cell phone chirped a chorus of Jimmy Buffet's "Margaritaville."

"Dr. Quinn, it's Tom Little."

Declan felt his hand tighten on the tiny phone.

"I'm at the Shippey house. You need to get over here. Now. And bring your friends from Atlanta."

"On my way."

"What's going on?" Markie asked.

He looked into Kato's eyes before turning to her. The dog seemed to know already. "I think somebody just died."

5

Declan called Marshall Wilcox from Markie's driveway, then climbed on his bike, waved a distracted goodbye to Kato and headed back to the Shippey house. *What could have happened?* he asked himself. After all, she'd been fine just a couple of hours ago. It didn't make sense.

He parked his bike across the street and strode over to where Tom Little was interviewing a middle-aged woman and her husband.

"Kathy and Larry Bridges," Tom said, by way of introduction. "They were bringing her dinner."

"She's still inside?"

"Yes."

Declan nodded. "Okay. They don't leave. You don't leave. CDC will be here in a few minutes. We need to lock this scene down. Nobody in or out."

"What's happening?" Kathy Bridges asked, fear evident in her eyes.

Declan considered how to answer. He decided on the truth.

"Ma'am, I honestly don't know. And until I have a better idea, we need to do things right."

"When can we go home?" Larry asked.

"Soon, I hope. But that's up to the doctors from Atlanta. They'll know what to do."

As if on cue, the CDC van rolled up the street and parked in the Shippeys' driveway. Declan nodded to Wilcox and summarized what little he knew.

Wilcox turned to the Bridges. "Did you touch her?"

"I…I might have," Kathy said. "I thought she was asleep at first. I don't remember."

"You didn't," Larry cut in. "We called to her, remember? She didn't answer. Then her dog nosed at her hand, and it fell limp beside her chair."

"That's right," Kathy said. "That's how it was."

Declan didn't know if they were telling the truth or simply trying to hide from the reality that they might have touched an infected body. Regardless, Wilcox wasn't buying it. He reached into the van and pulled out a green squirt bottle.

"Hold out your hands please," he said.

"What is that?" Larry asked.

"It's ordinary Lysol. If you don't have any cuts, and you haven't put your hands in your mouth or around your eyes, this ought to kill anything on your skin. It's for your own protection."

They held out their hands, and he sprayed them liberally, until the liquid foamed as they rubbed their hands together.

"We'd like to admit you overnight," he said, passing them sterile towels. "For observation."

And to quarantine them, Declan thought. Lysol would indeed kill any pathogens that were still on their skin. But it wouldn't do anything for microbes that had already been absorbed. What would? That was the million-dollar question.

While an assistant accompanied the Bridges back to their home and then to the hospital, Declan and Wilcox donned biohazard suits and made their way into the house.

"I was just here," Declan said as they entered the living room.

"When?" Wilcox asked.

"A couple of hours ago. I stopped by to see how she was doing. She seemed healthy then."

Wilcox nodded. "We'll need to quarantine you, too, then. Overnight, at least."

Declan shook his head. "I already attended Carter Shippey. Without any protection. If I were going to get sick, it would've happened already."

"You might be a vector. Do you want to pass this on to your patients and friends?"

That gave Declan pause. He was willing to take the risk for himself. But what if he were simply immune to whatever bug this was? Still…

"Look," he said, "Carter had contact with a hundred people, if not more, in the last week of his life. A quarantine, at this point, is an exercise in futility. Anyone who hasn't been exposed yet will be within a couple of days, regardless. It makes sense to keep an eye on Larry and Kathy Bridges, to see if they go symptomatic. But I have to keep working. The people here expect to see a familiar face when they come in for treatment."

Wilcox seemed to weigh the point for a moment, then finally nodded. "Okay. But you work for me, at the hospital. No private patients."

"I can live with that," Declan said.

"Let's hope so," Wilcox replied. "Or we can all die with it."

Marilyn Shippey was in a dining room chair, already turning flaccid. She seemed to sag lower with every second that they looked at her.

"Damn," Declan said. "Whatever this is, it works fast."

"We need to get her out of here and into post," Wilcox said, using the medical shorthand for postmortem. "And the dog."

The Shippeys' dog hadn't budged from its post beside the woman's chair, not even when they moved around the body. From time to time, he turned and chewed at his own leg.

"I should get him to the vet," Declan said.

"No can do," Wilcox answered. "We can't lock down the people on this island, but we sure as hell can lock down one dog. There's no reason to risk putting him in a kennel where he can infect other people's pets."

The logic was inescapable but terrifying.

"All right," Declan said. "Let's get this done."

* * *

Just before ten the following morning, Declan was summoned to a press conference. The island's lone TV station had brought a crew to the hospital's conference room. The station usually broadcast town commission meetings, educational programming for the schools, and a handful of locally hosted arts, crafts and fishing shows. The programs were more often an exercise in vanity for the hosts than a source of information for the viewers. On most days, nobody watched the island station, preferring instead the satellite feed of mainland U.S. programming. Today, everyone would be watching.

Tim Roth hosted a fishing program. No one else from the station had wanted to come near the hospital, so the job had fallen to him. He didn't look to be relishing his role. Joining him was Steve Chase, president of the territorial senate. Apparently Abel Roth, the governor, didn't want to flirt with danger, either.

Chase, who held his job by virtue of his membership in one of the island's elite families, wasn't looking very healthy this morning. Declan studied the man's ruddy face and wondered if his blood pressure had broken the bonds of beta blockers to hit the roof somewhere around 180 over 110. He would have to check on that.

And Tim Roth was looking like a man who needed to be in a hospital bed. His face was pale, despite his perpetual tan, and beads of perspiration glistened on his forehead.

He wore a white cotton shirt and shorts, the island's interpretation of daytime formal, and kept fussing at his neck as if his open-throated shirt collar was too tight.

"Okay," he said, turning to the camera. "In case anyone on the island hasn't heard by now, Santz Martina was placed under quarantine yesterday before noon. If anyone doesn't know what that means, it means that nobody gets on or off this island. If anyone tries to leave, the Coast Guard is going to stop them. So don't even head for your boats, friends."

Declan waited, saying nothing, knowing the best strategy was to see how things unfolded before jumping in.

"This decision," Tim continued, "was made by one of our local doctors, Declan Quinn. As most of you know, Dr. Quinn is also the Territorial Medical Examiner and head of Emergency Preparedness, Medical Section. Apparently, the Centers for Disease Control, represented here by Dr. Joseph Gardner, agree with Dr. Quinn's decision."

"Yes," Joe Gardner said. "At this point in time, we do. We can't afford to take chances."

Joe was a young hotshot—thirty, maybe—who'd made a point of letting Declan know he'd graduated from medical school at nineteen and specialized in rare communicable diseases of the Biohazard Level Four variety. The awful, terrible bugs, like hemorrhagic fever. Ebola. Marburg. The stuff of nightmares.

"But," said Tim, stabbing his finger at Joe, "do you know it's a disease?"

Joe took a moment to reply. "No," he said finally, "we don't. We don't know *what* it is. But we have two people dead, and the symptoms don't fit with any chemical exposure I've ever heard of. That leaves disease.''

"Is it contagious?"

Joe seemed to bite back anger at being challenged by a layman. "At this time we have no idea."

"But if it *is* contagious, does it make sense to keep us all here so we might get exposed to it?"

Declan intervened, sensing that Joe's patience was wearing out. "Tim, let me explain, please."

Tim nodded, making an impatient gesture with his hand. "An explanation would be very much appreciated, I can tell you. You should have at least approached the Senate before you did this."

"There was no time to waste. I'm sorry, Tim, but I had to act immediately. Now, if I can explain…" He cocked a brow, and Tim nodded.

"Very well. We don't know what killed Carter or Marilyn Shippey. I *can* say with absolute confidence, and I'm sure Dr. Gardner will agree, that whatever killed them is something we've never seen before. *Never.*"

Joe Gardner nodded. "That's a fact."

"That's comforting," Tim said sourly.

"I know it isn't," Declan agreed. "Frankly, it terrified the hell out of me, too, when I started the autopsy yesterday. The thing is, we don't know what it is. But what we do know is, if it's contagious, a lot of people have already been exposed. Cart volunteered at the high school woodshop. Marilyn taught English there. That's a couple of hundred kids they'd have had contact with. Plus they were active at church, and Cart was in the Rotary. Add in all the people they came into contact with there, and all their families and friends, and the odds are that if you live on this island, you've been exposed already.''

"You're not making us feel any better, Dec." This time Tim's voice was less belligerent. Quieter, as if unhappiness was overtaking anger.

"I know I'm not. I wish I *could* be reassuring. But the simple fact is, if this is a contagious disease, this is the best place in the world for all of us to be.''

That evidently shocked Tim, and even Joe Gardner looked a little surprised.

"Think about it," Declan continued. "If we find out it's a disease, it's only a short step or two to finding a cure or a treatment.'' Gross exaggeration, but he didn't want to start a riot. "If we're all here, we can receive treatment quickly. If we're scattered all over hell and gone, that won't be true.''

Amazingly, Tim was nodding.

"Moreover," Declan said, "we have a moral responsibility here. If this is a contagion, we can contain it here. So any way you look at it, the smartest thing we can all do is hunker down on the island and get through this together.''

Tim nodded again. Then he looked at Joe. "You agree, Dr. Gardner?''

"Yes, I do. I've treated outbreaks of some of the worst diseases known to man. I can assure you, even with Ebola, if you get treatment in time, you can survive. So it's important that everyone remain here on the island. We will bring in whatever resources are necessary to solve this problem.''

Tim's choler was fading a bit. ''Why aren't you wearing one of those fancy protective suits, Dr. Gardner? Aren't you afraid?''

Joe Gardner smiled. ''We've found no evidence the disease is airborne. The best analysis we can make right now is that it seems to spread by direct human contact.''

''How can you know that?''

''There've been two cases. The victims were married. We have no other patient reports. If it is a disease, it's apparently hard to spread.''

Tim sank back in his chair. ''I think that's the best news I've heard since yesterday morning.''

''I agree,'' Gardner said. ''But it seems quite clear to me that if this disease were airborne or waterborne, we'd have other cases by now.''

That wasn't entirely true, and Declan was sure Joe Gardner realized it. So much depended on incubation periods, as well as type and duration of exposure. Gardner was betting, a very dangerous bet indeed.

Outside the conference room, Dec took a minute to warn Steve Chase about his blood pressure and to tell him to come by that afternoon. Then he caught up to Joe Gardner, who was walking back to the lab.

''You're a fool,'' he said.

''Maybe,'' Gardner replied. ''But Carter Shippey hasn't been off this island in months, has he?''

''No. He and his wife were planning a vacation,

but they'd had to do a lot of work on their boat. It was banged up in a tropical storm last year.''

''And you don't get a whole lot of strangers here?''

''Just occasional houseguests at the other end of the island. Deliveries at the airport and the harbor, but everyone there checks out clean.''

Joe nodded. ''Then whatever it is started here. And it's my bet that it can't be highly contagious. No way. Anything highly contagious that had been introduced on this island over the past couple of months would have affected other people besides a retired fisherman.''

Dec nodded thoughtfully. ''Do you have any ideas?''

''Not yet. So far we haven't found a single living or partly living thing in Shippey's body. Not so much as a prion.''

''What about chemicals?''

''Nothing unusual so far. But we'll keep testing.'' Joe yawned and stretched. None of them had slept since the previous morning. ''So tell me again how this island works. If you had an outbreak of say, influenza, what kind of epidemiology would you expect to see?''

That was an easy question. The other doctors at the hospital had often talked about that, since they'd had an influenza outbreak two years before. ''We all live pretty closely on this end of the island. I'd expect to see a number of cases reporting simultaneously, and then a rapid spread through the town and schools. It'd hit the other end of the island somewhat later, carried over there by household employees."

Joe nodded. "How long?"

"Last time it was flu, and it only took a week for full contagion."

"I would have expected that." Joe yawned again. "Between you, me and the fence post? This isn't going to be an easy solve."

"Do you have to sound so damn happy about it?"

Joe laughed. "Admit you're intrigued, doctor."

Declan was. But he wasn't happy to admit it. Not at all.

Tim Roth wasn't happy, either. He'd cornered Steve Chase on the way out of the hospital.

"Let's take a drive," he'd said, his hand tightening on the man's forearm.

They'd climbed in his Land Rover and wound their way up into the hills, where he pulled off onto the shoulder. To their right, six hundred feet below, a white beach was empty despite the picture-perfect teal expanse of the Caribbean. To their left, a handful of blackened, chiseled stones fought a losing battle with the underbrush. They were the sole remains of a plantation house that had been burned to the ground two hundred years before.

"Why here?" Steve asked, shifting uncomfortably in his seat. "Why here, of all places?"

"You need to calm down," Tim said. "Quinn had his eyes on you. You're a public figure."

"Declan Quinn is my doctor," Steve said. "If he was concerned, it was strictly medical."

"Maybe. Probably. But we don't need the attention." Tim pointed to the ruins. "It's rubble, Steve. Dust and ash, just like she is."

Steve's chin set. "Carter Shippey said he saw her. Carter wasn't the type to make up stories."

Tim hesitated, then met his gaze. "Carter was a fisherman. He'd spent his life at sea. Tall tales are as much a part of a sailor's life as salt spray."

"You're a fisherman."

"I'm a businessman," Tim countered. "I send rich people out for day trips with a bottle of champagne, a case of beer and the hope that they'll catch a marlin to hang on a wall. The sea isn't a mystery. It's a cash cow."

He paused for a moment. "And Annie Black isn't a ghost. She's a legend you tell to make people feel like they're buying a slice of the supernatural with their five-thousand-square-foot Colonial Georgian with verandah and pool. She's an extra five grand on the asking price. That's all."

"And the Shippeys are still dead. Of unknown cause."

"Exactly." Tim sighed and repeated the words. "Of *unknown* cause. Could be a virus. Could be some chemical he got hold of at the high school shop. There's just no reason to assume they were killed by a two-hundred-years-dead murderer."

Steve shifted uneasily, eyeing the blackened stones again. "I didn't say that."

"No, but it's crossed your mind ever since Cart opened his damn mouth."

Steve nodded, and Tim pressed on.

"Look, we've lived on this damn island most of our lives. If the ghost of Annie Black were hanging around, don't you think somebody would have seen something at some time? But *nobody ever has.* So relax. Besides, ghosts are bullshit, and you know it."

"My sister saw one in our house in New York."

Tim sighed. "Yeah. Right. A twelve-year-old hysteric home alone at midnight sees a ghost. That's one for the headlines."

Steve flushed, but this time it wasn't an unhealthy color. "Okay. Okay."

Tim clapped Steve's shoulder bracingly. "Annie Black's ashes were strewn all over this island two hundred years ago. That's a lot of time for wind and rain to work. There couldn't possibly be enough left of her to do anyone any harm."

At that Steve laughed nervously, and the two men headed back into town. Steve even managed not to look over his shoulder as the burnt-out husk of the old plantation fell away behind them.

But he felt Tim was somehow lying to him. And he felt someone watching.

Jones and Perlman bought it today. Shit, this is starting to be like Nam. Nobody will say anything. But I know. Hell, everyone knows. Jackson said he saw it happen to Jones. One minute he's sitting in his barracks room, working his damn crosswords. The

*next minute, he's shaking like a leaf. Then he's dead.
Flat dead.*

*Word is the CO called Washington last night. Of
course, he's not going to tell us anything. We're just
peons. Bunch of damn draftees who'd rather be sitting home, smoking some weed, listening to Jimi Hendrix and painting flowers on the VW minibus. That's
how they see us. Worthless.*

They're going to kill us all.

6

The day turned out to be extraordinarily busy for Markie. She'd half expected that most of her appointments wouldn't show because of the fear of contagion. Instead, she was overrun by pet owners worried about dogs that had begun to chew their own fur off.

After the fifteenth time Markie had prescribed an antihistamine and said, "It's just nerves. This will calm him down and stop any itching that may be contributing," it suddenly struck her: the island's dogs were having nervous fits. Out of the blue. She usually only saw this kind of thing with separation anxiety or in an extremely high-strung dog, and never this many cases in a single day.

Looking at case sixteen, she heard herself asking, "Was Candy barking last night?"

"She went crazy," Candy's owner, Celeste Worthington said. Her beautiful cocoa-skinned face was creased with concern. "All that barking. Did you hear how the dogs started up?"

Markie nodded. "I sure did."

"They did that the other night, too. But this time…" Celeste shook her head. "It was worse, Markie. Candy barked until she was hoarse, but she didn't calm down like she did the other night when the dogs stopped barking. She started running in circles, like she was chasing her tail, bouncing off the furniture. Then, when she was too exhausted to do it anymore, she curled up and started nipping at her hind leg. At first I thought she had a flea, but when I got up this morning… Well, you can see what she did."

Indeed. A huge patch of fur was missing from the inside of Candy's thigh, and the skin beneath was scabbed and bleeding. The worst one yet. "There's a lot of this going around all of a sudden."

"I know." Celeste's gaze reflected uneasiness. "I talked to some of the others in the waiting room."

Markie nodded again and began to apply salve to Candy's irritated skin. "I'm doing scrapings to see if there's some kind of fungus going around among the dogs. It'll be a few days before I know for sure, though. In the meantime, we'll try to calm her and keep the itching down."

Celeste and her pet left a few minutes later. Candy didn't seem happy with the cone Markie had put on her and was howling mournfully. Kato, who'd been nearly invisible all day, watched the poor animal leave.

Markie squatted down, stripping her rubber gloves and tossing them in the waste pail before scratching him behind the ears. "Where have you been all day, big boy?" Usually he would have been out here with her playing nurse to all the dogs. Instead, he'd vanished.

Kato answered, a deep almost mournful sound. It didn't last long, but Markie felt it carried a huge portent of some kind. "Do you know what's going on here?"

Wolf eyes held hers steadily, but Markie couldn't read what was behind them.

She scratched him for another minute, then straightened. Her assistant, Donna, came into the cubicle. "Four more of the same," Donna said as she began to disinfect the steel examining table.

"Great. Do me a favor, will you?"

"Sure."

"Run down Dr. Declan Quinn. I need a word with him."

Donna looked at her, as if sensing something, but merely gave a nod. "You got it. Your next patient is in the other room."

"Who is it?"

"Sparky Vasquez. Same complaint."

"Jeez."

"Yeah," said Donna. "Jeez."

It was evening before Declan finally called Markie at home. "I'm sorry," he said. "I just got your message. I've been out all day, and my receptionist didn't page me. Is something wrong?"

"Something's definitely wrong. I don't know if it's related to this epidemic, but you need to know about it."

Dec was silent for a couple of beats. Then he said, "How about we get together somewhere? I'm on a cell."

And cell transmissions on this island were anything but secure. Not that anyone would listen in on purpose, but the signals sometimes got crossed. "Sure. Where?"

He thought a moment. "Most everything is closed. My place?"

He gave her the address and said he would be there in fifteen minutes. She promised to meet him.

She pulled on a pair of sneakers and grabbed her purse, but Kato took it upon himself to decide that she wasn't going to leave the house.

Despite his customary stoicism, he still had his playful moods, and when he got into one, the word "persistence" took on an entirely new meaning. He planted himself in front of her as she headed toward the door. She tried to step around him, but he moved to block her way again.

"You wanna play, huh?" Bending, she grabbed his scruff and tugged lightly.

Ordinarily he would bow, the international canine signal for "playtime." But this time he didn't. Nor did he try to shake her hand off his scruff. He just stayed right in front of her. She threw his big fuzzy play ball. He didn't even glance at it. She found a rawhide bone and made as if to gnaw on it, then offered it to him. He merely huffed.

"Kato, I have to go out!"

As she moved, he once again planted himself in front of her, his golden gaze defying her.

Markie knew he was the gentlest wolf hybrid on the planet. She'd raised him from a pup. He slept on her bed, went nearly everywhere with her and not once in his life had he shown the slightest aggressive streak.

Until now.

His eyes went feral, pure wolf. She knew better than to argue with him.

"Kato?"

He favored her with the slightest twitch of his tail, but his expression was still fixed.

"Kato, I have to go see Declan."

A low, throaty moan answered her. Something clearly was disturbing him. There were times when she wished she could speak dog, or he could speak human.

Finally she squatted and looked him straight in the eye. "Okay. What will it take for you to let me go?"

He headed straight for his leash by the door and nosed it. Then he returned to his guard posture in front of her.

"Okay," she said, giving in. "Okay. I just hope Dec doesn't mind you shedding all over his furniture."

With that, Kato let her move. He stood docilely while she put the leash on him and trotted at heel to the car with her. In the front seat, he sat erect, with his head out the window testing the breeze.

And his eyes were still feral.

*   *   *

Tim Roth made his way around the coastline toward the north end of the island where his family lived. He knew his father wasn't going to welcome him, but that didn't matter anymore. He was going to show the old man up very soon. The thought filled him with anticipatory glee.

The sun was just beginning to set, a vision of reds and golds that made him decide to detour inland to the old Black plantation. Give Annie Black, the bitch, credit for knowing where to build a house. She'd picked a hillock at the crest of a spiny ridge that stretched like a gnarled root from the base of the dormant volcano to dominate the southern peninsula. There wasn't much she wouldn't have seen from this hilltop.

It was a piece of property he wished he could sell. His father, of course, would never permit it. The indigenous peoples considered the place taboo, and old Abel Roth wasn't about to trample on their sensibilities. Tim thought his father was way too considerate of such things. After all, these people hadn't been slaves since the Revolution of 1809, when they'd cast off British rule. But they had long memories and told Annie Black's story as if it were yesterday. Hence, Abel left the land untouched. A big chunk of the island.

Tim planned to change that once the old man was dead.

He pulled his car up to the burnt-out ruins and planted himself on one of the tumbled stones, enjoying the peacefulness of the deserted place and the glories of the tropical sunset.

He wasn't immune to the beauties of nature, and it occurred to him that he might someday build his *own* house on this spot. After all, he would owe a lot to Annie Black.

He almost laughed out loud with delight. All those people down there who still feared the woman's ghost. Even Carter Shippey, apparently. And Steve Chase. A woman dead nearly two hundred years, who'd been so terrifying in life that people still feared her in death.

He envied her style.

He patted a nearby stone and said, "You were a great girl, Annie. Times have changed, though. No slaves. Or not so they notice. But if you were here now, you'd turn that amazing intelligence to the problem. Yes, you would. You'd own the island instead of my dad, for one thing."

He laughed again. "I'll find your treasure, old girl. Don't doubt it. I'll make sure people never forget you."

The wind swept across him, chillier now, even though the sun hadn't quite disappeared. "Patience, girl," he said almost absently.

Then he climbed back into his car and drove around the base of the mountain. Time to see the old man.

Markie arrived to find Declan in his garden, up to his elbows in potting soil. At least he didn't mind

Kato's chaperoning her. In fact, he seemed glad to see the dog. They even roughhoused a bit before Declan greeted Markie.

"I'm sorry I can't offer you the kind of dinner you fed me last night. I just got home, and the cupboard is bare. I've been too busy to catch up on shopping."

"It's not a problem," she assured him. "I had dinner a few hours ago."

"Maybe not a problem, but it's still embarrassing." He held out his hands. "I can grow things. I just can't cook them."

Markie smiled. "Different strokes."

His blue eyes sparkled. "In the meantime, Doctor, I offer you gourmet PB and J."

"Gourmet, huh?"

"Only the best," he agreed, leading the way into his kitchen. "Imported. From the States."

"Wow!"

Laughing, he scrubbed his hands clean, then pulled a jar from the refrigerator. "Actually," he said, "if you like blueberry preserves, this stuff is awesome. My sister made it and sent me a few jars."

After the sandwiches were made, they sat at his kitchen table, a piece that looked almost as old as the island's history.

"Where did you get this?" she asked him, running her palm over the scarred surface. "It's beautiful."

"At an estate sale, when I first got here. The auctioneer said it had been used in the kitchen for more than a hundred years."

"It's gorgeous. Did you refinish it?"

"A little sanding and a lot of oil. It was pretty dried out when I bought it."

"I'm glad you didn't sand it smooth."

"That would have been a crime." He paused from his sandwich and looked at her, his eyes saying the small talk was over. "So what's up?"

"I'm not sure. I just know that today I treated eighteen dogs who had chewed themselves raw."

"Mange?"

She shook her head. "No way. This was nervous chewing. I took samples for testing, but this isn't mange. These dogs were fine until the barkingfest last night. Afterward they started chewing themselves raw. God knows how many others have done the same thing but haven't been brought to my attention."

He gave a low whistle and sat back, sandwich forgotten. "What could have scared them that much?"

"I don't know." She picked at the crust from her bread. "Maybe I'm wrong. Maybe it isn't anxiety. Maybe there's some link with whatever killed Cart."

His head cocked, and his face darkened. He reached out for her hand, covering it and squeezing firmly. "That call I got last night? It was about Marilyn Shippey."

Markie drew a breath so sharp it sounded like a drowning person's last gasp. "Oh, my God," she whispered. Her face turned as white as chalk. "I'd heard she got sick, but...not..."

"Unfortunately, yes. I did the post last night. Same kind of deterioration Cart showed."

"Oh, sweet Lord." She closed her eyes, clearly trying to absorb this new horror. Her hand turned over and she linked her fingers with his. "I knew Marilyn." Her eyes popped open. "Where's Shadow?"

"Their dog?"

She nodded.

"CDC quarantined him. He was chewing his leg, too."

"Oh, my God," she said again.

Silence stretched between them for long minutes, a silence filled with foreboding. As if he sensed it, Kato sat up and put his head on Markie's lap. So naturally that she probably didn't even realize she was doing it, she began to rub his scruff.

Declan finally spoke, needing to brush away the chilly cobwebs of disquiet that were trying to wrap around him. "You said you took samples?"

"Skin and blood from every dog."

"I'd like CDC to look at them."

"Of course." She shook her head. Her color had improved a bit. "My initial microscopic exam didn't show anything unusual. I'm waiting for cultures to grow now."

"None of the owners were sick?"

"None seemed to be. But they all had the same weird story about how it started last night." She pushed aside her plate. "I'm sorry, I can't eat. It's just…the timing is wrong for an infectious disease. Why would they all go symptomatic at almost exactly the same time? And if it's some chemical irritant, how did it get to them all at the same time, with some inside and some out, and none of the owners affected?''

Declan nodded, his blue eyes thoughtful. "We need an epidemiological map. Where every affected dog lives."

"Okay. I can put that together from my files."

He put up a hand. "First I'll finish my sandwich...and yours, if you don't want it. I haven't eaten since early this morning."

She looked at him, feeling a twinge of concern. "A lot of patients today?"

He laughed. "Actually, nary a one. I think they're afraid of getting infected. Steve Chase even cancelled. No, I was doing some work for CDC. Questioning people. Trying to track Cart's movements over the last couple of weeks."

"So they *do* think it's infectious."

He shrugged. "At this point, Markie, nobody knows a damn thing. But the dogs might be a clue."

Abel Roth scoured the spreadsheet on his computer with the eye of a falcon circling a field mouse. Hyoko Akagi would be calling in an hour, and Abel knew he would expect an answer. Renovating and shoring up Kansai International Airport—built on an artificial island in 1994 and already sinking—would be a very complex, very expensive project. Roth Financial had a solid record with venture capital, and this loan could reap vast rewards. But it carried equally vast risks. Abel Roth had no doubt he could put together the capital to fund the three-billion-dollar project, but the risk-benefit analysis was edgy.

He was in no frame of mind to deal with his prodigal son when Timothy sauntered through the door of his study and plopped himself in a chair across the desk without so much as a by-your-leave. He refused to spare the boy even a glance.

"What?" Tim said, as if reading his father's mind. "No fatted calf?"

"You've had your share of the fatted calf, and you've chosen to waste it."

Tim shrugged. "That's a matter of opinion. I built a successful business."

Their respective ideas of business success were so far apart that the chasm couldn't be measured. Abel was banker for the world. Timothy took tourists on fishing excursions. There was no comparison.

"I'm expecting a call from Tokyo," Abel said. The implication was clear: *I have bigger fish to fry.*

"No surprise," Tim answered. He knew he was being dismissed, but he didn't move. It gave him pleasure to defy his father. "Have you heard about the Shippeys? Carter and Marilyn?"

Abel moved impatiently. For a man who could be carved stone in a business discussion, he was a deliberate open book with his son. "I approved the quarantine." It was the word of a man who governed by more than mere popular vote. He waved his hand at Tim. "Your mother's in the living room."

Another dismissal. "I'll go see her in a minute."

Finally Abel looked him straight in the eye, the

steely Roth glare that made men quake and women swoon. "What do you want? More money?"

His son shrugged off the look. "Actually, I don't need any money at all. I have quite enough."

"Well, that's revolutionary."

"No. I'm a successful businessman, whether you think so or not. And you know what, Dad?"

"What?"

Tim rose. "Soon I'm going to be richer than Croesus."

At that Abel laughed. "You? Not possible."

"You'll see."

The boy stalked out. Abel shook his head. So much potential. So little ambition. He wasn't merely a disappointment. He was a disgrace.

"My dear!" Lenore Roth said, rising from the sofa and opening her arms to her son. "I've missed you! Where have you been hiding?"

"Business." The word flowed easily off his tongue. In this house, that was always an acceptable excuse.

"How's Dawn? Why didn't you bring her along? I've missed her, too."

"She has some charity thing tonight."

The butler appeared, and Tim ordered a Scotch, neat. Lenore wanted another cup of tea.

She sat again and patted the couch beside her. "Tell me everything. How's the business going? What charity is Dawn involved with now? She's such a generous woman, that wife of yours."

"Yes, she is." So generous that Tim felt totally on the periphery of her life. Which was fine. Like his father, he had bigger fish to fry. "I think they're raising money for an addition to the public playground. Something about replacing the wood with a safer material."

"Oh, yes, I've heard something about that. I must make a donation. And you? How is your business?"

Funny how that was the first thing his family asked about on his infrequent visits, as if it were the beginning and end of existence. Not, *How are you feeling?* Not, *Are you happy?* Always, always *How is your business?*

"It's going well, Mom. My charters are all booked. I'm thinking of expanding."

"Wonderful!" She beamed at him.

It had been a mistake to come here. He'd been feeling so good, so full of himself, that he'd made the mistake of thinking he could tread safely here. He should have known. His father ignored him, and his mother cared only for his bottom line. They made him feel small. In fact, they made him feel downright angry.

He rose from the couch and looked down at her. "It's nice of you to enquire after my health and my emotional well-being."

Lenore looked confused. "You'd tell me if you were ill or if something was going wrong in your life. I just assumed…"

"No, Mother," he said harshly, "you'd probably be the last person on earth I'd tell."

With that he stalked out of the house, past a butler holding his whiskey on a salver, and climbed into his Jeep. As he sped down the coast road, dodging the detritus of last month's flooding, he cursed himself silently.

Idiot. Don't you ever learn?

He would show them. He and Annie would show them all.

Markie and Declan decided not to wait until morning. With two deaths, they couldn't delay. They drove up to Markie's clinic, where they found Alice Wheatley, one of the kennel's night attendants.

Alice was a tiltyish widow with hair the color of snow and one of the kindest faces Markie had ever seen. Alice loved animals, any and all animals, and supported herself by looking after the kennels three or four nights a week. Many nights she had to sleep here, on a cot, because one animal or another was seriously ill or injured. Other times she checked in every few hours to make sure the boarders were doing all right.

Tonight she appeared frazzled, and the instant she saw Markie, she opened her arms and said, "Boy, am I glad to see you, Doc!"

Markie dropped her purse on a chair. "What's wrong?"

"Damned if I know. We've got six boarders and they all went haywire, barking fit to be tied. That wound up the Laneys' dog, and it was all I could do to keep him from tearing his stitches."

Markie glanced at Dec. "He was hit by a car three days ago. We're keeping him under observation."

"He's going to need more than observation if he keeps this up," Alice said darkly.

"I'll check him out," Markie said soothingly. "The rest of them sound quiet now."

"Oh, sure, but take a look at them."

Markie looked oddly at Alice, then pushed her way through the green door that led into the kennel area. It was a huge cement building, filled with indoor-outdoor runs for the animals. Sometimes, especially around holidays, the place was overrun with pets. Tonight there were just seven lonesome dogs.

Not a one of them came to the kennel door to greet her. Not a one of them barked or wagged its tail. Instead, they sat huddled in corners, shaking.

"My God," Declan said. He was right behind her.

Markie lifted the latch on the first kennel and entered it, squatting down in front of Bonzo, a normally friendly golden retriever, a doggy-dog of the best kind.

"Bonzo? Here, buddy." She reached into her shorts pocket and took out one of the bite-size treats she was never without. Slowly, she held it out to the retriever. "Treat, Bonzo? How's my baby doing?"

He looked at her, shuddering, his tongue lolling.

Then he leapt at her.

7

Wendy Morgan rolled over and lit a cigarette. Beside her, Gary reached for a bottle of water, then whispered through parched lips, "Thanks, babe. That was…amazing."

For one of us, Wendy thought. She gave him a smile, confident he couldn't see through it in the near darkness. "Yes, it was."

The truth was, her husband was at best a mediocre lover and often not even that. His frenzied grunts and ragged breaths had been a huge turn-on when she was twenty-one and convinced that no man could find her attractive, back when it was enough to know that her body could actually elicit such a response. If she'd climaxed back then, and she wasn't sure she ever had, those climaxes had been born of validation, not stimulation. That was then.

Now she knew that her body could not only give pleasure but receive it. Exquisite pleasure, of the sort that made every nerve ending tingle, of the sort that left her gasping for air, floating away, anchored to this world only by the persistent flicking of her lover's tongue on her most sensitive nerve bundle, or the grind of his pelvic bone against hers, or the way his hands kneaded her breasts right at the edge of pleasure and pain. This, she had come to realize, was what sex was meant to be. Exquisite, explosive pleasure for her, as well.

She took another drag of her cigarette. Gary was already sliding off into sleep, his head heavy on her shoulder. Part of her wanted to scream in frustration, roll him over and say *I'm glad you had fun, but now it's my turn!* Part of her knew that would be pointless. He was who he was, not much different from the grad student he'd been twenty years ago. Still bookish. Still wearing glasses to try to distract attention from ears that were too large and a chin that was too narrow. Still buying her presents that were too expensive. Still doting on her like a wide-eyed, floppy-eared, wagging-tailed puppy. In many ways, he was still a child.

She had been his first love and he hers. She was his one and only. But, blessed be, he was not hers.

She chuckled silently, stubbing out her cigarette. Her husband was a child. But her lover...now *he* was a man. He had a man's rough hands, a man's sun-weathered skin, a man's penetrating eyes, a man's casual arrogance. He didn't hint, plead or even ask when it came to his sexual needs. He *took* her, as a conquistador must have planted a proud foot on this island almost five hundred years ago and proclaimed it the property of Charles I, the Kingdom of Spain and the Holy Roman Empire. And a man, a real man, did not take that which was worthless, no more than that conquistador would have claimed a useless spit of land. No, when a man claimed something that way, he did so because he valued it, even treasured it.

Her lover treasured her. Not in the simpering, pleadingly devoted way of a child, but in the proud and proprietary way of a man. The mere thought of him pinning her wrists to the bed, devouring her with his kisses, teasing her to the point that she begged, plunging himself into her as if planting a flag...it made her loins twitch and moisten.

Perhaps he was free tonight.

Gary's breathing had fallen into the easy, measured pace of sleep. In a few moments, when she quietly made as if to stretch her arm, he would roll over like the docile puppy he was. And she would slip out of bed. She would pad silently into the closet and shrug on some clothes, then out to the living room for a quick, whispered phone call. Then out to the car and over to her lover, her owner, captor of her heart and soul. He would ravish her until her body was limp and glistening with sweat.

And she would feel like a woman.

Gary felt the bed shift as she eased out, heard the clacking of plastic hangers as she chose her clothes, the soft *fup fup* of her footsteps on the tile floor of the hallway. He heard her breathy whisper, and while he could not make out the words, he didn't have to. A few moments later, the muted *shushump* of the front door being closed, and the quiet purr of the car as she drove away.

His heart squeezed.

The stale tang of her cigarette still hung in the air, mixed with the musk of her belated arousal, the only remnants of her presence. As if she had been here even then. He knew he wasn't enough for her. It wasn't her fault. It was his.

He wasn't a stud. He wasn't the man women fantasized about. He wasn't the mysterious stranger riding into town, or the dashing officer dancing with the ladies, resplendent in his uniform, before he set out to do battle with the forces of darkness. He wasn't the savvy business shark, or the rakish riverboat gambler, or the graceful athlete. He never had been and never would be.

He was a historian. A bookworm for whom the present held interest only as it reflected and fulfilled the past. He knew he could never hold a candle to the great men whose lives and exploits he presented to a classroom full of sleepy, distracted students. He wasn't one of those great men. He studied them. He taught them.

Those who can, do. Those who can't, teach.

In his younger years, when Wendy's love had buoyed his heart and given wing to his dreams, he'd resented that old aphorism. It wasn't true, he'd thought. Teaching was an ancient and honorable profession. After all, Socrates had been a teacher. As had Christ. Wendy taught psychology at the university, when she wasn't busy doing research in parapsychol-

ogy. Teaching *was* doing. And he had seen himself
as continuing that line, helping to assemble and even
contribute to the wisdom of the ages, then pass that
on to the next generation. A noble calling.

Somewhere along the way, assembling and contributing to the wisdom of the ages had given way to
simply living in the past. What had been noble was
now merely nerdish. The dreams had crashed into the
mountainside of Wendy's late night assignations.
Who had he been kidding? He wasn't an heir to the
legacy of Socrates and Christ. He was simply one of
those who couldn't *do*. So he taught. And, judging by
the glassy eyes he saw in his classroom, he didn't
even do that very well.

He would never leave Wendy, of course. It wasn't
her fault. It was his. In the thousands of times during
his childhood when he'd chosen to read a book rather
than join the other kids outside, in the thousands of
moments when he'd privately lauded himself for his
intelligence and derided others for their silly ambi-
tions and petty talents, he'd doomed himself to this
fate. He'd made of himself what he was: a tired—and
tiring—historian and teacher. He would never leave
Wendy, because he deserved his life, to pour out his
love on the woman whose merest smile could still
make his heart glow, only to listen in the darkness as
she slipped away into the arms of another.

He climbed from the bed, looking at the damp spot
on the sheets with self-disgust. He walked into the
bathroom and grabbed a washcloth, then scrubbed his
member clean. Deciding that wasn't enough, he

climbed into the shower, the water turned to an icy blast, and used a loofah to work his skin almost raw, until the soap stung. This had become a habit. Every time he made love to her, he scrubbed another layer of himself away. Sooner or later, his love for her would erase him entirely.

And that, too, was what he deserved.

In the meantime, there was work to do. He wrapped a thin cotton robe around himself and strode to his study. A quick check of his research log, and he reached for the next box of cassette tapes. An oral history of Santz Martina, as told in the local Creole dialect, by the descendents of those who had seen it all happen. He penciled *Volume Six, Tape One* on the log, plugged in the cassette, hit the Play button and closed his eyes. Wendy was going to be surprised by something, at least.

Annie wadda be gran bad wam.

Annie was a very bad woman.

"You're going to her," Dawn Roth said, her voice almost too soft to be heard.

"That's right," Tim replied, reaching for the car keys. "I'll be late."

"You do that," she said.

With that, he was gone. Again. He'd come home that evening, still fuming over the brush-off he'd received from his father. As Dawn saw it, he'd gotten about what he had coming to him. She hadn't offered much in the way of comfort or sympathy. Let him find his comfort and sympathy with Wendy Morgan, the lovestruck dreamer who still believed that some-day Tim would leave Dawn and be hers.

As if.

Dawn had long since resigned herself to the affairs. Tim's ever fragile ego needed his conquests. Wendy hadn't been the first and wouldn't be the last. He hadn't been welcome in Dawn's bed in years, and, truth be told, she didn't miss that. He was too ag-gressive a lover, adept but empty, in her opinion. No, she didn't miss that.

What she missed were the long evenings on the boat, watching the sun paint brilliant metallic red and orange and gold across the sky while they sipped wine and talked about the life they wanted to build. A life without the heavy thumb of business, where their true spirits could soar. Where he made a living doing what he loved and she made a difference doing what *she* loved.

Perhaps the worst thing that had ever happened to them was that dream coming true.

His fishing business had finally taken hold. He no longer had to trade on his family name. And she had her dogs, and the community theater, and her chari-ties. And they'd lost each other.

Tim had it in him to be a good man—if only he would stop trying to be a better man than his father. The simple fact was that he and Abel were too dif-ferent, and yet too alike, to ever appreciate each other. Lacking that, Tim was always looking for a way to put himself over the top. And the good man that he could have been gave way to the hard man that he was.

Caught in the middle, loving both of them, Dawn had buried herself even more in trying to make a difference. Let the men chase their inner demons. Lost dogs she could rescue. Lost men she could not.

"Isn't that right, Brindle?" she whispered to the massive beast beside her. The mastiff looked up at her with deep brown eyes that almost brimmed tears. "Oh, I'll be okay, sweetheart. And so will you. Not much longer now, and you'll be a momma."

The dog's tail swept from side to side, then stilled. Her ears perked, then flattened. She sniffed, let out a great, shuddering *huff,* and tasted the air again.

"What is it, honey?" Dawn asked.

Brindle gave a single bark, sniffed again, and settled back onto her bed, still alert, as if the puppies in her belly left her too little energy to do more than fret.

She'd been fretting a lot, Dawn realized. Maybe it was just the pregnancy. Dawn had never seen a bitch so unsettled before, but every dog, every pregnancy, was different. Yes, maybe it was just the puppies.

And maybe not.

For a terrifying instant, Markie thought she was about to be savaged. She braced, preparing for the worst. Then Bonzo hit her. She was aware of Dec's shout.

But the dog didn't attack her. Instead, it scooted up between her legs, pressing desperately against her, seeking sanctuary. The impact pushed Markie onto her bottom, but she managed to stay upright.

In an eyeblink, she had her arms around the dog. He licked her face, but these licks weren't loving. They were pleading. He wanted her to take him out, and he wanted out *now*. Every whimper he made nearly broke her heart.

"Alice?" she said, talking around the frantic licks she was getting. "I'm going to need sedative injections for these dogs. Valium."

"I'll get 'em."

"What the hell is going on?" Declan asked. He stood in the kennel door, as if still poised to come to her rescue. "What did this to them?"

"I don't know," Markie said, stroking Bonzo soothingly. "I've seen dogs get like this over thunderstorms or fireworks. Noise phobia is common in canines. But…"

"But there's no thunder and no fireworks."

She looked over her shoulder at him while Bonzo continued to lick her cheek and ear. "Exactly."

Kato returned with Alice, his ears pricked, his tail down, as he observed his fellow canines. He joined Markie in the kennel with Bonzo and licked Bonzo until the retriever turned his attention to Kato. The wolf's attention seemed calming.

Twenty minutes later, all the dogs were sedated.

While Alice stayed in the back with Lefty, the dog that had been hit by a car, Dec and Markie settled in her front office. The files from the day were still out, in a neat stack, waiting to be returned to their proper place so Dec pulled out the map of the island he'd brought along, and together they started plotting the addresses.

"It's just so weird," Declan said.

"What is?" As if she didn't know.

"I could see some infectious agent, or some irritant, being swept across the island on the breeze. I could even see the dogs detecting it and being so annoyed by it that they bark themselves silly. But…"

"The fear afterward doesn't make any sense."

"Precisely."

She looked up from the sixth file. "Unless…the agent, whatever it is, instills fear, at least in dogs. Their owners don't seem too upset."

"Maybe they should be. The Shippeys' dog was a mess, just like the dogs you saw today. He was chewing on his leg in frantic bursts last night."

She mulled that over, trying to ignore the disquiet she had been feeling all day in favor of logical thought. "Maybe the military is using us as a test site for some new weapon?"

Even as she spoke the outrageous suggestion she wished she could call it back. It sounded almost insane. Yet, given what was going on, could they afford to overlook any possibility?

He looked at her, eyebrows raised. "Now that *would* be terrifying."

Markie sat back in her chair, forgetting the files for a moment, rubbing her tired neck. "It's been a long day."

"Yes." His gaze said he would rub her neck for her if she wanted. She wanted, but didn't give him an invitation.

She shook her head a little, clearing away unwanted cobwebs of desire that for a moment had seemed to wrap around her. To distract herself, she changed subjects. "Did you know that the Inuit bred huskies *not* to obey perfectly?"

"Uh…no, I didn't. Why'd they do that?"

"Because a dog's senses are so much sharper. If the musher tells the dogs to go right, but the dogs sense a crack in the ice or a crevasse buried under the snow, they'll go left anyway. That's one of the reasons most people discover that they can't handle huskies. That and the fact that they're talkative. Howling and whining all the time, and we're too stupid to understand them, even if they understand a fair measure of English."

"I'm beginning to feel substandard here."

Markie smiled and spread her hands. "That's why we team up with dogs. But it's true. Consider what it means that they can understand so much human language. Or so many body cues. They have language centers in their brains. It stands to reason that they have languages of their own. Huskies and wolves sure seem to."

"I hadn't thought of it that way. And this is going where?"

"I'm thinking maybe we'd better start listening to the dogs. They seem to know something we don't."

In an instant, the sense of doom returned, a dark miasma in the brain.

He nodded slowly, not quite agreeing. "How would we listen?"

"I think we'd better start paying very close attention to their behavior and where it's happening." She paused for a moment, thinking. "You know, dogs can hear much higher sounds than we can. It's possible they're hearing something very high-pitched, a sound at a frequency that's driving them to distraction."

His expression said he didn't like that at all.

"What's wrong?" she asked.

"Well, the dogs were barking the night Carter died, right? And last night around the time Marilyn died."

"Right."

"So if they're hearing some kind of sound that's inaudible to us, and it's in any way linked to the Shippeys' deaths, then…maybe we *are* looking at a weapon of some kind."

Her heart gave a thud at hearing her own crazy suggestion echoed with all seriousness by Dec. "Exactly what happened to them?"

"I'm not supposed to say."

She arched a brow at him and pursed her lips. "Did it look like a disease?"

He sighed heavily, almost impatiently and shook his head. "What the hell. To tell you the truth, Markie, I've never seen the like. Everything inside them was dissolved, including bone."

"Oh, my God…" She tried to imagine it and couldn't. It exceeded belief. "But…then it couldn't really be linked with the barking, could it? I mean...why aren't the dogs dying the same way?''

''Unless it's a weapon.''

''I'm not buying that. I refuse to buy that. How could any kind of weapon be invented that would only kill people and not have the same effect on a dog standing right there? They're not *that* different biologically.''

''I don't know. What I do know is that I can't imagine why anyone with that kind of technology would want to kill Carter and Marilyn Shippey.'' He shook his head, a scowl settling over his features. His next statement was laced with bitterness. ''But maybe they were just collateral damage.''

They sat for a few minutes in silence, files forgotten, each of them lost in rumination about who or what might be doing all this, or whether the events were even linked.

Markie knew for certain that she didn't like the paths her thoughts were following. It was horrifying enough to think a terrible unknown disease had killed Carter, worse to think it might have been a weapon.

''Okay,'' she said finally. ''Skip the sound idea.'' Despite the comfortable temperature of the room, she wrapped her arms around herself and began rubbing her hands over her upper arms as if she were cold. And she *was* cold. Somewhere deep inside. Someplace that didn't respond to the ambient temperature.

Glancing up, she looked out the front windows of the clinic and realized that night had settled its obscuring blanket over the world. The outside security lights were even dimmed, as if a rare fog had crept around them. Her scalp started prickling, as if there were unseen eyes on her.

"Dec?"

"Yes?"

"I feel…" She couldn't bring herself to say it.

"Feel what?" He shifted on his chair and leaned toward her.

"My sister's fey," she said after a pause.

"Fey?"

"She…senses things. I hate it. I hate it when she tells me something is going to happen and it does."

"I can imagine." His voice had taken on a low, calming tone.

She looked at him, the corners of her mouth drawn down tightly. "I…sometimes get those feelings, too. I always ignore them."

He nodded slowly. "What are you feeling?"

"It's…" She shook her head.

"Go on. You can trust me."

She squeezed her eyes shut and felt the coldness inside her, like an icy toothache. "It's evil," she whispered. "I just sense…evil." Bone-chilling evil. As if Satan were standing just inches away.

All of a sudden, Kato, at their feet, lifted his head and howled.

8

The hair on Markie's neck stood on end as Kato howled. Declan rose from his chair, looking around. Evidently he felt it, too. For a horrifying moment, an icy breeze seemed to blow over her. Goose bumps raised the hair on her arms.

They were not alone. The feeling slammed into her, as real and certain as any feeling she'd ever had. She felt eyes on her, felt a presence. Then, as if a switch had been thrown, the feeling was gone.

"Jesus," Dec said.

But Kato didn't give them a chance to say more. He rose to his feet—head tipped back, hackles raised, ears flat against his skull, nostrils flaring—and let out another long, mournful howl.

As the last plaintive note faded in the night, a scream came from the kennels.

"Alice!" Markie jumped to her feet, but Declan beat her to the green door leading to the back. He burst through it. She was right behind him, catching the door before it swung halfway back.

Alice stood in the middle of the row, kennels to either side of her, her back to them. She stood frozen, as if carved from ice.

"Alice," Dec called.

The woman didn't turn.

Markie reached her and touched her arm, turning her to face them. She stared blindly, her face ashen.

"Alice?" Markie asked. The woman's skin felt cold and clammy. "Alice, what's wrong?"

Slowly Alice's eyes began to focus.

"What's wrong?" Markie asked again.

Alice shook herself, as if trying to free herself from a nightmare. "I'm…I'm losing my mind," she said, her voice cracking.

Markie glanced at Dec. His furrowed brow spoke volumes about his concern. She turned back to the Alice. "Why do you say that?"

"Because…because…I'm seeing…ghosts."

Markie found a sweater that she kept at the office and wrapped it around Alice's shoulders. She and Dec encouraged the woman to sit in the front office in the bright lights, and Markie put on a fresh pot of coffee.

"I'm scared," Alice insisted. "I've never felt so cold in my life, not even when I visited my son in North Dakota. He was in the Air Force then…." She trailed off as another shudder ripped through her. "I feel frozen to my very bones."

"The coffee will help," Markie said reassuringly. "And I'm going to call Buddy to stand in for you tonight."

Alice looked at her, her face still ashen. "Don't tell him about me, about what I... I'll stay."

Markie shook her head. "I'll just tell him you're not feeling well. It will be okay."

Dec nodded, giving Alice's shoulder a squeeze. "You've had a shock. You're still too pale. Markie's right. And if you won't take her word for it, I'm also a doctor, and I'll insist."

Alice's head sank for a few seconds. "Okay," she finally said quietly. "I think I can breathe again."

"What did you see?" Markie asked gently.

Alice looked at Markie, her gaze almost pleading. "It didn't feel like I was imagining it. God, I thought I could reach out and touch her."

"Who?" Dec asked.

Fear mixed with shame played over Alice's face. "Annie Black."

Markie stiffened. "I'm calling Buddy right now."

Buddy was young, but he was responsible. His goal was to save enough money so that he could go to veterinary school, and when Markie reached him, he was only too eager.

"Alice doesn't feel well," Markie explained. "I want her to go home. Do you mind coming?"

"Heck, no, Doc. I'll be there in fifteen minutes."

"Thanks, Buddy."

"No problem, mon."

The Jamaican lilt was suddenly strong in his voice, though he hadn't lived in his home country since early childhood. His parents had moved here fifteen years ago to open a shop that sold colorful Jamaican clothing and Blue Mountain coffee. The store was popular with everyone.

"He's a good kid," Alice said when Markie hung up the phone. "He'll go places."

"I think so, too." The coffee was ready, and Markie poured three cups. Alice cupped her hands around her mug as if to absorb every little bit of heat.

"Where's Kato?" Markie asked, suddenly realizing that her dog was nowhere to be seen.

At the sound of his name, there was a skitter of claws from the area of the exam rooms, and Kato emerged. His tail was down, and his ears were back. His hackles had settled, but he didn't look like a very happy animal.

"Looks like he saw her, too," Alice said. Her voice was steady again but still conveyed strain. "God. She looked as solid as you two do. Dressed all in black, with some kind of white cap on her head. Long dress. And her eyes…" A shiver passed through Alice. "I hope I never see eyes like that again."

Declan spoke. "Are you sure it was Annie Black?"

"Yes," Alice said, lifting her eyes to his. "We have that portrait of her in the library. I always wondered how it was that didn't get burned during the uprising."

"So you've seen it?"

"Of course I have." Alice looked at him as if *he'd* lost his mind. "Hasn't everyone?"

"The mind can play some nasty tricks."

Alice didn't cringe from the suggestion. "Sure it can. Didn't I see my own Henry three days after he died, clear as if he were standing there? Didn't I hear his voice, telling me he was happy and he wanted me to be happy, too?''

Dec nodded. "A lot of people have that experience."

"I know." Alice spoke emphatically. "I didn't imagine it. But this time...well...it's not the first time. I saw her at home yesterday."

"What?" Markie asked. She pulled up a chair and joined the other two in the huddle, sipping her coffee to drive the chill away. Kato curled at her feet, for once in his life seeming to need comfort. Outside, in the distance, dogs were barking. Markie reached down and rubbed his ears gently. Studiously, she avoided thinking about the sense of evil she had felt just before Kato howled and Alice screamed.

Dec spoke. "Would you be offended if I suggested a complete physical?"

"Not at all. In fact, I'd appreciate one." Alice held out her hand, looking at it. "Just as real as that. I swear. Right in front of me, she was. Looking at me with this smile. You know how her portrait seems to have no expression at all? She's almost blank. When I saw her...it wasn't a nice smile."

"I'd have been scared, too," Markie said comfortingly. Whether or not she believed Annie Black's ghost had appeared didn't matter. If she'd seen it, she would have been as disturbed as Alice.

Alice sipped coffee quietly for a while. "Thanks, I'm starting to warm up."

"You're welcome."

Alice looked from Markie to Declan. "Trust me, this is one ghost you don't want to see. She looked every bit as evil as the stories about her. Like she could skin you alive and enjoy every minute of it."

Markie made a sound of disgust. "Every time I read those stories, my skin crawls."

"I haven't read much about her," Declan said.

"Call it a hobby," Markie said. "When I was a kid, in upstate New York, I loved the local legends. So wherever I've lived, I've looked up the folklore of the area. But Annie Black is...not just a legend."

Declan nodded, and Markie continued.

"Annie Black was born into a poor home in England. Her mother died giving birth to her, and apparently her father and older brothers were, well, pimping her out to local miners by the time she was twelve. She got pregnant very young but lost the baby, either a miscarriage or more likely a botched abortion, and nearly died. While she was recovering, she met up with an older prostitute, and together with the woman and her pimp, she murdered her father. The details were...horrific. She was thirteen years old."

"Wow," Declan said. "Bad seed or bad start?"

"Who's to say?" Markie replied. "But if she thought she'd won her freedom by killing her dad, she was wrong. The woman's pimp just added her to his stable. She was supposedly sold as a sex slave in 1786, to a man named Jamison Black, and he paid a crooked priest to make it a legal marriage."

"Out of the frying pan," Alice whispered.

Markie nodded. "Black brought her here, to Santz Martina. He was a privateer, with letters of marque from the British Crown. The king gave him two hundred troops and five vessels, with orders to take this island from the Spanish and use it as a raiding base against the newly independent United States. He took Santz Martina, then decided there was more money and less risk in molasses and rum. So he expanded the island's cane plantations and became the first governor of Santz Martina. Annie was miserable, but he didn't care. She had affairs with slaves. He caught her and threw her in jail. Turns out the jailer was one of her former lovers. Together, they murdered him. Of course, she'd set it up so the jailer took the blame."

"Ruthless and clever," Declan said. "A dangerous combination."

"And rich," Markie added. "As Black's wife, Annie inherited the sugar plantation. That accounted for the bulk of the island's revenue, so of course she was on the next governor's A-list. Legend says she was also sleeping with him, but nobody knows. All we do know is that she killed her next husband, though his death was written off to yellow fever. And she kept the plantation, of which she was a brutal mistress. She had slaves hanged, or beheaded, for her dinnertime entertainment. She caught one of her maids stealing food. She marched into the maid's quarters, pulled her baby out of the crib, took the baby into the kitchen and plunged it into a pot of boiling soup."

Declan winced. "I had no idea."

Markie nodded. "And she ate the soup.

"And so it went, until 1807, when she married Frederick Glass. Glass was something of an abolitionist. Allowed slaves to earn their freedom after thirteen years' service. Wanted to end slavery altogether. He had no stomach for Annie's cruelty, nor for her affairs. He threatened to divorce her and have her arrested. Under the laws of the time, the plantation would have gone to him. She murdered him in 1809. And that's what triggered the Rebellion. Her household slaves bound her with wire, and burned out her eyes, ears and tongue so she couldn't see, hear or speak any curses against them. Then they covered her body with pitch, burned her to ash and spread the ashes all over the island, so she could never again have physical form."

Markie held up her hands. "And that, in a nutshell, is the legend of Annie Black."

Alice shuddered and looked from one to the other of them. "What I want to know is why I saw her."

For that, Markie had no answer.

9

After Buddy arrived, Declan and Markie escorted Alice home, watching from Markie's car until the older woman was safely inside and waved from a window. Kato whimpered, just briefly, then quieted as they pulled away from the house.

"Let's go to my place," Markie said. The files they'd been working on were in her trunk, along with Dec's map. "We can work on the map there."

"Sure."

But the truth was, she didn't want to be at home alone. Never in her life had she felt so...exposed. Somehow at risk. Telling herself she was being silly and overreacting wasn't helping. She just knew that if she were home alone with Kato and he started howling like that, she was going to become as much of a basket case as Alice had been.

The realization shamed her, but there was no denying the truth of it. She was possibly more unnerved than she had been in her entire life. Kato's strange behavior wasn't helping a bit. He was still on alert, his golden eyes flitting around, ears perked.

As if reading her mind, Declan said, "Kato sensed something back there."

"Yes."

She pulled into her driveway, set the brake and turned off the ignition. "You know what's really ironic?"

"What?"

"I moved to this damn island to get away from my sister's premonitions and feelings. She was driving me nuts with them."

"You mean telling you what to do all the time?"

"No, it wasn't like she was my personal horoscope or something. She'd have these dreams or visions about earthquakes, tornadoes, plane crashes, car crashes… Anything and everything, and not one thing anyone could prevent." Markie shook her head, trying to shed the chill that wouldn't leave her.

"Was she right?"

"Too often for comfort. I couldn't take it anymore. What good does it do to know there's going to be an earthquake in Asia in the next twenty-four hours? Who's going to listen?"

"I see your point."

"And now I'm cooped up with a dog who's doing the same thing." She looked back at Kato, who was still sitting up in the back seat.

"Did you come here just to get away from your sister?"

She sighed and shook her head. "No. That was just

a small part of it. Jeez, she can still call me on the phone when she gets upset, although she doesn't do it as often."

"These visions upset her?"

"Of course they do. And then she upsets me."

"Does she tell anyone else?"

"She's working with someone at the Rhine Institute. I don't know much about it."

That shivering sense filled her again, and the desire to get into the house nearly overwhelmed her. Behind her, Kato whimpered briefly, quietly. "Come on, let's get this stuff inside and see if we can't figure something out."

Declan hefted the files from the trunk and carried them inside. She let Kato off his leash. Ordinarily he would dash around to the back of the house and relieve himself while she retrieved the mail and went in the front, then wait for her by the kitchen door. Tonight, he simply sat by her left heel, still sniffing the breeze warily. She led him to the door.

"C'mon, Kato. We'll walk later."

Once inside, she offered Dec coffee, but he declined.

"I'll be up all night," he said. "I'll take a bottle of water, though."

The island's only fresh water source had a sulfurous taste to it, something even purification couldn't quite remove. So, like most folks, Markie bought bottled water. She retrieved two bottles from the fridge, poured a third into Kato's bowl and joined Dec at the counter.

Apparently Dec wasn't ready to get back to work, however. "You said your sister wasn't the only reason you came here."

Markie's heart sank. She didn't want to get into all this. It would have been so easy to deflect the question, change the subject. But she'd opened the door, and it seemed rude to slam it closed in his face.

"I'm sorry," he said, with a quickness of perception that surprised her. "I shouldn't have asked."

She could have let it slide then, but somehow his understanding made that impossible. "Actually, the biggest reason I came here was so I wouldn't have to euthanize so many animals."

His eyebrows lifted as the corners of his eyes creased with something very like sympathy. "How do you mean?"

"Well, I had to put down a lot of dogs and cats that could have lived if only the owners could have afforded surgery or to have a leg set. It's not like that here. Nobody has to pay for vet care. I'm on salary through the territory. So if an animal is ill, I can treat it without having to worry about how much it will cost and whether the owner can afford it."

He nodded. "That's one of the things I like, too. Universal health care. But I never thought about it in relation to your profession."

"I have. Too much." She bit her lower lip and tried to push away memories of too many patients who were now gone. "I feel guilty when a patient dies, Dec. Even if I've done everything I can. Even if I know it was just that animal's time. One of God's cruelest tricks is how animals can worm their way into our hearts, yet they have such short lifespans compared to ours.

"Now imagine how I felt when I *knew* I could have saved an animal, but the owners couldn't afford it. I couldn't adopt them all, nor could *I* afford to treat them all for free. That wasn't something I'd thought much about when I was a student. It wasn't until I was working for a group practice that I was really forced to face it. After a few years, it was a constant weight on my heart."

Unexpectedly he reached out and squeezed her hand, holding it. "I can understand that."

She looked straight at him.

Declan held up a hand. "Yes, I can. I don't have to euthanize anyone, obviously, but I used to work in a city hospital E.R. I saw plenty of senseless death. It weighs on you even when it isn't your fault. Having to actually do it, put the patient down, must be even worse."

She drew a deep breath, trying to steady her emotions. Tears were so near the surface, and she hated that. "I was starting to feel like a sham. I guess I was just too naive when I started down this road."

"But at least you have a place now where that doesn't happen."

"And I have every intention of keeping it."

He smiled, the corners of his eyes crinkling in a way she liked. "Good."

She felt raw, as if she had stripped away some of her own skin. But even more tumbled out of her. "I know a lot of people thought I was overreacting. The doctors I worked for kept telling me not to get personally involved with my patients. But it wasn't personal involvement. I didn't know these animals. I didn't have to. They were living beings, and I felt like an executioner.''

Kato was suddenly there, resting his head on her thigh. She reached out to stroke his head. ''Anyway, how can you not get attached? It's like he reads my mind and heart.''

''He does seem to.'' Dec released her hand and waited patiently, apparently aware that she was dealing with an inner storm.

But she'd been through this and had tried to put it behind her, and she had the strength to do so again. It was just that his question had made it fresh again for a few minutes.

''I'm fine,'' she said briskly. ''Now let's finish up this map.''

Eighteen dogs. Eighteen addresses. They sat staring at the map, and Dec felt a distinct unease. The marks followed a pattern, as if something had blown in from the northwest, over the Plantation Hills subdivision, over Harbor Street and Carter Shippey's house, across to La Puerta and Markie's clinic, finally stopping just north of the cathedral cemetery.

''I wish we knew what happened when,'' Dec said. ''A timeline would help.''

''It happened fast,'' Markie told him. ''I heard the

dogs barking. It was like a wave passing through. Well, you heard it, too. It didn't last all that long.''

"But Kato sensed it long before the dogs started barking."

Markie nodded thoughtfully.

"I'm trying to remember," he said, closing his eyes for a moment. He remembered Kato's reaction. He remembered how the barking had started, and how it had driven him to step outside. And then it had passed away.

He opened his eyes, suddenly certain. "It came out of the northwest."

"There's nothing out there. It's wilderness."

He felt a twist deep inside. "Nothing out there except..." He pointed at the map with his index finger. "Except the old fort."

Markie stared at the map, then slipped off her stool and began pacing. "That place has been abandoned since when...the 1920s?"

"They reopened it for a couple of years during the mess with Cuba. I guess they put up a few Quonset huts, installed some radar and antiaircraft stuff."

She leaned over to see the map better. "Unfortunately, that could support the weapon idea."

"Yeah."

All of a sudden she reached out and clutched his shoulder. "Oh, God!"

"Why?"

"The dogs are barking again."

He nodded, his eyes narrowing. "I know, but there's no way to know—"

She put a fingertip on the map, just above the cemetery, just a block and a half from her house. "Alice lives here."

He didn't argue with her, even though she expected it. If she'd sounded crazy earlier when she'd voiced the idea of a weapon, she knew she must sound like a lunatic now. But lunacy or not, she couldn't resist the compulsion.

Not one word of argument passed his lips, however. He simply nodded and stood.

But Kato had different ideas. Once again, he blocked Markie's way, his lowered head saying there was no way he was going to let her pass.

"Kato, for Pete's sake," Markie said impatiently. But before she could finish her reprimand, the chilly sense of foreboding trickled once again down her spine.

She knelt, taking Kato's head between her hands and looking into his incredible golden eyes. Her voice was little more than a whisper. "That's what you're feeling, isn't it?"

For an instant she felt a preternatural connection with the dog, as if some part of each of them melded in complete understanding. She'd had the feeling before, but not to this degree. For long moments she continued to squat, perfectly still, letting the feeling fill her.

When she rose, she faced Dec, expecting to see skepticism. Instead, she saw only a query.

"Kato's going with us," she said quietly. "He thinks I'm in danger."

* * *

Wendy always met Tim on his boat. Tonight, however, the marina wasn't a welcoming place. In fact, she found herself reluctant to get out of the car. All the streetlights in town had gone off as she had driven this way, and the lights at the marina were out, too. Some sort of power outage, she supposed. All she could see were the shadowy, dim shapes of piers and masts past her headlights, headlights that seemed unable to penetrate the darkness. It was almost as if there was some kind of invisible fog out there.

For a minute she toyed with going home, gallon of milk in hand, so if her husband woke, she could claim she'd gone out to the convenience store. But Tim was here somewhere, and the craving for him overwhelmed her caution.

Besides, nothing bad ever happened in Martina Town. This place might have started as a pirates' haven, but over the years it seemed to have inbred to placidity. She had nothing to fear from the dark, other than tripping.

A knock on her side window caused her to jump and squeak, but then she saw Tim's face grinning at her. Suddenly the lack of light seemed romantic, not threatening at all.

He opened her car door and waited while she climbed out. "What's with the lights?" she asked, trying to act casual. She'd already learned that Tim didn't like any hint that their affair was anything more. Time would change that, she promised herself.

"I don't know." He shrugged, his teeth the brightest thing in the night. "Inside lights are working. They must've blown something on the circuits for the streetlights."

He slipped his arm around her waist and gave her one of those demanding kisses that thrilled her all the way to her toes. "Come on, baby, the bunk's waiting."

Sometimes she wished they would take more time to talk first, but Tim wasn't like that. At times she thought he must be a pirate reincarnated. Another thrill shuddered pleasurably through her. They could talk later. They always did.

For a little while, at least.

Kato's presence made Markie feel a little better—until they stepped outside and saw that the streetlights were out everywhere, casting the town into a darkness it had rarely known since the advent of gaslight.

Lights still burned in the houses, but that was it. And nobody was driving the quiet streets. *Ghost town.* The crazy thought popped into Markie's head and caused her to shiver, even though the night was warm and balmy.

Tim rutted her with a eerie, alien passion, his hips grinding against her, his fingers clenched tight in her hair, pulling her face to his, mauling her lips with hard kisses. Wendy had never seen him like this. This was beyond the conquistador claiming his prize. This was…battle.

Her legs hung over the side of the bunk, splayed,

and she could already feel the bruises forming on her buttocks as he drove her again and again into the hard teak rail. Her sharp yelps only seemed to spur him on, and in fleeting moments between stabs of pain, her own sex quivered and shuddered in reply. But more and more, arousal gave way to rising discomfort.

Finally, trying to break his focus and bring his attention back to her, she raked her nails down his back, hard, knowing she was drawing blood.

For a moment, he paused and looked at her, an almost inhuman fire in his eyes. "Yes," he hissed.

An unearthly quiet seemed to settle over Kato as they approached the house. He could see other dogs in the neighboring yards, barking, clawing at fences and windows, but their voices were silent to him. His shoulders and neck tensed as his hackles rose to attention, and he lowered his head, eyes narrowed, trying to see the darkness within the darkness. The leash was taut, and a distant part of him registered Markie's command to heel. But there were times to obey and times to mind his own counsel. This was one of the latter.

He lowered his hips and shoulders and lunged forward, feeling the leash go slack as it flew from her fingers. "Kato!" she cried, but that was behind him. His attention was fixed ahead, on the black, burned, sickly sweet scent that seemed to rise from the house like a cloud. Legs driving, muscles rippling, ears flared back, teeth bared, he charged toward the door.

* * *

Wendy clawed him again, harder, digging deep into skin and muscle beneath, tearing, pulling, until she felt the sharp, icy snap of acrylic breaking away from her nail. Now his eyes seemed to darken, almost losing focus, then clenching shut as he shuddered deep within her, grinding her bruised bottom even harder on the teak until the last flutters of his climax ended.

She tried to push him away, to ease the awful pressure beneath her. Her hands left shiny, black, wet smears on his shoulders. His blood, in the light of the full moon. Bile rose in her throat, and she struggled, pushing, until finally he sagged to the floor.

''What the hell was that?'' she asked.

''God damn,'' was all he could reply.

Markie watched in horror as Kato crashed into and through the French door of Alice's house, glass shattering in moonlit sparkles. She broke into a run.

''Kato!'' she called.

Declan was already moving, easy long strides carrying him past her and to the door. He, too, yelled for the dog.

''Kato!''

Markie reached the door two steps behind him, as he reached inside and opened the dead bolt, then swung the door open. Flecks and smears of blood marked the dog's path. The veterinary mind in Markie registered that Kato must have cut himself as he broke through the glass. The other mind—owner, companion—quailed in fear as she followed Declan down the hall. He froze in a bedroom doorway.

"What the hell?"

"Tim!" Wendy snapped, slapping his face. "What the hell were you doing?"

His eyes turned up to her, a dark glow deep within the pupils. "Now," he whispered. "Now I understand."

We're leaving. The order came down today. Pack up fast, we're outta here. I just hope I get away in time. Those damn bones...

10

Declan watched in horror as Alice Wheatley's body shuddered and spasmed. Kato was snapping at the air around her, low, feral growls emanating from deep in his belly. And yet the awful dance continued, her feet scraping across the painted wood floor. Her hands flailed at the air, clenched at her throat, tore at her blouse. And her eyes...her eyes...

A silent scream creased her face, but it was her eyes that Declan would see in his nightmares. Wide with terror and pain, unfocused, seeing beyond the veil of reality into eternity, as she skittered across the floor.

Finally, finally, the spasms ended and she slumped to the floor with a wet thud. Declan crossed the room in two steps, then paused as Kato whirled, his teeth bared.

"Kato, no!" Markie yelled.

The wolf's eyes flickered over to her for an instant, then returned to Declan.

"Kato!"

The last scream seemed to reach the dog. He froze, looked at Markie, at Dec, then turned to sniff Alice. His haunches sagged to the floor, and he turned up his face to utter a long, mournful wail.

Hoping it was safe to approach, Declan walked over and knelt beside Alice's body. He took her wrist in his hand to search for a pulse, but he already knew what he would find. There was no pulse, and the wrist bones seemed to give way beneath even that soft touch.

"She's dead," he said, turning to Markie.

Markie's face seemed frozen in time, her lips parted in a gasp for breath that would not come. Then her entire spirit seemed to sag.

"Oh, no. Not Alice."

Death was stalking too close. The residents of Santz Martina were, by and large, a healthy lot. The mortality rate was usually very low. He might see one or two deaths a month. Now he'd had three in a week.

And he'd watched Alice Wheatley die.

In his time as an E.R. surgeon, he'd watched more than a few patients leave this world. Car accidents, gunshot wounds, drug overdoses, heart attacks. He'd watched people fight with every last reserve of energy for that final breath, and he'd watched people seem to just let go, accepting their fate with an eerie peace. He'd seen a young man slide into tachycardia as the last of his life blood drained onto green sheets, muscles fluttering with the last expulsions of electrical impulses from a dying brain. He had seen death.

But he had never seen anything like this.

Wave after wave of revulsion swept over him as he made what he knew was a useless search for vitals. This woman was not simply dead. She had been savaged, from the inside out, and he had watched it happen. Now, with every touch, he felt bones turning gelatinous beneath his fingertips. And with every touch, he silently cursed any God who would permit such a horror.

Finally he rocked back onto his heels, staring at his hands as if wishing they could somehow possess and transmit a magic powerful enough to undo the terrible damage that had been wrought on Alice Wheatley's body. Whatever that magic might be, if it even existed, he knew one thing with an awful certainty.

He didn't have it.

He couldn't do a goddamned thing.

Kato's golden eyes glittered in the disquieting swirl of red and blue emergency lights. He was by no means relaxed, but he was at least compliant enough that Markie could dab at his wounds with alcohol swabs.

"You are one lucky pooch," she said, trying to sound reassuring and cheerful.

She could only imagine what the stinging scent of alcohol was doing to his canine nose, not to mention what the liquid itself was doing to the myriad tiny lacerations around his snout. Still, he did not move.

"You could have died crashing through that glass."

If he had an answer, he kept it to himself. Instead,

his eyes simply bored into a space inside her head. If a dog were capable of a thousand-yard stare, this was it. She had to remind herself that he had sensed something beyond what she had seen.

And what she had seen had been horrific enough.

She knew she was in denial, focused on Kato as a way to avoid her own grief and horror. On the other hand, as a vet, she had long since internalized the old cavalryman's creed: "First the horse, then the saddle, then the man." Kato needed the attention, not only medically but also emotionally.

He'd known Alice most of his life, and animals feel shock and grief, too. There were countless stories of dogs who would run away from a new owner's home to sit at their old owner's grave, or by their old owner's house. She recalled stories of rescue dogs working the Oklahoma City bombing, and how their handlers had to deal with the dogs' growing depression at finding one dead body after another. The handlers had taken to covering a fireman with a bit of rubble and leading the dog to him, just so the dog could experience finding a live person. It was hardly surprising that Kato had a thousand-yard stare.

"How's he doing?"

Markie turned to see Declan standing beside her. His eyes looked as haunted as Kato's.

"Minor cuts on his snout. And he's pretty shaken up."

He nodded. "And how about you?"

That was a question she didn't want to answer, or

even consider. "I'm hanging in there," she offered with a great deal more courage than she felt.

"Me, too."

At some point, they would have to talk about it. But not now. Right now it was too fresh, too raw. It was as if her soul had been scraped with a metal rasp, disbelief and pain oozing from the wound like bloody lymph. It would need to scab over before she could touch it.

She looked around, occasionally catching a glimpse of a face in a window here, another there. At the corner, old Loleen Cathan stood next to a lamppost, eyes closed, ebony skin almost invisible in the dark, lips murmuring, hands shaking a bead necklace. Loleen was something of an island institution. No one was quite sure how old she was; the guesses ranged from ninety on up. Hundreds of islanders called her "Gram," though Markie had no idea how many of them were blood descendants and how many simply saw her as the matriarch of the island's native population.

"What's she doing?" Declan asked.

"Praying," Markie said quietly. "The rattle of the beads is supposed to help guide the soul to heaven."

He nodded. "Can't hurt."

The sound of wheels scrunching on grit drew her attention away from the old woman. The CDC van arrived. Finally. As Marshall Wilcox led a team of biosuited technicians into the house, Joe Gardner walked over to them. His eyes spoke of all too rare sleep, interrupted by Declan's call earlier.

"Another one?" he asked.

"Alice Wheatley," Declan said. "White female, age fifty-four."

"You found her?"

Declan looked at him for a long moment. "I watched it happen."

Joe pulled out a pocket cassette recorder, checked the tape and clicked the record button. "Tell me everything."

Markie felt the wound in her soul tear again.

"She was seizing when we got here," Declan said. "Or that's what it looked like."

It was the closest medical explanation for what he had seen. But seizure patients usually collapsed to the floor almost immediately, as the brain lost control of the body and balance gave way to gravity. Alice hadn't. It was as if something had been holding her up.

Joe nodded. "How long did the seizure last?"

"I don't know. It seemed like forever. I'd guess thirty seconds."

"After you arrived."

"Yes. I've no idea how long she'd been seizing before that."

"Of course." Joe paused for a moment, as if reluctant to voice the next question, although it had to be asked. "Why did…what brought you here?"

"She worked for me," Markie said. "I'd sent her home from work earlier. I wanted to check on her, see how she was feeling."

It wasn't the whole truth, but apparently Markie wasn't ready to tell the Centers for Disease Control about ghosts in the night and dogs that seemed to sense evil around them. Neither was he. The steady parade of death and ugliness in the E.R. had left him with an empty space where his belief in God had once resided. He wasn't about to replace that with a belief in evil spirits.

Joe looked at her. "And you are…?"

Declan watched her spine stiffen at his ever-so-subtly dismissive tone. "Markie Cross. I'm the island's veterinarian."

He nodded. "And what did the victim do for you, Ms. Cross?"

Declan had had enough. "Alice Wheatley was one of *Dr.* Cross's technicians."

He knew the emphasis on the word "Doctor" had dripped more bile than necessary, but he would be damned if some hotshot CDC weenie was going to disrespect Markie's education, experience and expertise.

"My apologies," Joe said. "So you sent the victim home. Was she ill?"

Markie seemed to weigh her words carefully. "I don't think so. More…spooked."

"Spooked?"

She nodded. "Needless to say, people are a bit edgy here. The dogs seem to be feeling it, too. We'd had a long day. I treated eighteen dogs who were chewing themselves raw. Then, last night, all the dogs erupted in a barking frenzy. Alice got...nervous. She'd had a long day. So I sent her home.''

"Tell me about the dogs," Joe said.

"I was planning to do that today," Declan answered. "She called me yesterday. She thought it might be related to this...whatever it is. You know how busy we were at the lab. I couldn't get over here until tonight. I guess I was too late."

"Don't," Markie said. Her eyes said the rest: *Don't protect me. Don't blame yourself.* "Dr. Gardner, I took blood, skin and hair samples from all the dogs. My initial labs didn't show anything. No indicators of mange or fungal infections. Histamine and white cell levels were normal. I called Dr. Quinn and suggested he forward the samples to your lab for testing. He came over, and while we were discussing my findings, the dogs went berserk. Alice got nervous, and I sent her home. Dr. Quinn and I talked over the cases some more. He mentioned that the Shippeys' dog had shown the same symptoms. I...decided we should go check on Alice."

"What about him?" Joe asked, looking at Kato. "The victim's dog?"

"No," she said. "He's mine. I live a couple of blocks from here, so we walked over. He came along."

"And his wounds?"

"I guess he heard her seizing. He crashed through her French door. Minor cuts and scrapes. He'll be fine."

It was close enough to the truth, Declan thought. It

might even *be* the truth, for all he knew. It was certainly better than making fools of themselves with tales of Annie Black's ghost. Or a secret government weapon.

"We'll need to quarantine him," Joe said. "For testing."

"I don't think that's possible," Markie said.

"He had an open wound, and he touched the victim. He could be infected. Or a disease vector. We either quarantine him or I'll have to order him destroyed."

She rose and looked him in the eye. Her voice was low and even, but there was no mistaking the anger. "And what…exactly…*Doctor*…are your facilities for quarantining an eighty-pound wolf hybrid?"

"We usually—" he began, but Markie cut him off.

"CDC usually calls on local animal control or veterinary hospitals to quarantine animals. Well, my clinic is that local facility. I'll quarantine him."

"I…"

"Dr. Cross is the expert on animal medicine," Declan said. "Her clinic is licensed. I'm sure it meets federal standards for animal quarantine."

"This is my profession," Markie said. "I'll keep Kato in quarantine, isolated from the other animals in the clinic. If he shows any symptoms, I'll take samples and forward them to you. Unless, that is, you and your team have the training, experience and resources to deal with an adult wolf?"

"No," he said, glancing at Kato's golden eyes.

"No, you're quite right, Dr. Cross. You handle the animal patients. We'll handle the humans."

He turned and walked away.

"Jackass," Markie muttered.

"He's a bit full of himself," Declan agreed.

"He's not the only one," she said.

"What?" Dec felt a shudder of shock hit him.

"You're a good man, Declan Quinn. And a good doctor. But please, don't patronize me. I've handled my share of bureaucratic assholes in my life. I don't want or need a protector."

"I'm sorry," he said. "I didn't mean to…"

"I need a friend, Dec. Not a knight in shining armor. A friend. An equal. Please."

The look in her eyes hurt almost as much as anything that had happened in the past week. In that instant, he realized how much she'd come to mean to him. And how much that frightened him.

"I'm sorry, Markie. I was wrong."

She seemed to weigh his words for a moment, studying his eyes, then looked down. She reached out to touch his hand. "You had honorable intentions. I overreacted."

"We're both a little wired," he said.

"More than a little." She looked at Kato. "And I need to get him home…into quarantine."

"I'll walk you," he offered. "There's nothing more I can do here, and my car's there, anyway."

"Thanks," she said. "I'd like that."

After picking up Kato's leash, she tapped her thigh, and Kato came to heel. As they passed Loleen Cathan at the corner, Declan heard the woman whisper almost soundlessly.

"Annie wadda be gran bad wam."

The streetlights came back on.

Steve Chase was almost blessedly asleep when the phone rang. His wife's snore broke off in midroar, then resumed its sawlike rasp. He loved that woman, but there were times when he wanted to put a plastic bag over her head and let her snore herself into oblivion permanently.

Like tonight. Sleep was dancing at the far edges of his consciousness, stubbornly darting away nearly every time he caught it. Tonight his wife's snoring was a major irritant. When the phone rang, it at least gave him an excuse to leave the bedroom and go to the living room. An excuse, maybe, to fall asleep on the couch, which approached the comfort of a medieval rack but which was at least silent.

"Hullo," he said, sounding more asleep than he was.

Abel Roth's voice boomed angrily into his ear. "What the hell is happening on this island?"

Steve blinked, no longer even hopelessly flirting with sleep. His entire body stiffened to rigid attention, and he stood in the dark, listening to a friend and colleague talk down to him as if he were a troublesome neighborhood brat.

"I beg your pardon?" he said. This wasn't like Abel Roth. Yes, he held the power on this island— not so much because he was governor as because he was Abel Roth, banker to the world—but he didn't usually need to demonstrate it directly. A subtle word here. A shake of the head there. This…this was…

"Does the Governor's office have an issue with the Senate?" Steve asked, his tone stiffly formal.

"Oh, don't get on your high horse with me, Chase," Roth said. "You're the Senate President. What the hell are you guys doing about this mess?"

"If you could give me a clue…"

"Alice Wheatley just died. I got a call from Bill Thomas." Bill Thomas was a member of the island's police force, a man who was bucking for a promotion by whispering in influential ears. Steve cordially disliked the man.

"What did she die from?"

"That's what I mean!" Abel bellowed. "Why the hell aren't you on top of this?"

The last of Steve's strength seeped away. "I didn't know…." But he sounded weak and apologetic even to his own ears.

"Three deaths in less than a week from a cause unknown! Why aren't you people all over the CDC? Good God, do you know what this is doing to property values? Not to mention that the locals will be calling for our heads before long."

If Steve hadn't been so unnerved himself, he might have heard the merest hint of fear in Abel Roth's own voice. Fear because the deaths were spreading, fear because he couldn't get off his own damn island.

And fear that the delicate balance of power that was Santz Martina might crumble. As things stood, the

Roth, Chase and Morgan families had a virtual license to print money…so long as they took care of the people who did the grunt work. The territory was ostensibly a democracy, with an elected governor and senate, but no one ran against the handpicked candidates from the three families. Even if someone had, he would have lost. The people were happy with the way things had been running. Everyone got a slice of the good life, so why complain?

But if this epidemic spread and the government seemed powerless to stop it, all of that would change. Opposition candidates would rise up, perhaps even win. And the island cash cow might well disappear.

But at that moment Steve Chase was beyond such thoughts. Terror washed though him in hot and cold waves. Another one. Just like the Shippeys.

"I'll…I'll look into it, Governor," he stammered finally.

"You do that." Abel Roth slammed the receiver down.

Steve didn't hang up his own phone. Instead, he stood staring at the receiver in his hand, thinking that just yesterday Gary Morgan had suggested Alice's yard as another possibility. At Tim's behest, Steve had issued a permit for the water department to dig there.

Just today. And now Alice was dead.

His knees buckled, and he sagged onto the couch, shaking all over.

11

"It's got to be a weapon," Dec said. In the fluorescent light of Markie's kitchen, she looked as pale as a corpse. At the moment, he wasn't sure he had much more color himself.

Whatever Kato had sensed still had him spooked. The dog had stationed himself at the sliding glass door, staring steadfastly into the dark, twitching not so much as a muscle.

"Oh, yeah," Markie said, her voice sarcastic even though the idea had been her own suggestion. "A weapon. Sure. It makes dogs bark and chew at themselves, and kills individuals with pinpoint precision. Something that Kato was trying to bite. My God, Dec, if it was a weapon, how come it didn't kill us both when we got there?"

He wished he had an answer, but there wasn't one.

"You heard what Loleen said. You heard what Alice saw tonight!"

"Oh, for the love of Pete! There's no way I'm

going to swallow a ghost. There's a physical cause for this, including for the hallucinations. We just have to find it.''

She sagged onto one of the stools and released a long, unsteady breath. ''I hope you're right.'' Then she burst into tears. ''Alice…oh, Alice…''

It wasn't much, but at least it was something he could *do*. Drawing close to her, he wrapped both arms around her and held her tight, letting her tears flow over both of them.

And in his mind's eye, the horrific vision of Alice in her final, deadly spasms played over and over.

Over Markie's head, he saw Kato, posted like a sentry at the last line of defense, painfully alert. That dog knew more than he did. More by far. And Dec was quite certain that when he discovered the truth himself, he wasn't going to like it.

He had a feeling that he was being forced through a door to ideas and beliefs that he'd long ago shut out. His brain had recorded images he could not accept and it refused to let them go.

Markie stretched and yawned, and in the way of such things, Dec's own body cried out for a yawn.

''You're tired,'' Markie said.

''So are you,'' he replied. He wasn't sure where this was going, nor where he wanted it to go. ''Are you going to be able to sleep?''

She nodded. ''I don't think I'll have much choice. However I feel otherwise, I'm exhausted.''

He could see the tension in her face. He had no doubt his own face bore the same strain. Part of him wanted to stay here with her. Part of him knew better than to ask. And another part of him was too afraid to.

"I'll see you tomorrow?" she asked.

"Of course," Dec said. "You're sure you're okay?"

She looked at Kato. "I'm well protected."

Somehow, he didn't doubt that.

"Tomorrow, then."

"Yes," she said. "Tomorrow."

Dawn was still up when Tim returned home. She was sitting curled up on the living room love seat, turning the pages of a hardcover thriller. She looked up as he entered, gave him a smile and said, "Steve called. He sounded upset. Something about your father."

"Yeah."

Tim never quite knew how to react to his wife these days. She knew he'd gone out to meet Wendy Morgan, and she didn't say a word. Instead, she continued to smile at him as she always had, continued to care for him as she always had, all except for the sex. She'd turned off that tap years ago. But nothing else had changed.

This wasn't the reaction he'd expected, those long years ago when his eye had begun to stray. She ought to be furious, brokenhearted...*something*. Something that would make him feel like a heel. Something that would tell him she cared. Instead, she just smiled and went on. And he was left wondering exactly what he was to her. The thought made him angry.

She nodded and started to go back to her book. Then she looked up again. "Oh! Your mother called. She wants to know if you're coming to your father's birthday party."

"Oh, hell, she knows better than that."

"Well, that's what I told her, but I promised to come myself." Her head bowed again, her attention returning to the book.

For some reason tonight he didn't want life to go on the way it had been. He wasn't willing to let her be sweet and selfless and go back to her own activities, even though his back was raw from Wendy's nails and his shirt betrayed him with blood streaks.

"Every damn streetlight went off in town," he said.

She looked up, her expression pleasant. "Really? I didn't notice anything here."

"It was just the streetlights. Nothing else."

"How strange." She waited.

Sometimes he wanted to shake the passivity out of her, and now was one of those times, but he restrained himself. "Yeah. Could hardly see to get on and off the boat."

"But you managed?"

And there it was again. Intellectual curiosity, without a hint of emotional involvement. Had he *managed* to have sex with Wendy Morgan, despite the power failure? As if she were asking if he'd *managed* to pick up a gallon of milk at the store on the way home. Well, fuck that.

"Oh, yeah, we managed. God, did we manage," he said, and gave a sniggering laugh that sounded as if it had issued from someone else.

The memory of what he'd done with Wendy crept through him like the hot glow of heroin. It was as if some other presence had taken him over. Powerful. Strong. Ruthless.

Dawn's smile faded. "Is something wrong, Tim?"

Part of him wanted to tell her the truth, to describe the scene in vivid detail, to see shock and horror crease her smooth, sweet face. Somehow he held the words back. There would be an opportunity to deal with this unfeeling bitch. But this wasn't that time.

"Did Steve say what was going on?"

"No," she said, shaking her head. "But he sounded really upset. You know your father."

"Yeah," he said again, laughing harshly. "Oh, yeah, I know my father. I better call Steve."

He strode past her to his home office. The bland smile was still fixed on her face when he shut the door. He never heard her start to cry.

Gary, too, was awake when Wendy returned. He was in his study, wearing headphones, eyes closed, listening to the lilt and flow of the local Creole dialect, occasionally jotting notes on a yellow legal pad, but more often simply sitting, nodding, the occasional smile dancing across his features as he listened to the history of an island he had come to call his home.

The image left Wendy feeling empty. Or perhaps it was the fuck-and-duck way Tim had claimed her tonight. For the first time in the year-long affair, she hadn't come home feeling satisfied in body, heart and soul. Instead, she'd come home feeling…dirty.

A part of her longed to say something about it, but she guessed that was part of any relationship with any man. It couldn't always be wine and roses. Sometimes, with any man, it was vinegar and thorns. She supposed it was that way for men sometimes, too. Making love couldn't always be that shimmery, sparkling, neural fireworks display of adolescent romantic fantasies. Once in a while, it just didn't click. Tonight was one of those times. It didn't mean Tim didn't love her, or that they weren't soul mates. Really, it didn't.

She walked past the door of Gary's office, neither furtively nor lingeringly. She figured either would draw attention. Instead, she simply walked past as if she'd been right there in the house with her husband for the past three hours, instead of out on a boat, her thighs clenched around another man, clawing his back until he bled, making his eyes shine and his face contort in climax.

She tried to concentrate on that part, and not the aching, swollen crease across her buttocks where he'd ground her onto the bedrail. She turned on the shower and winced as she kicked off her shoes, then again as she bent over to slide her jeans down her legs.

"You're hurt," Gary said behind her.

Wendy nearly jumped out of her skin. "Damn. You scared me, honey!"

"You're hurt," he repeated, his eyes flicking down to her bottom.

"I fell," she said.

Gary shook his head slowly, sadness in his eyes. "No, you didn't. He hurt you."

She didn't know what to say. A million glib lies flickered through her mind, but she knew he would see through any and every one of them. She looked at the floor. Took a slow, deep breath. Saw his feet as he approached, saw his hand rise toward her face. She flinched, but he simply raised her chin with his fingers until their eyes met and she saw his tears.

"I love you, Wendy Marie Morgan."

Of all the things he could have said, that hurt the worst. Because she knew, absolutely without question, that he meant it. And because she knew, absolutely without question, that she couldn't return those words. She would be lying. And he would know it. From the quiver in his jaw, he already did.

"You want me to leave," she said softly.

"No. I don't." He paused for a moment, as if studying her features. "Wendy, if I wanted you to leave, I'd have said something months ago. I've known. I've known all along. I accept the way things are with us. I know I'm not like him, whoever he is. I know I can't do for you what he does. I can live with that."

She didn't know what to say and tried to stammer

out words, but he put a fingertip to her lips and pressed on.

"What I can't live with, my darling, my Wendy, what I can't live with is you being hurt. Those bruises. That's what hurts me. That he's hurting you, and you're going to take it and lie about it and let it keep happening. That hurts me, because I wonder what I did wrong, how I made you feel so small, so insignificant, so unworthy, that you would let some-one hurt you like that. I can't live with that."

The words tore through her heart like a ragged shard of glass, leaving a wound deeper than she could ever have imagined. She knew that someday he would find out. She'd planned on it, sooner or later. She would leave him, and Tim would leave Dawn, and she and Tim would be together. She'd rehearsed all the ways she might break the news to Gary. She'd rehearsed all the ways he might reply. But never had she imagined this.

"Gary…" she began.

"No," he said. "Just promise me this. Don't let him hurt you again. That's all I want you to say. Nothing else. Not one word more. Just promise me that."

She nodded. "I promise."

He turned and walked back to his study. And she stepped into the shower, feeling lower than she ever had in her entire life.

Gary sat in the study, listening to the wavering but rapturous voice of Loleen Cathan. Yet not listening.

He knew a better man would have handled it differently. A better man would have thrown her out. A better man would have left. At the very least, a better man would have demanded that she end it. He was not that better man.

He heard her sobbing in the shower, despite the rush of the water. He felt guilty, but he knew there wasn't a damn thing he could do about it. He'd seen it in her eyes when he'd said "I love you" and she couldn't answer. He'd known her body was no longer his. Now he knew the rest. Her heart was no longer his, either. All that remained was a shared house. A shared closet. A shared bureau. A shared bed.

Lost in his thoughts, he almost didn't hear the phone ringing. Finally the persistent chirp dragged him out of his well of self-pity, and he picked up the receiver.

"Hello?"

"Gary? It's Steve Chase."

"Yes," he said.

"It's Alice Wheatley," Steve said. "She's dead. Just like the Shippeys."

The shock and fear were apparent in Steve's voice. Well, that was Steve. He would be shocked and afraid. For such a powerful man, he was practically afraid of his own shadow. But Gary felt something entirely different. Gary felt...vindication.

"Then she is real," he said.

"That's it?" Steve asked, incredulity in his voice. "Three people dead, and that's all you have to say?"

"What else is there to say?" Gary replied. "We knew from the beginning that this was a possibility."

"It was a *legend,*" Steve pressed on. "Like the Loch Ness monster or Bigfoot. That's hardly what I'd call a *possibility.*"

Hardly surprising. Steve could believe in the power of ones and zeros in a bank's computer, but not the power of an evil soul, caked on this island like residue on a pot after water boiled away. An evil soul like Annie Black could not be expunged merely by killing her body. Tendrils of her black heart clung to the people, to the folklore, to the black, crystalline soul of the island itself. She was as much a part of this place as the volcano. He wouldn't be surprised if it was her fire that churned deep within that mountain.

"Well," he said, "now you know."

"Yes," Steve said. "And this can't go on. We have to stop the search, before more people die."

No, Gary thought. That wouldn't do at all. Some things were more important than life itself. Knowledge. Accumulated wisdom. And they were parties to a knowledge, to a power, that most people could never imagine. To harness that knowledge, that power...that would make a life spent in the dusty corners of libraries worthwhile.

He couldn't remake the child he'd been or the man he'd become. But neither could he walk away from this.

"We'll have to discuss this," he said, a cold calm in his voice. "We'll find a way."

"It's insanity," Steve said, and hung up the phone.

No, Gary thought as he hung up. *It's not insanity. It's destiny.*

If Wendy wouldn't love him, perhaps Annie would.

Markie lay in her bed, watching the glowing red digits on the clock: 4:00 a.m. Beside her, Kato sat on the bed. He hadn't slept, either, and had only left his post beside the kitchen door when she'd called him to bed. Normally he would curl up beside her, his head tucked on his haunches, his warm breath on her face as she dozed off. Tonight he sat erect, looking at her window, stopping only to nuzzle her face when thoughts of Alice came to her mind and the tears flowed.

"She didn't deserve to die, Kato."

He glanced at her, golden eyes whispering, *I know.*

"I don't know what to do."

His brow furrowed a bit, as if he was sorting through her words and her expression to find her meaning. Then he turned and carefully laid a huge paw on her shoulder.

Sleep. I won't let anything hurt you.

She put a hand over his paw, felt the rough pads with the stiff tufts of fur between them, the delicate strength of the fine bones in his foot, calm and still.

"I love you."

His nose lowered to hers, and his tongue darted out for a quick kiss. *I love you, too. Sleep now. I'm here.*

She felt her thoughts float away, carried on a dark wind to a distant night. Ebony faces flared in anger around a burning pyre, chanting, spitting into the flames, flames that rose and danced until liquid gold poured out and flowed over the black earth. Through it all, she felt a distant anchor, soft and firm, holding on to her soul with vigilant, golden eyes. Those eyes were all that stood between her and the hissing, crackling pyre. So far, they held it at bay.

So far.

12

Markie woke abruptly from sleep, her heart hammering. Kato was lying beside her, head up, as if he hadn't slept a wink. Beyond the window, the faintest hint of day grayed the sky.

"God!" What had she been dreaming? Something awful, she was sure. She was soaked in sweat, her sheets tangled around her legs.

Kato gave one of his quiet whimpers, one that indicated he felt her distress.

Markie threw back the sheets, struggling to pull her legs free, hardly aware that Kato trotted after her as she went into her small bathroom.

She splashed cool water on her cheeks, then looked at her gaunt face in the mirror. *Alice…*

The memory of what she had seen last night was dancing on the edge of her memory like some ghastly puppet, just as Alice—

She jerked her mind away from that and looked down at patient, protective Kato. "Let's go for our run."

His tail gave a single whisk across the floor, indicating approval. She dressed swiftly in shorts and a cotton tank top. Bare feet slid into her running shoes, and she tied them snugly.

Kato was becoming eager, his claws clicking happily on wood flooring. Apparently whatever had kept him so disturbed last night had faded from his memory. Or had faded away. The last thought caused her to stop just as she was reaching for the handle of the front door, Kato's leash in her other hand.

It had faded away. It wasn't that Kato had forgotten. She closed her eyes, drawing a deep breath of air and realized that the morning felt lighter somehow. As if some oppression had lifted. Apparently Kato felt it, too.

Uneasiness returned, but different from what she had been feeling last night. Different because last night it had seemed to surround her from without. Different because this time it was definitely coming from the course of her thoughts. Self-generated.

Shaking her head, trying to dislodge thoughts she didn't want to have, she opened the door and stepped out with Kato.

The sky had lightened some more. Still night, still predawn, but not for long. She patted her thigh to remind Kato to heel, and the two of them set off south down the tree-lined street leading toward the marina. Toward the water.

Kato loped easily beside her. Her pace didn't even begin to test his speed, but it was a good pace for her, enough to work up a sweat and make her muscles burn a bit by the time she got home. Kato probably could have run twenty miles with barely a pause, and it touched her that he tolerated these brief, tame outings when he probably would have preferred to be allowed to roam free all over the island.

"I guess that's the price you pay for hugs and regular meals," she murmured to him, her feet pounding a steady rhythm on pavement.

He looked up at her briefly, his golden eyes seeming to agree.

By the time they reached the marina, the first pink streamers were beginning to glow above the eastern water. It always thrilled Markie to see sunrise here. Unlike back in the States, where it was a dusty sort of red, here the clouds gleamed with colors that looked as if they were made of metal. No dust, no exhaust fumes, dulled them. Nor could any camera truly capture them.

Near the marina, she and Kato turned right and began to pass Federal Plaza and its imposing stone structures—the police station, administration building and Government House—to the boardwalk and the park beyond. The masts of sailboats caught the first reddish light and stood out against the dark gray southern and western sky. The water itself, far from its usual blue, looked like beaten silver with just a hint of fire. It was calm out there this morning. Calm enough to be a lake rather than an ocean.

At the park they turned again, heading toward the beach and its wide strip of faintly pink coral sand. Once there, Kato would be free of his leash to romp as much as he pleased. While there was no one about, Markie didn't have to worry about someone becoming frightened of the unleashed wolf. Kato seemed to understand and accept the rules: stay on the sand and at the water's edge, avoid people.

Sometimes he treated the sand as if it were snow, and this was one of those times. He rolled in it, then plowed his nose into it, flinging sand everywhere. *Someday,* Markie promised him, *I'm going to take you someplace with snow to play in.* A silly promise to make to a dog who had never seen the stuff and seemed quite happy to play in sand.

His burrowing nose brought up some sand crabs, and he stalked them playfully, never hurting them, never getting his nose close enough to feel one of those clamping claws. It was just a game to him. Markie could only guess how the crabs felt.

The red was beginning to seep through the water as the sun rose higher, now a sliver of yellow-red metal above the water, with an arc of fiery clouds above it. The color oozed across the sand like spilled water paints, running into peaks, rolling away from deep depressions. The water, too, was changing color, becoming darker, less gray, more mysterious.

Kato tossed another snoutful of sand into the air, then sneezed, clearing out the rest of it. Looking back at her over his shoulder, he gave her a happy grin.

That was when she realized she was crying. Crying for Alice. She would have loved to be here....

It was a long time before Markie could force herself to head back home. By then the sun was higher, stinging her delicate skin with its strength.

Here the sun was always powerful, never weak. But now the night seemed powerful, too.

It was just after nine when Dec rang her doorbell. She came to the door, Kato at her side, her features looking much the worse for wear. She smelled fresh, though, from a recent shower and shampoo.

"Rough night?" he asked.

"Is it that obvious?"

"No worse than it is on me, I'm sure."

She looked at him for a moment. "No, you look fine. Um, would you like to come in?"

"Thank you." He held up a brown paper sack. "I come bearing bagels."

She smiled. Even haggard, it was a beautiful smile. "I have coffee. And I might have some smoked salmon in the fridge."

"Sounds like a feast."

She closed the door behind him and led him to the kitchen, where she promptly began digging through her refrigerator. Even through the shapeless house-dress, the curves of her hips and long lines of her legs were obvious.

"I'll be just a minute."

"No rush," he said. "And don't put yourself out on my account. I can eat them plain."

"If you're kind enough to bring bagels," she said, "the least I can do is find something to put on them."

She emerged with a package of smoked salmon, a

tomato and half a red onion wrapped in cellophane. With swift, efficient movements, she guided the knife through the tomato, leaving slices so thin he could have read through them. The onion was next, transparent pink rings accumulating on the cutting board as if by magic. She took down two plates and poured a small circle of olive oil in the middle of each, then added quick shakes of dried basil and oregano, a sprinkle of horseradish, and a dash of freshly crushed black pepper. Humming an idle, haunting melody, she arranged twists of salmon, tomato and onion around the dressing.

"Breakfast is served," she said, sliding a plate across the island to him.

"Amazing," he said. "I'd have just slathered on some cream cheese."

She smiled. "This is healthier for you."

"And beyond my culinary skills," he replied. "Especially first thing in the morning, when I only have one eye half-open. I don't know how you do it."

"Practice, I guess," she said. "I'm still on automatic pilot."

He cut his bagel, then swirled the salmon and veggies in the sauce she'd prepared and piled them atop a half.

"Wow," he said around a mouthful, the bright blend of flavors having left his manners in an untended synapse far from his taste buds. He swallowed and offered a sheepish smile. "I'm sorry."

"For what?" she asked.

"For talking with my mouth full."

"Oh, that," she said, tossing a hand. "I'll take it as a compliment."

"It certainly is."

"Well, thank you."

"You're welcome."

They ate in silence for a few minutes, until she lowered her plate to the floor for Kato to clean. As his pink tongue lapped up the last of the oil, she looked up. "So, to what do I owe this honor? I'd have thought you'd be busy at the hospital."

His lips tightened for a moment. "Apparently Joe Gardner has decided my services are…superfluous. CDC doctors only in the lab, he says. If he needs me, he'll page me."

"In short, he's peeved about last night and playing the petty tyrant."

"That's about right."

"I'm sorry," she said.

"It's not your fault, Markie. And in a sense, he's right. They certainly know more than I do about these kinds of things. I'd just be in the way."

"But you still hate to be out of the loop."

He nodded. This woman was far too perceptive. "Yeah. I do. But there it is. So I thought maybe we could go up to the fort. Have a look around. I doubt we'll find anything, but…"

"But it's better than stewing and fretting."

"Exactly."

She paused for a moment. "Okay, I'm game. But I need to swing by the clinic first. Check on my patients. And I was thinking I'd go to Mass today."

"Mass?"

She nodded. "It's Sunday. We're all scared. I thought it couldn't hurt. You're…welcome to join me."

"Sure," he said. "I guess."

"You don't sound very enthusiastic."

He looked down as Kato finished licking the plate. "I guess I'm not. It's been a long time since I've been inside a church."

She smiled and patted his hand. "I'm sure God will remember you."

If there is a God, he thought. Oh, well. It was, as she'd said, better than sitting and fretting. Or maybe it was just something else to sit through, something else to fret about.

"Make yourself at home," she said. "I'm going to get dressed."

"Take your time," he said.

Preferably, enough time that Mass will be over when we get there.

But of course Markie was ready in plenty of time. For the first time in many years, Dec found himself sitting in a church. Worse, he was sitting in a wooden pew in the front, unsure if he even remembered the prayers or the times to sit, stand or kneel. He supposed God could forgive an almost-atheist.

The thought amused him, leavening for a few brief moments the sorrow of the past hours and his discomfort at being swaddled in the lingering aroma of frankincense, a smell so much a part of his childhood and youth that even the merest whiff could carry him back twenty years in time. This old church, however, was so permeated with it that it seemed to rise from the pews and sink from the rafters. The odor would probably still be there another hundred years from now, even if incense never again burned within these walls.

Rituals that had once engaged him mind and heart now left him unmoved. His mind wandered, working through all that had happened last night, trying to come up with some logical reason for Alice's horrible death dance. Kato's behavior could be explained away, but not Alice's seizure. He'd seen a lot of seizures in his day, but never one that looked so much like it ought to be a scene in *The Exorcist.*

He struggled, trying to find a way to categorize it, to make it finite and graspable. And for some reason his eyes kept going back to the crucifix behind the altar.

Back to the infinite.

Back to the same old question: If there was a God, how could he or she allow such terrible things to happen to people? Oh, he knew all the standard explanations. But he still didn't know why a God would send his own son to such a terrible death as a ransom for the sins of the imperfect people he himself had created.

The priest tried to offer a rationale during his homily, a discourse on fear, illness and the need to turn the heart toward God and our loved ones. None of us knew how long we have on this earth, he was saying, no matter how healthy or fortunate our present state.

How often we neglected a fleeting opportunity to show love and kindness because we were caught up in our plans for the future. The current epidemic, he said, frightening though it was, ought to be an occasion for each of us to remember that life is brief and only love is eternal.

On one level, it made sense, Dec supposed. On another level, he had often wondered why people who had just escaped crisis or tragedy talked about how the experience had taught them to cherish what was "really important." It said something about the human race that we would ignore each other for most of our lives, then suddenly grieve the lost time when we were separated. A dog, after all, leaps in joyous greeting whenever the owner comes through the door, even if the owner has only gone to the mailbox. It seemed to Dec that an omniscient, perfect God would have recognized that canines were a better bet than humans and folded the human hand long ago.

Instead, he allowed humans to go on neglecting and hurting and killing each other in the most senseless ways and for the most senseless reasons, convincing themselves that they were at the top of the evolutionary ladder, when in truth they usually showed less "humanity" than their nonhuman companions. If God's purpose in this epidemic was to teach the people of Santz Martina to value one another, it seemed to Dec a shocking and terrible lesson wasted on a genetically incapable audience. Why invest so much in such a brutish species to begin with?

The corpus on the wooden crucifix returned his stare in utter silence. As always.

Relief nearly overwhelmed him when the Mass was at last over. There might be no answers to his questions, but that didn't mean he liked being reminded of the silence that always greeted them. The silence of the stone markers in the cemetery, mankind's tribute to those who had gone before, most of them probably pondering the same futile questions en route to their destiny as worm fodder.

As he and Markie made their way out of the cathedral, he was surprised to see Loleen Cathan kneeling in front of the statue of the Blessed Virgin, murmuring quietly, her fingers counting off the beads of a rosary. The old woman seemed to sense his stare and looked up to meet his eye.

"Di you wan summin?" she said, having caught up to them in the street outside. Her deep brown eyes held no malice, only curiosity. "Saw you starin'."

"I'm sorry," Dec said. "I guess I just didn't imagine you being Catholic."

"Make us even," she said. "I din figure you Catholic, neider."

He nodded. "I was raised in the church. But it's been a long time."

"Don' make it so long next time," she said. She studied his face for a moment. "You tink I'm odd."

"I wouldn't use that word," he said.

Loleen reached into her bag and pulled out her rosary in one hand and the beads she'd been shaking the night before in the other. "God know which prayer he hear which way. God have an open min'. Not like you.''

He stopped in midstride, taken aback by the woman's forwardness. ''I'm sorry?''

''Saw you last night. Saw you dis mornin'. Scared as de last chicken in de yard when de farmer come. Not scared coz what you saw. Scared coz what you din' see.''

In a few words, she had summarized every feeling he'd had in the past eighteen hours. He had no trouble seeing why so many of the locals looked to her as a juju-priestess-cum-grandmother. The rational part of his mind announced that she was merely an astute observer of human behavior, mannerisms and body language. The other part of his mind—the part he tamped down at every opportunity—whispered that the locals just might be right.

''So what didn't I see?'' he asked.

She smiled. It was an enigmatic smile, the sort that hid far more than it revealed and virtually dared him to press the issue.

''What didn't I see?'' he repeated.

''Dat's de wrong question,'' she said. ''You already know what you din' see. De question is, are you gon' let yourself see it, or go on chasin' dem bugs dat don' exist?''

''Okay,'' he said, growing impatient. ''What did you see that I didn't?''

She tapped her temple. ''Ol' eyes. Dey don't see so much of dis,'' she said, sweeping an arm around the street corner. "But de ol' eyes, dey see dis." She touched her small, sagging breasts.

Then she put her hand to his chest. "You wan see what hap'nin, doc? You gots look in here. Not out dere. Like de father say today. De real world not out dere. De real world in here."

It would have sounded like so much superstitious hokum but for the deep intensity of her eyes. Eyes that held his gaze paralyzed. Finally she looked away, over at Markie.

"You ask her, Doc. Trust her. She gots de eyes dat see. She gots de eyes dat see," she repeated.

With that, she turned and walked away. Only then did he notice the thudding in his chest, the cold sweat trickling down his back despite the tropical heat.

She was right. He was afraid. In so many ways.

13

Kato had taken the opportunity to nap, and yawned hugely when Markie and Dec returned to the house for him. As soon as he was in the back of Dec's borrowed Range Rover, he turned in circles, then flopped down on the back seat and closed his eyes.

"I thought we'd need four-wheel drive to get to the fort," Dec said. He nodded toward Kato. "I guess he was up a lot last night."

"I don't think he slept at all," Markie agreed, remembering how alert his eyes had been when she'd awakened just before dawn.

"I'm taking it as a good sign he's comfortable enough to sleep," Dec replied. "And I'm not kidding."

The day was turning into a tropical standard for this time of year, temperatures headed to the mid-eighties, the breeze steady and balmy. It was, upon occasion, possible to grow sick of sunshine, a fact that sometimes still amazed Dec.

This morning the sunshine seemed like an insult

after last night. The sight of some dark clouds on the western horizon almost cheered him. It ought to be a stormy day, a wildly stormy one, after what had been going on around here.

He steered around a pothole, then returned to his lane. No one else was out and about on this end of the island. None of the usual sunbathers or swimmers or picnickers. It was still early, but it was also Sunday. The tropical storm a couple of months ago had taken out a lot of the beach, but there was still enough to be usable. Beyond the narrow strip of white sand, the water glowed a gorgeous shade of aquamarine. There was so much beauty on this island that no camera could ever capture.

And now so much ugliness that didn't bear thinking about.

"I talked briefly to Joe Gardner this morning," he said, just to hear the sound of his own voice and banish the demons that were chortling evilly at the edges of his mind, whispering of ghosts and ghoulies and other unnatural things.

"Yes?" Markie's biting tone conveyed her opinion of Joe Gardner with perfect clarity.

"Well, he may be an arrogant son of a bitch, but he's a reasonably smart one. I told him I thought we might be seeing the effects of some kind of weapons test."

She turned on her seat to look directly at him. "And he said?"

All of a sudden he was aware of two days' worth of beard stubble on his cheeks. He had to force himself to focus on the matter at hand and not Markie's closeness. "He says that if the army were testing something here they wouldn't have sent him. USAMRIID— the Army's biological research agency—would have been here instead."

"Like we'd even know."

"What do you mean?"

She gave a short laugh. "That's a fairy tale, Dec. CDC would be here, all right. And we'd never ever know USAMRIID was here, too. Not if this was some kind of weapon driving the dogs nuts. No, they'd let us think CDC was handling it so we wouldn't start to wonder about weapons."

"You have a very devious mind."

She shrugged. "Well, I grew up knowing my country would put a virus in the New York subway system to test dispersion." She gave another laugh, this one a little easier. "You want the truth, Dec? I can't believe I'm thinking the things I'm thinking. The Shippeys and Alice died from a cause unknown. It wouldn't be the first time in the history of the world. For all we know, some ship at sea disposed of something it shouldn't have, something that's made a few people sick and is annoying the dogs."

"I like that explanation. I'd like to buy it. But the back of my neck won't let me." Again he felt her gaze on him.

"The back of your neck?"

"Yeah. My gut instinct. My bullshit meter. My early warning system. Whatever you want to call it. I won't rest until it quits."

"You could get awfully exhausted."

He laughed then, and it felt good to laugh. For a while his mood didn't feel quite so dark. "At the very least, I'm going to enjoy a day with a beautiful woman and her cute wolf in one of the greatest places on earth. So today is very worthwhile."

She studied him for a moment, as if weighing his words. As soon as they came out of his mouth, they seemed to him to clank against the mood of the day, utterly out of place given what had happened and what they were out here to do. He wished he could snatch them back.

Then her laugh answered his, a wonderful cascade of sound. "Sounds good to me, as long as I can nap afterward." Then she chuckled again. "Yeah. Laughing in the teeth of death. I can't think of a better way to handle it, can you?"

"Unfortunately, no."

She turned to face front again and added almost grimly, "It sure fits the history of this damn island."

The fort on the west end of the island had started life during the Spanish period, as protection from pirates. It had been built in the customary star shape, with jutting sentry and cannon towers to be able to rake fire directly along the walls. It was built of coquina, a wonderfully durable, almost indestructible, mix of shell and limestone. But later it had been upgraded, first by the British, then by the Americans during the Spanish American War, and a little more during World War I, only to be deserted from 1926 until the Cuban Missile Crisis. A considerable amount of work had been done then, both in restoration and in additions. In 1969 it had been abandoned yet again.

After more than thirty years, the tropical forest had encroached mightily. The road surface had become little more than a track through thick growth. Dec felt fortunate that he and some of his friends had come out here to explore a couple of years back, or he might not have been at all sure of his way.

From time to time, though, the rough road emerged from the densest growth to give a glimpse of the Caribbean. And finally it yielded a view of the fort.

Dec stopped the Range Rover, giving them a chance to soak up the view.

"It's amazing," Markie said. "It almost looks brand-new from here."

It did. The coquina, imported from St. Augustine three centuries ago, had withstood the years as well as solid granite would have. Here and there, even at this distance, they could see vines climbing the walls, and inside the fort somewhere a palm tree rose higher than the walls. Otherwise, it might have been built yesterday.

"I'm surprised nobody's built out here," Markie said.

"I think it's all still federal reservation. Maybe someday they'll turn it into a park."

Federal reservation. They were on it now, this close to the fort. He glanced back at Kato, who was still dozing on the back seat, his head in a puddle of sunlight. Apparently all was right with the world, at least for now.

Dec released the brake and restarted the cautious drive toward the fort.

"I wonder what it was like here back then," Markie mused. "At one point, pirates pretty much ran the island."

"Yeah. I imagine it was a rough-and-tumble place, and the decent people tried to stay as far from the harbor as they could."

"Oh, of course. Some of them worked for the crown. Jamison Black, for example. But…"

He nodded. "Didn't mean they were nice people. Or that their crews were. I'll bet they were hell on wheels when they pulled into port after battling the Spanish. They didn't have military police then. And, of course, some of 'em were just plain outlaws, fighting for nobody but themselves."

She laughed. "A lot of them got their letters of marque as an alternative to prison or hanging. Not many were patriots or idealists. Just opportunists. It's a fascinating period of history."

He nodded. "I've been too busy since I got here to think much about history."

"After we get done here, I'll race you to the library."

"You know," he said, his voice turning serious, "that might not be the worst idea in the world."

"Den dey bur' it buv de boneyar, out de wall. Out de holy groun', in de black eart'."

Gary Morgan's attention snapped away from thoughts of Wendy and his lot in life. He rewound the recorder and played it again.

Then they buried it above the boneyard, outside the wall. Out of the holy ground, in the black earth.

Finally, after weeks of poring through tape after tape filled with tired tall tales of family doings that might have interested him as a graduate student, after hour upon hour in this chair with these headphones, cut off from Wendy and the rest of his life, finally, a solid clue.

He pulled out a sheaf of maps, cartographical snapshots of Santz Martina at various stages in its history. It was easy to place the cemetery, across the street from the cathedral. Neither had moved since the late Spanish period, although the cathedral had been rebuilt after a fire in the late nineteenth century.

Above the boneyard, outside the wall.

Like most settlements of the period, Martina Town had originally been a walled village. And, like most settlements, it had outgrown its walls, torn them down, built new ones, and torn those down yet again. Today, only the east and west gates, at either end of Avenida La Media, remained. The question, then, was where was the wall in 1809, at the time of the Rebellion, at the time of Annie Black's death?

He leafed through delicate parchments, excitement building, hardly mindful of how fragile the documents were. They were supposed to be stored in the archives at the junior college, but he'd checked them out months ago. No one else made a study of the island's history. They hadn't been missed.

Ahh. This was probably the best source. Jamison Black's original survey, dated 1791. Black had been a sailor, a pirate, then a sugar plantation owner. What he had not been was a surveyor or a mapmaker. The coastline and cartography bore only a general resemblance to the current detailed U.S.G.S. maps. But the United States Geological Survey had access to aerial and satellite photography, GPS locators, laser measurement and computers to hash it all together. Black had relied on landmarks, paces and his sailor's eye. Still, he hadn't done all that badly, and within the relatively small dimensions of the town itself, his work ought to be accurate enough.

Black's map had no scale, but Gary could make reasoned estimates based on the dimensions of the cemetery and the way towns grew. Houses and properties tended to extend up to a wall. When the wall came down, it was most often replaced by a street. Often enough, that street acquired the obvious name—Wall Street—as had happened in New York City, for example. But not always, and not in Santz Martina.

The fledgling United States had claimed the island in 1815, under the treaty that ended the War of 1812. At the height of the Enlightenment, when science and reason rose supreme, Thomas Jefferson had devised a new, grid-based surveying system, to be applied throughout the new territories of the United States. Thus, when the U.S. Army Corps of Engineers arrived to improve the island, they laid out the geometric gridwork of streets that still marked the old town. And, in the spirit of pure reason, the Spanish and English names for most of the east-west avenues were dropped and replaced with numbers.

Gary's best estimate was that the old wall ran along what was now Second Avenue. Which meant Annie Black's treasure was buried somewhere north of there.

Above the boneyard, outside the wall.

The cemetery lay between Cathedral and Marina Streets. Cathedral Street ran along a low ridge that rose a few feet as it passed Second Avenue. On Black's map, it had ended at the wall. If Black's rough cartography were to be trusted, there had been a low hill, just outside the wall, to the northeast of Cathedral Street.

It was at best an educated guess. Black's map might be grossly out of scale. The hill symbol might be purely decorative. And Gary might be misunderstanding the words of an old woman, taking literally what might well be mere folklore. But it was the best guess he could make.

He took the street address from the modern map and logged on to the court clerk's computerized deed and tenant records. Out came the name.

Cross, Margaret, D.V.M.

"Okay." Tim looked at Steve with distaste.

He didn't much like Steve, who was, despite being President of the Senate, a weak-willed, spineless man.

The fact was that Steve Chase held his position by virtue of his last name. It was, simply, the Chase family's turn in the rotation for Senate leadership. And that meant Tim needed Steve Chase. For a little longer, at least.

Paying Carter Shippey to let them dig beneath his house had, in retrospect, been foolish. Tim had conceived of a better way. Routine public works projects—such as maintenance—did not require the approval of the Senate as a whole. The signature of its president was enough.

"I don't think this is a good idea," Steve said. Steve was always saying that.

"Why not?" Tim asked, careful to keep his voice even.

"Look, you may think the Senate runs this island, but that's not entirely true. The U.S. government is looking over our shoulders, and if I get involved in anything shady, the FBI is going to be all over me."

"Who said anything about shady?" Tim smothered a sense of indignation. "We're not doing anything shady. We're trying to recover artifacts of great historical importance to the territory."

Steve's face reddened. "Then why not just hire an archaeological team? Why keep pretending we're repairing water lines? Jesus, Tim, one permit for Alice Wheatley's house I can explain. But when they start to pile up…"

Tim couldn't believe that they had come full circle back to this argument, an argument he had thought they'd settled several weeks ago. "Jesus, Steve, don't you understand anything?"

The comment had the desired effect. Steve was jovial, well-liked, reasonably intelligent, but as malleable as a snail without its shell. Push hard enough, and Steve caved. He always caved.

But the task was getting tiresome.

"We agreed to this weeks ago," Tim reminded him. "It's for everybody's good to keep this quiet. I told you, the Feds would just jump in and take it all."

"What makes you think they won't take it anyway?"

"They're never going to find out that we have most of it. I told you. We'll pick out the pieces that would be good for the local museum and keep the rest."

"I don't know...."

"The rest," Tim said impatiently, "is our finder's fee. We're entitled to it, just like when someone salvages a boat." Everyone knew about the laws of salvage on an island like Santz Martina.

"The laws of salvage only apply at sea."

"Right. But when there are no heirs to an estate, what happens? Who gets it? Annie Black didn't leave so much as one little baby behind her. If she had any family, they never turned up. Neither did Jamison Black's. So...it's finders keepers, Steve."

Steve was beginning to nod. The law was on their side.

"It's not even like she really owns the dirt under her house," Tim argued. "It's subject to the same easement as every other property on this island. All mineral deposits belong to my family.''

''You mean they belong to your father,'' Steve said.

Tim bristled. He was tired of hearing that argument, too. ''My father, my family. The old goat isn't going to live forever, and I'm his oldest son. He may not approve of me, but I doubt he's cut me out of the will. And he can't be bothered with every niggling detail on this island. He's too busy being banker to the world. So I'm entitled to look.''

''I guess.''

Steve was caving again. So easily, really. Tim just wished he didn't have to shore him up again and again. That weakness that Tim found so useful also made Steve unreliable.

Get rid of him.... The thought wafted through Tim's mind. A cold shiver seemed to pass through him with it, then was gone. Later, he thought. Later he would have to get rid of Steve, but for right now, he still needed him.

''So we'll get the permit?'' he pressed.

''Let me think about it,'' Steve hedged. ''You can't be digging up people's yards without their getting curious. And Abel was all over me last night about these deaths. If he catches a clue that they're in any way linked with the permits...''

''Linked with the permits?'' Steve's jaw dropped. Then he laughed. ''Oh, my God, don't give me that hoodoo nonsense. The utility company has dug all over this island at one time or another. What the hell makes you think our digging is related in any way to these deaths?''

"Well, Carter saw—''

Tim cut him off ruthlessly. "I don't want to hear that shit, understand me? Do you really think a ghost could *kill* somebody? How would it do that, dammit? *How?* With its *hands?*''

Even Steve quailed at how ludicrous that sounded. "But a curse…''

"Dammit, there is no curse. The woman died two hundred years ago. If there was a curse, don't you think somebody would have mentioned it?''

Steve, who had held up longer than he usually did under a frontal assault, was rapidly caving again. Spoken out loud, the idea of a ghostly murderer sounded as silly as a child's bedtime fears.

"Still,'' Steve said, holding on to a last shred of his dignity, "your father… I don't want him getting wind of this.…''

Tim opened his mouth, ready to give Steve a tongue-lashing for his stubbornness, then abruptly changed his mind. He would start with one more permit. Before long, Steve would be handing them out whenever asked.

"Okay,'' Tim said smiling. "So we'll be discreet.''

"It'll take me a few days.''

"A few days?''

"Listen,'' Steve said, his face reddening again, "I've got to go through channels or people will get suspicious. Give me some credit for knowing my job.''

"Yeah. Sure. Sorry."

Not that he was really sorry, but over the years, he'd developed a fine-tuned sense of when to stop pushing Steve. He could wait a few more days.

"See ya," he said, rising from his chair, smiling at Steve, who sat on the other side of the desk. "I got a boat to take out."

It was a relief for Tim to get out of the stuffy lawyer's office that practically screamed Eastern blueblood and into the breezy sunshine of Santz Martina. God, he couldn't understand why anyone would want to spend his life living like a mole when there was a world outside like this one.

But he *could* understand the need for wealth. Wealth made all things possible, a lesson he'd learned while growing up. But he wasn't willing to become a mole to be wealthy. No, he had a better idea, one that would keep him in sunshine and champagne for the rest of his life, even if Abel did cut him out of the will.

And the old man damn well might. Right this very minute, Roth scions and trusted associates all around the world were hastening to do Abel Roth's bidding. Tim, alone of the Roths, was doing things his own way.

That was a dangerous precedent to set. Others in the family might get the heretical notion that their lives were their own.

Whistling, Tim shoved his hands in his pockets and headed toward the marina. He was definitely going to show them all that he could be his own man.

He felt a cool touch at the base of his neck, almost frigid, and he grinned into the sun. "That's what *you* wanted to prove, too, wasn't it, Annie? That you were your own woman. Did a damn fine job of it, too."

He knew Annie couldn't hear him, but he liked to talk to her. Of all the people past and present on this island, he had a feeling she would have understood Tim Roth the best.

14

Within the walls of the great fort, the waves were nearly silenced. Standing at its very heart, Markie felt the sunlight pounding down on her, felt the way the air barely stirred. Around her the ground was nearly barren, except for the lone palm that rose high above the walls. Small tufts of grass clung in stony, unwelcoming soil, perhaps once paved beneath so that roots had little room to grow.

It would have been an intolerable place to be on those rare occasions when the island's temperatures jumped from its average high of eighty to nearly a hundred.

Stifling. Men accustomed to dressing for colder climes, like the British, would have suffered in wool uniforms.

"How did they stand those uniforms?" she asked.

"I'll show you. Come on."

Bending, she let Kato off his leash to explore. He seemed to find dozens of interesting scents on the open courtyard—or parade ground, she supposed it was. He appeared impervious to the way the sun must be heating his black coat.

Declan led Markie to the edge of the parade ground, where doorways yawned at regular intervals in all the surrounding walls.

Stepping through one, Markie was hit by a cooling wind. A breezeway surrounded the entire parade ground, opening at points into rooms, some little more than large alcoves, some closed behind heavy steel doors.

"The steel doors are where the munitions were stored," Declan said, pointing. "I think they were put in during the Spanish American War."

"They're in amazing shape, considering the salt air."

"Yeah." He started walking along the breezeway, peering into openings. "Maybe they fixed them during the sixties. But still..."

"It's easy to understand why there are so few doors, though."

He gave a laugh. "Yeah. Between termites and salt, doors would have to be pretty much optional."

Even with the strong breeze it stirred up, the passageway seemed dark and dank. Forbidding. Any signs of habitation were long since gone, cleaned out, no doubt, when the last occupiers left.

"This would make a wonderful museum," she remarked.

"Yeah, if the Defense Department would turn it over to the Interior Department."

"I wonder why they haven't."

Dec shrugged. "I don't know. I'd think it was pretty much useless in these times."

Markie nodded, turning slowly around before resuming the walk through the breezeway. "Unless you still wanted to use it from time to time for secret things."

Which was the whole reason they were here.

Markie let her imagination roam, wondering what the early inhabitants of this fort had been like, wondering how they had lived. Had their families come with them? Or had they come alone, maybe fifty or a hundred strong, bearing muskets or rifles and a will to hold Spaniards at bay? Or, at an earlier time, to hold the English at bay.

Had they been much better than brigands themselves? What did they do with their time when no threat loomed?

The tour of the rooms offered no answers of any kind, except that it was possible to stay cool within these thick walls.

A crumbling stairway led up to the parapets. Dec took her hand in his, a comforting grip to steady her. At least that was what she thought it was, though some aching part of her suddenly wished it was far more.

As they climbed, Kato seemed to lose interest in the parade ground and dashed after them. When he reached the top, well ahead of them, he turned around and grinned down at them, apparently pleased with himself. Then he dashed off to explore.

Atop the walls, the view was breathtaking. The

blue-green sea stretched forever, calm and sparkling under the sun. In the other directions, the forest spread, a canopy that appeared uninterrupted most of the way toward the foot of the mountain.

"Look. There." Dec pointed.

Not too far from the northernmost wall, she thought she spied rust between some of the branches of the trees. "What is that?"

"I think it's the Quonset huts that were put here in the sixties. I'm not sure, but I've heard about them."

Markie strode closer to the edge, peering over the side. "I can't tell. I guess we'll have to walk over there." But she was surprisingly loath to do it. Coming out here had been an inevitable next step, and now something she had a truly personal stake in, but she found that all of a sudden she wanted out of here. She didn't want to find whatever secrets might be hidden out there.

She was afraid.

She looked straight down along the walls and saw what appeared to be rock fences squaring off bits of ground, now filled with growth. "What are those?"

Dec leaned over beside her and looked. "Probably the remains of gardens. If you wanted fresh food, you had to raise it. There are probably even pens for animals."

"I guess that answers my question about what the troops did when they weren't facing an enemy."

"They were pretty busy, actually. They not only had to feed themselves, but they had to keep their clothing in shape. So basically they were soldiers when needed and farmers the rest of the time.''

"But not in the sixties.''

"No,'' he agreed, his face shadowing. "Not in the sixties. Let's go check out those huts.''

She followed him, but reluctantly. Whatever uneasiness had settled over her seemed to grow with every step, until her legs began to feel leaden and unwilling to move. At the bottom, she stopped and looked around.

Dec turned, apparently realizing she wasn't following him. "What's wrong?''

"I...don't know.'' She tried to brush the feeling away, but, like cobwebs, it clung, refusing to be dismissed.

His face expressed concern. "Would you rather I check out the huts alone?''

"No!'' The words escaped her with startling vehemence, and before she realized what she was doing, she had grabbed his hand.

Almost at once, her face heated with embarrassment and she tried to let go of him. This time his fingers refused to yield.

"Markie, what's wrong? Are you having a feeling?''

How could he ask that so casually, as if it were normal? All her life she'd known it wasn't normal. And just as her sister had scared her and others, she had scared a few people herself. The sense wasn't as active in her, but at times it shocked her into blurting things that made others decide to avoid her.

Dec would want to avoid her if this didn't stop. She looked at him, feeling a crazy mix of emotions that she couldn't express, from fear that he would want to avoid her to   that this uneasiness she was feeling had a real

"Are you having a feeling?" he asked again. He tugged her closer, until her breasts brushed his chest; then he put his arm around her shoulders, while his other hand continued to hold hers.

"You know," he said, "I'm Irish. The Irish have a strong sense of such things, and if you're fey, Markie, I won't hold it against you."

She looked up at him, feeling uncomfortably exposed. "Do you read minds?"

"Sometimes." For an instant there was a devilish twinkle in his blue eyes, but it faded almost as soon as it came. "What are you feeling?"

"Just…uneasiness. Maybe it's my imagination at work. It's like…we're not alone."

He nodded, and nothing in his expression suggested that he thought she was nuts. Instead, he said, "I'm feeling it, too."

A chill poured down her spine, icy and sinister. Goose bumps rose on her arms, despite the morning's warmth. "Not a good place for a picnic, huh?" She tried to laugh, but the sound was pathetic.

"Maybe not. And maybe it's just these old walls remembering." He lifted his head and scanned the area. "There's no one else here. We know that. At least, no living person."

"Right." She said it firmly, but inside, she didn't feel firm at all.

"Let's go take a look at those Quonset huts. Maybe we can shake free of whatever this is."

Immediately she looked around for her wolf. "Kato?" Then she spied him. He was standing before one of the darkened doorways across the parade ground, peering into it with his head lowered between his shoulders. The chill along her spine deepened. "Kato?"

"He sees something," Declan said, following her look. "A rat?"

It was such a prosaic explanation, but it didn't seem to fit the mood. "Maybe." Her lips and tongue felt dry.

"I'll go check. You wait here."

There was nothing there, she told herself as Declan walked toward Kato. Nothing except possibly some poor frightened animal. No one could have approached the fort without being seen or heard. A rat, a mouse. It had to be.

Before Dec reached him, Kato gave a growl that made the hair on the back of Markie's neck rise. She'd never, ever heard such a sound from him. It even froze Dec in his tracks.

Then Kato seeped into the shadows, his hackles raised, and disappeared. They heard no more growling, no howling. Nothing.

"You go stay in the car," Dec told her.

"No! Kato..." Scared as she was feeling, she couldn't leave her dog behind. No way.

"I'll get him, Markie," Dec promised her. He was dragging her to the car. "I'll get him. But there's no reason to expose both of us to possible danger."

He was making sense, but she didn't want to admit it. "Kato!" She called over her shoulder, hoping desperately that he would suddenly bound out of the shadows and everything would be all right again.

"Come on," Dec said, propelling her steadily toward the Range Rover. Once there, he gave her the keys and told her to lock herself inside with the ignition running. Reluctantly, she obeyed.

Then he headed back into the fort, in the direction Kato had disappeared.

The sun had risen higher since they arrived. The courtyard was blisteringly bright under the hot tropical sun, but that only served to make the contrast with the passageways even starker. Dec felt as if he had stepped into an inkwell.

The contrast made the air feel cooler, too. Downright icy. Standing in the breezeway, he tried to let his eyes adapt to the pitch-darkness, all the while straining his ears for sounds of Kato.

Nothing. Not the merest whimper, breath sound or clatter of claw. No growling. That was at least some comfort. When Kato growled, as he had just minutes earlier, Declan understood the atavistic human fear of wolves. But where was Kato now?

They had to be alone inside the fort. They'd walked

this entire breezeway and peered into every open room. If anyone had come in while they were there, they would have heard something. A car or snippets of conversation. Dec hadn't heard a thing. But something had sure drawn Kato's attention.

Admittedly, he didn't know Kato all that well yet. It was entirely possible the dog had gone haring off after a lizard or something. But somehow, standing in this icy, dank, dim corridor, he didn't believe it.

The medical doctor in Declan registered that he was in fight-or-flight mode, adrenaline coursing, every sense on high alert, as he crept, peering into every corner. The place still seemed every bit as abandoned as it had before. The rational part of his mind knew there was nothing here to fear. But somewhere deep in his cortex, the warning flashed out regardless. *Danger.*

As he padded silently along the breezeway, the chill deepened. It seemed physically impossible that, with eighty-degree temperatures outside, it could feel almost like a refrigerator inches away. But there was no mistaking the iciness of the air.

Suddenly the steady breeze—born of the temperature gradient between the dark, cool interior and the sun-baked courtyard—simply stopped. Declan froze in his tracks, wondering what the hell was going on. It was as if the chill had solidified the air, holding the molecules in place. But he was still breathing. For some strange reason, he needed to remind himself of that. If he could breathe, the air was still moving. The beads of sweat that trickled down his back felt like icicles.

Cautiously, he moved toward the end of the breezeway, where it turned at a right angle. As he passed each alcove or room, he paused to look and listen. He began to wonder if his nerves were misleading him or if the shadows in the corners really were reaching out to him. He shook himself. He wasn't the kind of person to get scared of shadows, but even that didn't ease the tingling at the base of his neck.

When he turned the corner, he at last heard Kato. The faintest hint of a claw scraping stone. Worried that the dog had somehow been hurt, he hurried his pace, not caring any longer if he was silent.

Glancing into a dim side room, a deep one with a sloping roof, he thought he saw an inkblot.

Halting, he peered closer.

There was Kato, all but invisible given his black coat, six feet from the back corner, rigidly alert.

"Kato?"

Dec thought he saw Kato's ear flick, but the animal didn't move. What the hell was in that corner?

Dec stepped into the room, expecting to find a lizard, a rat or even one of the notorious but rare island insects that could reach nearly a foot in length. Even paradise had its glitches.

Instead, ice slammed him in the face. The temperature dropped at least thirty degrees as he took a step forward. He stopped, shocked and…unnerved. This simply could not be happening.

"Kato!"

The wolf answered with the briefest of whimpers, then again let out that ugly, deep, *I'm going to tear out your throat* growl. Once again, campfire stories told for millennia flashed through Declan's mind in an instant. *Wolf! Run!*

But he knew Kato wasn't growling at him and forced himself to move through the frigid air to the wolf's side. Peering into the corner, he couldn't see a damn thing. He fought the urge to rub his arms briskly against the cold.

Then the darkness moved.

It wasn't physical movement but rather a shifting in attention, laying open every feeling in the darkest niches of Declan's heart. Examining. Evaluating.

Then, as suddenly as if a light switch had been thrown, it was gone.

The air stirred and warmed. Kato whined once, then sat on his haunches and looked up at Dec with golden glow-in-the-dark eyes. Bit by bit, his hackles were lowering.

And Dec wondered what the hell he had just seen.

The reunion at the car was a joyous one, Kato licking Markie's face all over until she finally, laughingly, begged him to stop. "What got into him?" she asked Dec.

The wolf was standing on his rear legs, forelegs planted on Markie's shoulders while she rubbed his scruff and ears. Quite a sight.

"I don't know," Dec answered truthfully. That was all he wanted to say. He wasn't prepared to tell anyone that he'd walked into a cold spot and found a dog ready to kill a shadow, a shadow that had peered into the depths of his soul.

In fact, he was already coming up with logical explanations. Some draft through a hole in the stones was colder than the rest of the air. Kato had chased something into the corner, and it had vanished into a crack. The dog had remained, waiting for it to emerge again.

Yeah, that was possible.

But the back of his neck didn't believe it.

"He chased something," he told Markie. "I guess it darted into a crack in the wall."

"That's so unlike you," she said to the dog, grabbing his head in both hands and shaking him gently. Kato grinned with absolute delight.

She looked at Dec. "He's acting so weird lately."

"The whole town is going to start acting weird if we don't find some answers soon. I'm gonna go check out the Quonset huts."

"Okay. We'll come with you."

Part of him was still concerned enough to want her to wait in the safety of the car. Part of him wanted a reliable witness if anything weird happened again. A sanity check, at the very least.

But Markie forestalled his answer. "I'm going," she said, her chin thrusting forward just a bit. "I'm going with you. We both are."

He noted, however, that this time she attached Kato's leash.

"I'm not going to argue." He managed a smile he

was far from feeling. "That dog spooks me sometimes."

She nodded. "All dogs do, at times. But lately..."
She shook her head. "Lately, it's getting out of
hand."

He glanced back toward the interior of the fort and
wondered if those shadows were darkening again.
Then he realized he didn't want to know.

15

The huts weren't that far away, although forty years of undergrowth and tree growth had chewed up the pavement that led to them. They had stepped into triple-canopy jungle, dense and dark, which had swallowed even the Quonset huts themselves.

They were huge buildings, showing rust wherever the paint had flaked away, which was nearly everywhere. Not even galvanized steel could stand up to this climate. All were locked; only one had windows. Markie watched as Dec worked his way toward a window, and rubbed away years of salt and grime to peer inside. "Offices," he said.

Markie leaned forward and was surprised to see that the room inside was still furnished. "They didn't take this stuff away?"

"Maybe they planned to come back. Maybe it was too expensive to remove."

"Or maybe they left in a hurry," she said.

Creepers had found their way up the sides of the buildings, clinging to small crevices that defied ordinary vision. They worked their way through the vines and other undergrowth to the front of the building. There a rusty combination lock was visible beside the door.

"I wonder," Dec said, "what happens if I smash that thing?"

"As rusty as this building is, you might be able to punch a hole anywhere."

Dec gave the lock a hard jerk and it snapped open. Rusted through. He flexed his arm at Markie. "That's me, Superman."

She let out a brief, nervous laugh, but the sound was deadened. It was like being in another world. She looked around. They were alone. Or whatever presence she had felt earlier was hiding.

The heavy steel door opened with a groan. Behind it was a wooden door, covered with the signs of termites. One gentle shove from Dec caused it to collapse into a pile of dust.

"Busy little buggers," he remarked.

The termites had long since moved on to a better smorgasbord.

Markie followed Dec into the dimly lit space. They were in an anteroom occupied by a steel desk and a row of steel chairs for waiting. A phone, one of the old black dial varieties, still sat on the desk. Barely visible on it was the warning: *This line is not secure. Do not discuss classified information.*

Posters, nearly rotted through and mildewed black, still drooped on walls. Markie figured if she touched them they would turn to dust just as the door had.

Dec pulled open the desk drawers. A handful of black, government-issue pens rattled in the bottom of one. A spool of typewriter ribbon. A paperclip bound a stack of yellowed pages with delicate, feminine writing.

"Love letters," Markie said, glancing through them as Declan searched the other drawers.

"They probably took all the official paperwork with them when they left."

Markie nodded. "I'd be surprised if they didn't. God, this place feels like a mausoleum."

"Yeah."

Dust layered the floor, and every step they took disturbed it. In the next room, Kato sniffed at a small plate, then sneezed. Whatever had been on that plate was long since food for insects and the elements. Only a few crumbs remained. Once again, Markie was left with the sense of an abrupt departure.

"Nobody's used this building in recent memory," she said. "So...no weapons test."

"I still want to check everything out."

She shrugged. "I guess."

The rest of the building was the same. Offices, desks and filing cabinets stripped of official paperwork, yet casually littered with personal effects. A makeup compact and a pair of earrings. A coffee cup. Black shoelaces. A diary. A plastic comb. Half-used erasers. A wooden ruler with a peace symbol carved on the back.

"It doesn't make sense," Markie said. "Sure, people leave stuff behind in the corners of drawers when they move on. But earrings? Love letters from a girl-friend?''

The rest of the buildings, when they broke in, were more of the same. No documents. Not even the slightest hint of activity. But an old sock lay beneath a rotting bunk. Above another, faded family photos, held in place by once-transparent tape, which had since degraded to deep amber.

The post was well and truly abandoned. And either these had been the most slovenly and forgetful soldiers ever to wear a uniform, or they had been too rushed to gather up the bits and pieces of their lives.

''We're not going to find any answers here,'' Declan said, indicating that he'd seen enough.

Markie agreed. ''No. Only more questions.''

They released Kato to roam ahead and made their way back to the car, the return path somewhat easier because they could follow the track they'd already beaten down.

Kato seemed determined to lead the way, advancing a dozen paces, then looking back as he waited for them to catch up. He didn't detour once, Markie noted. He didn't want to linger. Neither did she.

''What happened back in 1969?'' she asked, as they settled into the car and headed back to the main road.

''Joe Namath won the Super Bowl in Miami,'' Dec answered. ''Richard Nixon was inaugurated in Washington. Ted Kennedy had a car wreck at Chappaquiddick. Neil Armstrong took a walk on the moon.

Jimi Hendrix played the national anthem at Woodstock. And a bunch of guys died in Vietnam.''

"Thank you, Mr. History-in-a-nutshell," Markie said, laughing. Then her face darkened. "But what happened *here* in 1969?"

His eyes mirrored her own. "That I can't answer. Maybe it's time to hit the library."

Senator Mark Maxwell leaned back in his chair, making no attempt to conceal the look of disgust on his face. "We need to do *something!*"

Maxwell was perhaps the only senator who was truly in a position to challenge Abel Roth on any issue, despite his diminutive size and soft blue eyes. The others were either members of the three blue-blood clans—Edward Perlman Roth, Alex Morgan and Steve Chase—or were handpicked toadies. Joe McGinley ran a fleet of eight commercial marlin boats and represented the interests of the harbor industries, but the profitability of those industries was based largely on the Roth-Chase-Morgan development cartel. Kevin Cathan was the token island-boy-made-good, a *cum laude* graduate of Yale Law, former clerk for the Ninth Federal Circuit in Atlanta, and rumored to be short-listed to replace the aging Gladys Shackmon as Santz Martina's lone Federal judge. Of course, Cathan would only remain on that short list, assuming he was truly on it, if he remained in Abel Roth's good graces.

That left Maxwell, whose membership on the Senate was owed to his position with the island's coffee growers. And while his candidacy had been vetted by Roth, Santz Martina's Fire Mountain coffee was coming to rival Jamaican blends in trendy New York, L.A. and European bistros. It was the only industry on the island that could and likely would continue to make money independent of the Roth-Chase-Morgan empire. That single fact gave Mark Maxwell the chops to rock the boat. And rock the boat he was.

"The people of Santz Martina are expecting a response," he said. "If we sit on our hands while people die, if we're afraid to lift a finger without permission from a bunch of mainland doctors, we may as well surrender any pretense of independent territorial rule."

"Those 'mainland doctors' are experts from the most respected epidemiological institution in the world," Cathan said. "When the World Health Organization handles a viral outbreak in Africa, it calls on doctors from the CDC. I'd say we're damn lucky to have them."

"I've no argument there," Maxwell said, holding up a hand. "They're good. The best. But three people are dead and who knows how many others infected. And those are *our* neighbors. They shop in the same stores we do. Their kids go to the same schools. They go to the same churches and walk their dogs in the same streets. And fifteen thousand other people on this island know that, and they expect—and they have a *right* to expect—*their* elected officials to take some action to protect them."

"And you think those people will sit still for an

internal quarantine?'' Abel asked, leaning forward. He rapped the bowl of his pipe on the table. ''No. I can tell you how they'll see that. They'll see that as the rich folks up north trying to wall themselves off while the people who do the real work—the folks who live here in town—are left to die. And I won't have it.''

''But—'' Maxwell began, but Abel cut him off.

''You had your say, Mark. Now it's my turn. This island works, and all of us have our fancy titles and make our fortunes, for one reason: the people who've sat around this table have always taken care of the people out there. It's as old as the Romans. Bread and circuses. Every time it's come down to an extra five points a share versus building a park or a community swimming pool, improving a road or building a modern hospital, we've made the smart choice. And y'know what? We've gotten rich anyway.''

''And I'm saying we *should* take care of them,'' Maxwell said. ''We need to close the schools and nonessential businesses. Impose a curfew. Take reasonable steps to limit the contagion.''

''In short,'' Alex Morgan said, ''put everyone out of work and fuel a panic, when we don't even know how this disease spreads. Hell, the last I heard, the CDC docs aren't even sure it *is* a disease.''

''What else could it be?'' McGinley asked. ''Something sure as hell killed those people. And my business is already shut down from the quarantine. My people are already out of work. So is everyone else at the docks. We're taking it on the chin and I've got to be honest, a lot of the guys aren't happy about it. Why should they be the only ones to make sacrifices?''

And that was the problem with a wild card like Maxwell in the room, Abel thought. It only takes one man to break the ice and others will follow. Maxwell's seat was up in eighteen months. Abel made a mental note to make sure that someone else filled it next term. In the meantime, there was a nascent rebellion to curb.

''I know it's unfair to your people, Joe. And I'm sorry. For what it's worth, I'm sure Steve would put in a word to the construction firms, take your people on as temp hires until this is over.''

''Sure,'' Steve Chase agreed after a brief pause. ''I doubt they'll earn as much as they do on the docks, but it's a paycheck.''

McGinley nodded. ''That would go a long way to pouring oil on troubled waters.''

But Chase's response hadn't been as immediate or as enthusiastic as Abel had come to expect. He considered the possibility that Chase might be making preliminary maneuvers toward a more independent role in island politics but quickly rejected the idea. Jellyfish don't turn into sharks. Something else was bothering the man. Still, it was an issue he would have to address soon.

''And this should only be temporary,'' Abel added.

''Isn't that a little optimistic?'' Maxwell asked.

''No,'' Abel said. ''We've seen viral outbreaks on this island before. Think about it. There's the flu. Or something comes ashore on a freighter, or some bird carries an insect in from Cuba or Colombia or whatever. It goes through the island and infects pretty much everyone it's going to in a couple of weeks. So figure ten more days and we should be out of the woods and back to normal."

"Except for the dead people," Maxwell said.

Yes, Abel thought. *Except for the dead people.* Like the soldiers who'd died thirty-five years ago, out at the fort, before the Army shut it down and left. That time it had been USAMRIID doctors who'd come down, and they hadn't found a damn thing. Or if they had, they'd never shared it with the civilians on the island. The disease, whatever it had been, and the names of the dead, had simply vanished into the background noise of a turbulent time. And Abel certainly wasn't going to bring it up now.

"I wish there were something else we could do," Abel said, suddenly weary. "I didn't know the Shippeys, but my wife knew Alice Wheatley from church. I met her a few times. She was a decent woman."

"Carter and his wife were damn good people," McGinley said. "I've known them for years."

"So," Abel said, turning to Maxwell, "it's hardly as if we're sitting here in an ivory tower, unaffected by it all. These were our friends, too. And if whatever killed them is contagious, everyone in this room has probably been exposed already. As has everyone else on this island. So a quarantine, shutting down businesses and the like…all that's going to do is frighten people even more. I'd have to veto it. I'm sorry, but there it is. I wish there were something we could do. I wish we could stop this, and no more of our friends and neighbors had to die. But I just don't know what we could do that wouldn't be more likely to make things worse rather than better. We'll just have to let Mother Nature and the CDC do their work.''

"I'll spare everyone the embarrassment of a vote," Maxwell said. His posture spelled defeat. "I'll withdraw the motion."

"In that case," Steve said, "is there anything else?"

Abel studied him again, wondering at Steve's eagerness to end this meeting. There was definitely something going on there.

And Abel was damn well going to find out what it was.

Late that afternoon, having found no sign of contagion, the CDC gave permission for the Shippeys' bodies to be released. Dec signed the official order, and Jolly Wells, the island's only undertaker, came to pick up the remains.

Jolly unzipped Carter's body bag and shook his head dolefully. "Ain't no bug dat did dat," he murmured.

"Maybe not," Dec answered, saying nothing more.

Jolly was a huge man, built like a defensive end: tall, broad and muscular. He wore the island's formal attire of white guyabera shirt, white slacks and white deck shoes. His skin looked as silky as the Caribbean night, and his brown eyes held a world of warmth and intelligence. Too many people who didn't know better made the mistake of underestimating him. It was a mistake they didn't repeat.

"Closed coffin. Ain't enough of dat man left to embalm. Mmm, mmm." Jolly shook his head, zipped up the body bag and motioned his two assistants to wheel the gurney out to the hearse. Then he looked straight at Dec, his dark brown eyes so intense they seemed to burn. "Somebody be stirrin' up somethin' bad. Real bad."

Dec leaned back against the wall and folded his arms. "You got any ideas, Jolly?"

"Ain't no disease."

One corner of Dec's mouth lifted upward. He liked Jolly, always had. "You said that."

"I'm repeatin' it for a reason."

Dec nodded. "You always have a reason. Care to share it?"

Jolly appeared to consider the question, but Dec sensed he was weighing a variety of responses. Considering how Dec would respond to each.

"Just lay it out for me, Jolly. I'm ready to consider anything.

"Are you?"

Sometimes Jolly sounded as if he'd been raised speaking the Queen's English—probably because he'd done a term or two at Oxford before deciding he missed the balmy island breezes too much.

Dec felt a quiver at the base of his skull, a warning, a hint that maybe he should back off. But he didn't. He was past the point of backing off anything. With what he'd seen in the past twenty-four hours, the unthinkable was growing increasingly more thinkable.

"Just tell me what you know," he said to Jolly.

Jolly shook his head, as if something displeased him. "I ain't sayin' I know sumfin', Dec. But I got a bad feelin'. A bad, bad feelin' dat sumfin' ain't dead what oughta be."

"How do you mean?" The quiver was turning into a full-bore chill.

"Ask Loleen."

"I'm asking you, Jolly." Dec hesitated. "I was out at the fort today. There was something strange...." He couldn't quite bring himself to say what had happened.

But Jolly's gaze seemed to say that he already knew. "Da fort. Now why you wanna be doin' dat for, Dec? Dat place be bad juju, mon. Bad juju."

It was the first time Dec had ever heard that word on Jolly's lips. He opened his mouth to press for more, but the two assistants returned to get Marilyn's body. Jolly helped them lift the bag onto the gurney.

"Closed coffin, fer sure," Jolly said. He paused as he was about to follow the gurney out. "Talk ta Mam' Loleen, Dec. When you be ready ta listen."

Martina Town had become an eerie study in contrasts. On the one hand, people weren't quite at the point of locking themselves in their homes, although there were fewer people on the boardwalk than usual. People were out, but it was as if each family, each couple, each lone individual, was moving in a plastic bubble.

Down on the basketball court, the customary three-on-three games were absent. Instead, a father and daughter shot baskets at one end, while a lone teenager practiced layups at the other. On a bench at courtside sat a woman, obviously the wife and mother, ostensibly reading a book. Yet whenever the teenager edged too near midcourt, the woman cast him a warning glance: *You stay on your end and we'll stay on ours.*

The beach volleyball pits were empty, the bottoms of the nets fluttering in the evening breeze, silent pennants of caution. Two women sat on a picnic table beneath one of the thatched shelters, hugging their knees, silently eating fried chicken from a paper box, their faces set with grim determination, their eyes fixed on the water yet darting around whenever someone passed. At the waterline, an older sister stood guard while a toddler built a sand castle. On the steps of the community center, a lone flutist played "Amazing Grace," an empty coffee can at his feet. The haunting melody mated to the surreal scene only added to Dec's sense of unease.

Throughout his medical career, he had always known what he was fighting. Now he didn't know, and he hated that feeling. If he could be sure that whatever it was had done its work and would harm no one else, he would find it a hell of a lot easier to be in the dark. Which was not to say he would ever stop wondering.

But this, this waiting for the ax to fall again and not being able to do anything at all about it…that was foreign to his nature. Although he recognized some of the people in the park as patients, none of them had said a word to him. They didn't have to. The unspoken questions were plain in their eyes. *What is it, Doctor? Will I get sick? How do I protect my kids? Is there a cure?* And he had no answers.

Jolly had been absolutely no help whatever. His hints had only succeeded in making Dec feel even more ignorant. Did Loleen really have the answers?

"Hell," he said under his breath, watching the gentle evening waves roll in.

He was a man of science. Jolly's talk about juju should have gotten his dander up. But after the last twenty-four hours, he couldn't bring himself to react that way. Jolly was hardly a superstitious man. He ran a successful business. He went to Mass and sang in the parish choir. He played a mean game of tennis and had helped Dec hook up to the island's Internet service. Jolly wasn't the sort to talk about juju.

But Dec had been out at Alice's house last night and at the fort today. He'd felt the evil, felt the juju crawl into his mind.

So where did that leave him?

16

Wendy Morgan was, frankly, sick to death of the crackly voice of Loleen Cathan and her incessant, singsong pidgin prattle. Gary had been listening to the old woman, hour upon hour, for the past three days. He *said* he was looking for more clues to nail down some historical hypothesis. But the rapturous look in his eyes whenever Loleen spoke of Annie Black was…eerie. She'd seen that look in Tim's eyes, more and more, in the past couple of weeks. And last night, he had gone wild.

The thought of Gary evidencing a similar animal-istic wildness filled Wendy with a mixture of excite-ment and comic disbelief. There was certainly no way her husband could be capable of such a thing. But if he were, if he turned that massive intellect to such a course…the mere thought sent shivers down her spine.

She didn't expect that thought to turn her on. He hadn't turned her on in years. And yet, Tim's fright-ening display last night and Gary's response when he saw her…something was changing within her. Gary's eyes had been a mirror held up to her soul. And not a harsh mirror, but a forgiving mirror. Echoes of a connection long since buried in the ebb and flow of life and offered anew, even in the face of betrayal. It had been perhaps the most humbling experience of her life, and she had awakened this morning to a bleak emotional emptiness that demanded attention.

And, of course, just about the time she would have liked to sit down with Gary for their first truly honest conversation in months, or even years, he had withdrawn to his study and that tape recorder. She fought down urges of jealousy and spite. Given what she had done, she had no right to be jealous. As for spite, well, that was for children and heads of state. As Tim would have put it, it was high time to fish or cut bait. To rebuild her marriage or end it.

Although his door was open, she knocked regardless. His response was an impatient grunt.

"Gary? We need to talk."

"I'm busy," he said.

"You're right. You are. And you can go on being busy for the rest of the day, and tomorrow, and the next day, and the day after that. And when you finally do come out, I won't be here."

He pushed the pause button on the tape recorder and turned to face her. "What does that mean?"

"It means we can't go on living separate lives. You with your secrets. Me with mine. Not if we're going to go on living together. If anything we ever had was real, we have to start to work things out. Right now. Or I start packing. *Right now.*''

It was harsher than she'd meant to sound. But she felt as if she were standing at a fork in a road, with a pack of wild dogs chasing her. She could go one way or the other, but she couldn't stand still. She watched his eyes as he realized she was serious. He pushed the Stop button.

''So what do you want to talk about?'' he asked.

''Us, Gary. You and me.

He rose from his chair, tossing his glasses on his desk. ''Maybe,'' he said slowly, a frightening fire flickering in his eyes, ''talking isn't what we really need.''

Impossibly, an instant later she was crushed against the wall, and his mouth and hips were grinding against her as if he wanted to come out the other side.

The thrill that shot through her pierced her very core. In another instant thought was gone and all that was left were two hungry animals. Just the way she wanted.

Or so she hoped.

''Hey, Dec.'' Footsteps crunched across the sand.

The sound of Markie's voice caused Dec to turn from the water and the steadily sinking sun. It was about to begin the dazzle of its nightly display, but as yet the light was still yellow. ''Hey,'' he said in reply, smiling. ''Where's your cohort?''

''At home.'' Dressed in a white sarong and a

brightly flowered blouse, she was the image of island beauty. "We needed a break from each other."

"He's still alerting?"

She nodded. "Acting uneasy. Pacing from the back door to the front window and back. I think we were feeding each other's anxiety."

"I can understand that." He waved toward the approaching sunset. "I was just about to go indulge myself at Cap'n Pete's. Care to join me?"

"Seafood and sunset? How could I turn that down?"

He chuckled and offered her his arm, thinking that any man could be proud to be seen with this woman. Not only was she beautiful, but she was brainy, too. And nice. Most especially nice.

She smiled up at him, eyes dancing, and tucked her arm through his. "I'm an ostrich tonight."

"Exceptionally pretty feathers."

She laughed. "I meant I'm pretending the world is just hunky-dory."

He looked around the park again, at the isolated clusters of humanity. "Just like everyone else. So long as nobody gets too close."

"Well, you don't see two ostriches sharing the same hole," she said.

"Except us," he said.

She winked. "Just don't rock the boat."

Cap'n Pete's, out at the end of a stone pier, had been a Michelin Pick of the Caribbean for nine of the past eleven years, and its reputation was well-deserved. On a typical Sunday night, Dec and Markie would have waited an hour or more for a table, if they could get one at all. Tonight, though, it was half-empty, and they were quickly escorted to a table overlooking the water. The light was beginning to redden a little, but it still dwarfed the candle on the table between them.

Their waiter arrived with menus and eyes tight with worry. "Good evening, Doctors."

Dec and Markie nodded, and Dec looked around the room. "Slow night."

"Yes, sir." He poured bottled water into crystal glasses as he talked. "Lunch was slow, too. People are nervous."

Markie sipped her water. "I can understand why."

"Well, that's the bad news," the waiter said. "The good news is tonight's special seven-course meal. The entrées are—fried grouper ratatouille with wild rice, seared chicken breast and grilled zucchini in a spicy Caribbean roux, and peppered roast tenderloin medallions and sautéd mushrooms with whipped burgundy, chive and parsley butter."

"Wow," Markie said. "Pete's pulling out all the stops tonight."

The waiter smiled. "Actually, he called it rewarding faithful patrons. But yes, ma'am, you're right."

They both chose the special. Neither was in the mood to fret over choices, and Dec nodded to the sommelier's wine recommendations: sauvignon blanc with the fish, chardonnay with the chicken, merlot with the beef.

The waiter brought fresh poppy seed rolls and

creamed butter. The sun had met the edge of the sea now, and wisps of clouds high above were turning a metallic orange.

"So," Markie said, surprising Dec with her bluntness, "have you ever been married?"

"Wanna hear me do my rendition of bawdy sea chanties?"

She looked away from the sunset and right into his blue eyes. "That bad?"

He shrugged. "It wasn't pretty. I was working trauma in a big city emergency room. My hours were, well, let's just say my ex started to think we didn't have a marriage at all. She wanted me to quit. I was addicted to the adrenaline. She finally decided a dermatologist's hours were more to her liking. Unfortunately, the dermatologist in question was my best friend."

"Ouch!" She winced for him.

"That pretty much summed it up at the time. I went through the usual period of self-pity, feeling I was gutted, thinking that somehow I was less than a man...." He shook his head. "I got sick of drinking the house whine, kicked my own butt and buried myself in work."

"Did that help?"

He gave a quiet laugh. "For a while. Then the job started to be a problem for me, too."

"How so?"

Her expression was sympathetic, gently inquiring. So he found himself answering, speaking words he'd never spoken to anyone.

"One night they brought in an eight-year-old girl. Multiple gunshot wounds. Drive-by, the cops said. Two entries anterior thorax, one at posterior C-One. Nine-millimeter, hollow-point rounds. One of the chest wounds had taken a lung. The other blew half her sternum through the descending aorta. Then, probably because she'd seen the shooter, and just to make sure, he'd walked up while she was facedown on the sidewalk and put the barrel to the base of her skull. The bullet shattered her spine. It was so damn hopeless. She'd been coding all the way to the hospital. We intubated. I opened her chest, stuck a finger in the lung and looked for the artery with the other hand. There wasn't anything to find. It didn't matter. Nothing mattered."

He paused to pick seeds off the roll on his plate.

"I saw too much of that, Markie. Innocent kids hurt in the worst ways. Car accidents were bad enough, but the shootings and the rapes and the abuse... That girl was the last straw. The detective came in later that night. The shooter?"

He waited until she met his eyes. "Her cousin. I finished the shift and quit with no idea where in hell I was going to go."

"And you wound up here?"

He nodded. "Three months later. And up until Carter Shippey died, I've enjoyed every minute of it."

"You needed a change of scenery," she said.

"That would be putting it very mildly."

She reached across and touched his hand. "I don't have to say it, do I?"

"What? That it wasn't my fault? No, you don't. My ex would've left me sooner or later, or I'd have hated what I became to keep her. And that girl would've died, no matter who was on duty that night. But that's cold comfort." He paused for a long moment, looking out at the water. "She had hazel eyes."

"Your ex?"

"The girl."

"Oh."

"Yeah."

Wendy lay on the carpet, sated beyond belief, sweat pouring off her in rivers. Dimly she realized that her bottom had been rubbed raw on the carpet, but she didn't care. Gary's heavy weight on her was like an answer to a prayer. He'd set off all the fireworks and more.

Raising a shaky hand, she smoothed his damp back with her hand. He lifted his head and looked down at her.

"I love you," he said hoarsely.

For the first time in a long, long time she believed that. The words hovered on her lips, too, but she wasn't quite ready to say them.

His face darkened, and he rolled off her, lying beside her on the den carpet. A feeling of loss unexpectedly filled her. She wanted to reach out to him, to tell him that she wanted to believe, wanted to hope for a future with him, but that she was feeling fragile and vulnerable. Too vulnerable to make promises just yet.

But before she could move or speak, a voice broke the silence.

"Dey nev buhn dem bones. Nev."

Gary sat bolt upright. "I turned that off."

"Maybe you just hit the Pause."

"No, I turned it *off*."

He scrambled to his feet, and Wendy sighed. Giving up, she rose, too, and padded over to his side. The tape was spinning again, Loleen's crackly voice filling the room. Except it kept saying the same thing over and over.

"Dey nev buhn dem bones. Nev."

Gary looked at her, his eyes dark and uneasy. "She didn't say that, Wendy. Not that many times. Not that many times."

Wendy looked down at the tape recorder, her parapsychologist's nature coming to the fore. "You're sure?"

"Of course I'm sure, dammit!"

Just then the tape recorder turned off.

All by itself.

"So what about you?" Dec asked. "Did you ever marry?"

"Never."

"Smart lady."

"I wouldn't say that." She was clearly reluctant to answer, and he watched the brief struggle on her expressive face. "I may not have married him, but I made pretty much the same mistake."

"He didn't like your hours?"

"Worse, he didn't like my brain. We worked in the same clinic for a while until I couldn't take it anymore. He had this way of...implying that I didn't know what I was doing, without ever coming right out and saying so. I started to lose my confidence in a lot of ways. Too many ways. Nothing I did was right. He always had a better way. And he did it in front of clients."

"He was a vet, too?"

"Yeah. He owned the place. So finally I took a hike to another clinic and moved out of his house. It was a year before I stopped running to the other doctors to verify my diagnoses or treatment plans."

He nodded. "It's terrifyingly easy to sink someone's self-confidence. A bit of unwanted advice here, step in to take over a case there. Next thing you know, you're paralyzed."

"Exactly." She sighed, then said bluntly, "That's the last time I let my gonads lead my brain."

A startled laugh escaped him. "I thought only men did that."

"I don't know about other women, I just know about me. He was so damn attractive. Not movie-star good looks. It was something else, some kind of warm charisma."

"And too full of himself."

"He was good." She thought for a few seconds, then said, "I'm not sure he was egotistical. I didn't really see that. I think he lacked self-confidence and made himself feel better by putting me down."

"I don't pretend to be a shrink." He reached out

and took her hand briefly, squeezing it before letting go. "Whatever his reasons, the bottom line is, he was being abusive."

"Yeah, that finally penetrated my dim brain."

"There's nothing dim about your brain," he said firmly. "Self-doubt grows easily. I know. Only an iron-clad ego can avoid it. I sure don't have one."

She smiled. "So what about those sea chanties?"

He laughed, but shook his head. "Later, maybe. I wouldn't want to shock the waiter."

She hesitated, turning her gaze back to the blazing sunset. He waited, sensing she was about to bring up something less cheerful.

Finally she asked, "Anything new from the CDC?"

"You know as much as I do. No, wait. There's one more thing. I know it sounds crazy, but it's the only new thing I've heard. Jolly Wells said someone had stirred up something very bad."

"Jolly said that?" Something in Markie's face seemed to tighten.

"Yeah, why?"

"You've lived here longer than I have."

He squashed a sudden sense of impatience. "Meaning?"

"Jolly came to my house when I first arrived on the island and put some kind of pouch over my doors. He said there was an evil spirit hanging around but the pouches would keep it away."

This was a side of Jolly Dec had never seen. "I had no idea."

"I thought he did that for everyone."

"He sure didn't do it for me. And nobody else has mentioned such a thing."

She gave a little shake of her head. "Well, he was so nice and so darned determined, I let him do it. I figured it was some kind of local greeting."

"Not that I know of."

Red light began to pour through the window as the sun dipped toward the sea. Everything inside the restaurant seemed to burst into orange flame.

"Do you still have the pouches up?"

Markie shook head. "They rotted apart recently, so I knocked them down rather than have them shedding whatever was inside them."

"Maybe you ought to ask Jolly to come give you some new ones."

She looked at him strangely, but said merely, "Maybe I should."

He wanted to dismiss the whole subject with an urbane laugh and put his feet squarely back on solid ground. But he'd seen Alice Shippey die, a sight so shocking that today he'd acted like a paranoid lunatic and gone running out to an abandoned fort to look for secret weapons. Why not witch doctors, medicine bags and evil spirits?

Or maybe… An uneasy thought began to nag him. Maybe Jolly knew something that didn't have anything to do with evil spirits. Maybe he should talk to the man more closely.

Wendy pulled on a robe and got two glasses of orange juice from the kitchen. Then she sat beside

Gary at his desk and watched as he carefully backed up the tape. He played it again, Loleen's crackling voice filling the room.

But the words they'd heard before weren't there. He hit Fast Forward. No. He hit Rewind. No. They weren't there at all.

Wendy felt her skin prickle with excitement. Gary looked at her. "Why do I think this is your area of expertise?"

"Because," she said, "maybe it is."

"Communication from the dead?"

It was something she'd always wondered about, yet never been able to devise an experiment for truly testing. Even the best attempt could be explained by ESP, by the supposed medium picking up telepathic messages from a family member who was present. How in the world could you really prove it?

But this...this was beyond weird.

"Play it again," she said to Gary. "Start back about five minutes and play it again."

He was quick to oblige. Loleen's irritating voice returned, but for once Wendy didn't wish it would shut up.

"Maybe we imagined it," Gary said.

"Shh."

If there was one thing Wendy was sure of, it was that they hadn't imagined those words, nor had they imagined the fact that the recorder had turned itself on and then off. Excitement and frustration grew in equal measure as they searched back and forth on the tape.

Suddenly the tape crackled, cutting off Loleen's voice. Another voice whispered.

"Dey nev buhn dem bones. Nev."

17

"**I** read through that diary today," Markie said. "The one we found at the fort."

The waiter reappeared with crystal goblets, their rims covered with steamed shrimp. A deep, thick red sauce lay within the goblets. Soup would follow as the next course, in the truly formal fashion that hardly anyone followed any longer.

When he was gone, Dec prodded Markie. "And?"

She speared a piece of jumbo shrimp but didn't immediately bring it to her mouth. "A bunch of soldiers got sick. Back in 1969."

"Tell me."

"I'm not sure what to say. Just going by the diary, I'd have guessed I was reading about a tropical disease. He mentioned three soldiers dying. He didn't say how. I didn't get the impression he'd…seen the bodies. Just that it left a big mess."

Dec nodded slowly. "So it might be related, or it might not."

"Exactly."

"Damn." He picked at his shrimp. "This is so frustrating. We're up to our ears in 'might be related, might not.'"

"Dec," she said, trying to offer a reassuring smile, "let's not think about it. Let's enjoy dinner."

"You're right." He dipped the last of his shrimp in the sauce and popped it in his mouth. After a moment, he said, "I wonder how they make this cocktail sauce."

Markie dipped a fingertip in the sauce and touched it to her tongue. "Tomato ketchup, horseradish, lemon juice and minced cilantro."

"You can tell that?"

She nodded. "It's the same recipe I use."

He shook his head. "I don't know how you do that. Just taste something and list the ingredients."

"I don't, either. Call it a talent. I've gotten better at it since I started cooking more, though."

"So how'd you learn to cook?"

She paused, studying his eyes. It was another one of those minefields. Fortunately, the waiter rescued her by arriving with their soup, a creamy chicken and garlic concoction that rolled and sparkled on the tongue and warmed all the way to her stomach. Dec seemed to be enjoying it, as well, and they sipped in silence for a few minutes. But he didn't let it go.

"So? What's in this?"

"Hmm. Cream, chicken stock, garlic, white pepper, a splash of white wine, parsley and a hint of rubbed sage."

He laughed. "Tell me you asked the chef for the

recipe. Or something. I just…can't believe you can tell that by taste. It's amazing.''

Markie smiled and drew her thumb and forefinger across her lips. "I'll never tell."

"No, really. How do you do it?"

She had to remind herself that he was not William, not the man who'd challenged everything she said and did as if she were incompetent to get dressed without his help. He seemed genuinely curious. In an appreciative, supportive way. Safe.

"When I finally left him, I didn't have a lot left to feel good about. I didn't believe in myself as a doctor, a lover or a woman. So I started cooking. I bought some cookbooks, the classics. *The Joy of Cooking.* A couple of the Betty Crocker books. Then some ethnic workbooks, for adventure. At first I treated it just like vet school. Study. Meticulous attention to detail. I did everything by the numbers."

She paused as the soup bowls were whisked away and replaced with their salads, which were a visual delight, with lettuce, cherry tomatoes, slivers of yellow bell pepper, red onion, crumbled bleu cheese and black olives. The dressing was fresh and snappy, a vinaigrette laced with garlic and lemon zest.

"You were saying?" he asked gently.

"Oh, yes. I followed the recipes exactly. Then one day I screwed up. A brain fart. I was making bulgogee—Korean marinated beef—and I flip-flopped the measurements for rice vinegar and rice wine. I knew I'd done something wrong as I was mixing the beef in the marinade. It smelled tart. I looked at the bottles on the counter and realized what I'd done.''

"And?"

"And I added a bit of brown sugar to take some of the tang out and cooked it anyway. And I loved it. It was…wow! I'd made a mistake, but I'd caught it myself and I knew how to fix it, so I did. And the end result came out…better.''

He smiled and touched her hand. "So that's what you meant when you said cooking is therapy."

"Yes," she said, squeezing his fingers gently. "That's what I meant. I learned that I don't have to be perfect. I just have to be the best that I am. And trust that's good enough.''

The moment hung thick, their eyes locked together. He returned the squeeze of her hand.

"Yes, Markie Cross. That's good enough. Very…good enough.''

Wendy was on her knees between his legs, her lips wrapped around his member. Wow. This was…wow. His fingers tangled in her hair, claiming her, forcing her down, forcing more of himself inside her, and she let out a low, animal growl. When he finally spilled his passion, she looked up at him with glazed eyes.

"Where were you hiding the last ten years?" she whispered. "My God, Gary!"

She was an incredible lover. He'd always known that. But now she was something more. She was *his*. His prize. His property. His to love, use or dispose of, as he pleased. The thought rushed through him with an electric charge.

Thank you, Annie, he whispered silently.

He knew Wendy wanted her turn. Wanted her climax. Well, she would just have to wait for that. He had other priorities, and she would have to get used to the new way of things. He looked down at her and reached for her cigarettes. Handed them to her.

His voice was flat, even, devoid of emotion. "You need to get to work."

"Yesssssssssss," she said.

He almost smiled as he watched the muscles in her loins twitch. He could get used to this. He could get very used to this, very quickly.

She lit a cigarette, inhaling deeply, as if the poisons were the very breath of the gods, and settled onto her haunches, staring at the blank sheet of paper before her. Her eyes were distant, unfocused. Gary realized she had gone into her own world. And yet it was a world *he* controlled. He could sit here in his chair, his member still half-full, a drop of his seed glistening at the corner of her lips, and watch. And she would perform.

Seconds stretched into minutes. That was fine. He had time. She wasn't going anywhere. And neither was Annie. Not until he dispatched her.

Wendy stubbed out her cigarette and lit another. Finally she began to draw.

Dinner had crept by at a luxurious, leisurely pace. Every course was exquisite. Now they were sharing a slice of raspberry cheesecake and sipping warm, rich, mocha cappuccino.

It felt like a dream. The moonlight glistening on the water. Muted candlelight. From a chair at the center of the room, an acoustic guitarist filled the room with island songs. And across the table sat a man with whom Markie felt safe. A man she could talk to. A man whose wounds made him better, not worse. A man who seemed to think her wounds made *her* better, not worse. It had to be a dream.

Without a word exchanged, they chose to stroll on the beach after dinner. The sky was a black velvet blanket sprinkled with diamonds. The soft lapping of the waves sounded like a lullaby, steady and soothing. The sand beneath their bare feet was cool and damp, soft.

Dec clasped her hand in his, and she squeezed back. Feeling really close to him. When the balmy breeze whipped her hair around, she wanted to laugh with unexpected exuberance.

It was as if the wind lifted the burdens and sorrow, and for a brief time she was willing to let them go. Life had to be lived, and it deserved to be appreciated.

Smiling, she looked at Dec and found he was smiling, too. They had the beach to themselves, lost in a rare moment that seemed to arise from another time, another place. This was not Martina Town as she had always known it. This was…heaven.

Dec tugged her hand, and, as if floating, she drew near to him until their bodies touched, breast to breast, hip to hip. Then, slowly, as if they had all the time in the world and not just a few stolen moments, he lowered his head to kiss her.

Electricity filled the night suddenly, zapping every cell in her body. Her mouth welded to his, and she never wanted to break away. She caressed his tongue with hers, drinking from him as if he were a fountain of life, wanting to stay in this place, in this moment, forever and ever.

She felt his hands pull her closer, gently crushing her against his firm body. Her fingertips curled into his back, grasping the fabric of his shirt.

"Markie," he whispered, his voice thick and heavy.

"Yes, Declan. Yes."

She didn't want to contemplate the moment. She didn't want to go back to the real world where every action had to be weighed and considered and pondered, every decision agonized over until analysis gave way to paralysis. Not again. Not ever again.

"Yes," she repeated. "Yes."

A sliding glass door. A patio. Teak deck chairs. A palm tree with a faded leaf hanging near a roofline. The images floated into Wendy's mind like the nicotine that coursed through her bloodstream, welcome, wanted, but not entirely within her control. All she could do was expose herself to the ethereal presence. It did the rest.

She was not an artist, and for a moment she had to quell frustration at not being able to reproduce on paper what she saw in her mind's eye. The trained scientist in her recognized that this was a common problem with remote viewing. The worst thing to do was to try to fight it. Instead, she simply had to accept that her subconscious would guide her hand, that the resulting images would be correct, however inexact, and regardless of their aesthetic qualities.

Golden eyes. Brooding. Watching. Measuring. Assessing. Patient.

The presence of those eyes almost unnerved her. The other eyes that hovered at her consciousness, blue and green and hazel and brown, might as well have been blind. She could have floated right up to those eyes and plucked them out, and their owners would never have known or missed them. But those golden eyes were different. Not blind at all. Somehow, she knew that if she reached out to touch those eyes, they would burn a hole in her soul.

Declan felt her hands on his buttocks, pressing him closer to her, grinding him against her pelvis. A part of him wanted to tear off her shirt and find her wings, for surely this woman was an angel.

Her lips brushed over his, lightly, teasingly, sending tingles through him, making the hair on his arms stand up.

He had not felt this in so long. Maybe not ever. This was beyond a mere meeting of bodies, a blending of pheromones, nerve cells transmitting electrical impulses that triggered a cascade of endorphins. The anatomical processes he had committed to memory in hour after hour of study were at best a pale, cold description of the moment. This was...spiritual. This was...a meeting of souls.

He felt her angelic presence enwrap his, melding into him as he melded into her. Their hearts drew closer, closer, until cells mated and shared and they beat as one heart, one soul, one being. The lips on his, the hands that squeezed his buttocks almost to the point of pain, the dance of their tongues, were merely a gateway into the beyond. A beyond where the concepts of *he* and *she, his* and *hers,* gave way to *we* and *ours.*

And yet the gateway was exquisite. Her touches, her kisses, were magical, as if she had peeked into his mind, seen every fantasy he had ever had and determined to make them real.

She teased. He moaned. She giggled, as if knowing that he wanted that frustration, craved it, needed it. He moaned again.

He responded by trailing his fingertips up her rib cage, knowing the touches almost but not quite tickled. Her nipples grew to hard nubs, pressing through the fabric of her bra and her blouse and his shirt, announcing their readiness, and hers.

He wanted to take her and be taken.

Here.

Now.

The golden eyes would not leave her alone. Wendy lit another cigarette. Somehow she would have to deal with those eyes.

"Do it," she heard a distant voice whisper.

Yes. Do it, echoed a voice within her mind.

Of course it was wrong. Of course it was cruel. But the course of human history was forged by acts that lesser men and women might call wrong or cruel. Cruelty was at the heart of life itself. Ask any lion. Or any gazelle.

She drew on the cigarette, pondering that thought. To the gazelle, it was cruelty. To the lion, it was survival. It was a pleasant, warming notion, stirring yet another contraction deep within her. Pain and cruelty were as essential to existence as pleasure and kindness. More so, in fact. It was, simply, natural.

She tapped the ash from the cigarette, rolling the burning tip against the ashtray until the ember glowed hot and exposed.

Then she reached for those golden eyes.

Markie heard the howl and knew immediately. *Kato!*

18

The half mile to Markie's house from the beach had never seemed so long. She ran it nearly every day with Kato by her side, a lazy ten-minute-mile round trip unless she chose to go farther. Tonight, although her legs and lungs burned with the strain of an all-out sprint, it felt as if she were running through molasses. Seconds seemed like hours.

Halfway home, Kato's howls stopped. Her heart slammed as even more adrenaline surged into her system. She kicked up the pace. Round the corner, two more blocks…

Finally, *finally*, she reached her front door. She hadn't locked it. Kato was all the security she needed. Or so she had thought. She had horrific visions of her dog injured or killed by some intruder.

She flung the door open and was hit squarely in the chest by a leaping dog. He knocked her down on the porch. She heard Dec calling her name.

Then Kato grabbed at her sleeve and tried to drag her toward the street. Disinclined to argue, she pushed herself up, reaching the sidewalk just as Dec reached her.

"Are you okay?" he demanded. "What the hell was that dog doing?"

Markie, trying to catch her breath, could only look down at Kato. His golden eyes looked back, everything about his posture trying to tell her something.

Then he looked at the house and growled.

"You stay here," Dec said. "I'm going in for a look."

The golden eyes winked out like lamps. Wendy shuddered and jerked back into the present, shuddering with a fear she could not explain.

Gary reached for the paper, snatching it from her hand. "What's this?" he demanded.

"I don't know. A house. Glass doors. Eyes."

She looked at the paper herself for the first time and saw what she had drawn. The house and doors were almost unidentifiable slashes on the paper. But the eyes...

She shivered again, cold to the bone. She wanted her robe. She wanted to bury herself in a heap of concealing blankets and hide from the chill.

The eyes were everywhere on the paper. Outlined in heavy strokes. Slanted eyes, dangerous eyes. Eyes that seemed to reach out from the page. She turned away.

"What are these eyes?" Gary demanded.

"I don't know. I saw them. Something told me to

take them. I tried to reach them and…they were gone.''

''Dammit.''

She wanted to quail. Gary was angry with her. And for the first time in a long time, that seemed to matter.

''Try again,'' he demanded.

She shook her head. ''I…can't. Not yet.''

For an instant she thought he was going to hit her. Never in their entire marriage had he ever raised a hand to her, but right now he looked as if he wanted to hit her hard enough to knock her silly. Perversely, the idea did not frighten her. It thrilled her.

''I need some time,'' she said, hating her own placating voice. ''I need to rest for a few minutes.…''

Slowly, the hardness seeped from his face. ''Okay,'' he said finally. ''Rest for a while.''

Then, still naked, he rose and left the den.

And Wendy wanted to cry.

Markie knelt on the sidewalk and hugged Kato close. He was shivering, she realized. He never did that. At once she leaned back and looked into his face.

''Oh, my God!'' There was a burn on his snout, small but blackened. Tears burned her eyes and tightened her throat. ''Who hurt you?'' she asked him.

He shook off her touch as if it were of no importance and looked toward the house.

''Dec?'' She called to him. He had just reached the porch.

He looked back. ''Yeah?''

"Be careful. Kato's nose is burned. It looks almost like a laser burn."

"Oh, cripes." He looked at the door of the house, hesitating.

"Call the police," she urged. *"Please."*

But Dec was apparently determined to check out the house. He took another step toward the door.

Kato let out a howl, leaving Markie in his dust as he raced for the porch. He beat Dec to the door and planted himself sideways, blocking entry.

"Dec! *Please!* Call the police." Markie, still on her knees on the sidewalk, didn't care that she was begging.

Kato growled, continuing to bar the door.

"I know you wouldn't bite me, you determined beast," Dec said to the wolf. "You don't fool me."

But he pulled out his cell phone and called the cops. When he'd finished, he snapped the phone closed and looked down at Kato again. "There. Happy?"

Kato's tail lifted a bit and wagged once. Then, with his nose, he started pushing Dec back from the house.

Dec returned to the sidewalk, muttering, "First time in my damn life I've been herded like a sheep."

Apparently satisfied, Kato sat on his haunches and continued to watch the house.

Shaking with effort, Wendy pushed herself to her feet and went to the bedroom to get her robe. Then she went hunting for Gary. She found him in the kitchen, frying a steak.

"A steak?" she asked. Gary almost never ate beef.

"I'm hungry." He looked in her direction, but his gaze seemed to be focused on something else.

"I am, too." Maybe a few calories would help her recover. She felt as drained as if every ounce of blood had deserted her body.

"Did I tell you to put that robe on?" he asked, returning his eyes to the range.

It was as if an electric charge had pulsed through her womb. She dropped the robe to the floor. "No, you didn't. I'm sorry."

"Very well," he said, still not looking at her. "When I want you dressed, I'll tell you."

"Yes," she whispered. "Thank you."

It struck her as odd that she loved him more in that moment than ever before in their marriage. She realized she ought to be offended, to feel belittled, dehumanized by his raw assertion of power and ownership. Instead, she felt beautiful, wanted and loved.

"I love you, Gary," she whispered.

He turned to her, and a smile flickered across his features. Momentary, but real.

"I love you, too, Wendy. Now set the table."

Tom Little arrived at Markie's house within five minutes. Dec waited with Markie at the curb, where she was examining the burn on Kato's nose. It was a small, round wound, of a type Dec had seen too many times before.

"Cigarette burn," he said.

She looked up at him.

He simply nodded. "I worked an E.R."

Her eyes seemed a well of infinite sadness. Without a word, she returned her attention to the wolf. What she had left unsaid hung in the air like the sulfurous residue of a struck match. Someone had been in her home.

Tom Little emerged from the house with a look of confusion. "I didn't see any sign of an intruder. No broken glass or obvious signs of burglary."

"Someone burned my dog," she replied. "And there would be no reason to break in. I don't lock my door."

"I'll dust the doorknob for prints," Tom said. "And we should go through the house together. You can tell me if anything's been disturbed. Bring the dog with you. He might signal something that would help."

Markie hesitated, glancing at Dec.

"It's okay," he said. "I'll wait here. I'd just be in the way."

"Don't leave, okay?"

"I'm not going anywhere," he promised.

He watched as they went into the house, Kato in the lead, and fought against the notion that all the problems he'd come here to get away from had followed him. Violent death. Cruelty. Pain.

He supposed he ought to think about the positive things he'd found on Santz Martina. A good practice in a top-quality medical center. Wonderful mountain roads on which to ride his bike. A climate to die for.

Friendly people, by and large. A woman he was coming to care about.

And he was going to lose her. He was as certain of that fact as he was of the sunrise. He would say the wrong thing, do the wrong thing, be the wrong thing. He always did, always was. Earlier, on the beach, for just a fleeting moment, he'd felt her desire. He'd felt like a desirable man. And he'd nearly lost himself in that, let them tumble over that cliff. But the simple fact was, once she really got to know him, she would find a million little things that bothered her. Including his hours. Always the hours. And she would leave. And he would ache. Again.

Just the way he'd looked at death and pain and misery before and was seeing it now. Again. Life was full of second chances. But to paraphrase the words of David Mamet, the only second chance we get is the chance to make the same mistake again. And here he was, about to make the same mistake.

Again.

Kato pointed his nose up into the air, sniffing, his cheeks fluttering as he puffed the air back out. He led them around the living room, then back to the dining room, where he sniffed at the back door.

"It's still locked," Markie said.

"You lock the back door and leave the front open?" Tom asked.

She nodded. "It's weird, I know. I've been locking it for a couple of days now. Ever since he started sitting in front of it and staring through the glass."

"So you've had the idea that something's out there before?"

"I guess," she said. "Kato certainly has."

He unlocked the door, slid it open, and looked at the catch and jamb. "I don't see any tampering. Let's look around the rest of the house."

There was nothing out of place in the dining room or her bedroom. The second bedroom could have been turned over by a tornado and she wouldn't have known. She'd only been there six months and it was full of boxes, some open and half-empty, others still awaiting her attention.

"Is this…yours?" Tom asked.

Markie smiled and blushed a bit. "Yeah. That's my mess. I couldn't tell you if anything's been disturbed. Most of it is probably junk I shouldn't have bothered to pack and move to begin with. Maybe I got lucky and the burglar took some of it away."

He laughed. "That's one approach to unpacking." After a quick glance in the closet, he added, "I don't see where I have a lot to report."

Markie paused for a moment, then nodded. "So who burned my dog's nose?"

He spread his hands. "I wish I had an answer for you, Dr. Cross. But I'm not psychic. I'm just a cop. I'll write up the incident, though. Maybe we'll catch a break and turn up something. No promises, though."

"I understand," she said, as they walked back to the kitchen. "I'm sorry I wasted your time. Can I offer you a cup of coffee, at least?"

He smiled. "No doughnuts?"

"Sorry," she said. "Kato ate them all."

He looked down at the wolf. "Somehow, I can believe that. But no, thanks. I need another cup of coffee like I need a second head. I won't sleep tonight anyway."

She walked him to the door and smiled as Dec came up the walk.

"All clear?" he asked.

"Seems to be." He seemed different, she thought. Unsure. "Would you like to come in?"

He looked down. "Are you sure this is a good idea?"

She caught her breath, understanding what he meant. Different answers surged to her lips, then ebbed away. She wasn't sure. Did she know him well enough? How much of a risk was she prepared to take?

Finally she looked down at her toes and spoke the clearest truth. "I may go to the hotel. I don't want to be here alone tonight."

He started to speak, no more than a syllable passing his lips before a shove from behind pushed Markie right into his arms.

A startled laugh escaped him.

"Kato!" Markie said sharply, both embarrassed and dismayed. Straightening, she turned from Dec and looked down at her dog. He grinned back at her. "What has gotten into you?"

"I don't think he wants you to stay here alone," Dec said, a devilish but wary twinkle in his blue eyes.

"So I'll camp on the couch. Or the two of you can come stay at my place. I don't know that the hotel would let him in."

And she certainly wasn't going to leave the dog alone again. Somebody had *hurt* him.

"I'll camp on the couch," Dec said, settling the issue. But even as he spoke, she could hear the subtle question. He was awaiting her permission.

"Thanks," she said, trying to sound gracious, although gracious wasn't at all what she was feeling. Her nerves were as taut as bow strings, and she was on the edge of screaming.

Why, she didn't know. Only that someone had hurt her dog, and the craziness on this island was beginning to drive her nuts. The north pole was beginning to sound attractive.

Turning, she waved Dec inside. She didn't know if she wanted coffee or something stronger. If it was something stronger, she was out of luck, because she didn't keep alcohol on hand. She settled finally on a bottle of water, tossing another one to Dec.

Kato camped himself by the pantry door, reminding her that he hadn't had dinner yet.

"He seems okay now," Dec remarked.

"Yeah."

His too-wise eyes studied her. "But you're not."

"No. I'm not." She reached for the pantry door, and Kato moved to let her open it. Using the metal scoop, she filled his bowl with kibble. When she closed the door again, she nearly slammed it.

"Sorry," she said, not looking at Dec. Grabbing

her bottle of water, she went into the living room, as far from the glass doors in back as she could get. Sitting on the easy chair, she curled her legs beneath her.

Dec sat on the sofa. "Want to talk about it?"

"What's there to talk about?" she asked. "Alice… I can't get that out of my mind, Dec. I try to pretend everything's okay, but I keep seeing her, jerking around like a fish held on a hook. And nobody knows why. And Kato. I can't believe he would let anybody close enough to him to do that."

Dec hesitated, then admitted the unthinkable. "I don't think he would, either."

Her face looked pinched and her eyes anguished. "Then what? *What?*"

He was afraid of the answer to that. Mortally afraid.

19

Tim finished hosing off his boats, trying not to think about the quarantine that was killing his business. Keeping these boats in harbor was an expensive proposition, since he was still paying most of them off. He had reserves, of course—he was a good businessman—but they could last only so long without income.

It was dark now, only the lights of the marina and his boat illuminating his way. He wound up the hose, grabbed a mop and swabbed the water in the cockpit toward the scuppers. Satisfied at last, he stowed the mop and the hose, and sauntered away from the marina.

He didn't want to go home. He rarely wanted to go home anymore, even though it was one of the few places in the world where he could have all his comforts around him. Dawn was there, and he didn't want to face the deep freeze.

So he climbed in his Jeep and headed up the mountains toward Annie's old plantation. From there he could look down on Martina Town and the lights of the harbor. Maybe even see a few of the cruise ships that were forever plying the shipping lanes to the west on their way to favored locations like Aruba.

Sitting on a burnt, broken column, he took in the dark, diamond-studded sweep of the Caribbean night. The air was fresh, free of human pollutants, perfumed faintly by exotic blossoms that bloomed only at night. Blossoms the names of which he could never remember.

Except for one, a bloodred hibiscuslike bloom with a black center. He had no idea what its botanical name might be, but he knew what the locals called it: Annie's Heart.

He almost snickered every time he thought of it, because it was a truly beautiful flower to his way of thinking. Yes, it bloomed only at night, and yes, it had a black center, but it was still beautiful.

Annie must have been like that, he mused. A beautiful sensuous woman. How else had she manipulated so many men?

He closed his eyes, and it was almost as if he could feel her touch, hear her murmurs.

Yes. One hell of a woman.

Steve Chase stayed late in his office, drafting the Senate resolution that would close the schools early for the Christmas holidays. A precautionary measure. Late, but still a decisive act, never mind that a lot of kids had been yanked out by their parents after the Shippeys died, anyway.

He was alone, working by the light of his computer and the green-shaded banker's lamp on his desk.

There was something about the beauty of drafting a legal document that always pleased him. The precision of the language, the careful choice of words, so that there could be no possible misinterpretation. The organization for the sake of clarity, the detailed explanations in support.

All of it pleased him, just as architecture pleased him. Details coalescing into a thing of beauty. It absorbed him as nothing else in his life did.

A chilly breeze blew across the back of his neck, and he looked up crossly, annoyed at the disturbance. Had his secretary turned down the air conditioning again?

She had an annoying habit of doing that, and he generally didn't notice it until after dark, when the sun no longer shone in his windows to warm him and his office.

Another breath of coldness, this one seeming to wrap around him.

Dammit.

Rising from his computer, he went to the door leading to the outer office, where he could reset the thermostat. He would have to get severe with her again. More severe than last time.

He flung the door wide, then stopped as he saw a shadow move in the dark outer office.

"Camille?" he said, thinking it must be his secretary.

Nothing answered him. The chill snaked over his neck again, reminding him of his irritation.

"Dammit, I told you not turn the air down anymore. I'm freezing in there."

The shadow moved again, looking like a woman's shape, but she didn't make a sound.

Uncertainty began to grow. "Camille? If this is some kind of joke..." Reaching out, he flipped a switch, filling the room with bright light.

But there was no one there.

It took him exactly two strides to reach the outer door, and exactly three seconds to pass through it and lock it.

He would finish that resolution in the morning.

Dec was deep in much needed sleep, dreaming of things at once dark and bright, amorphous and fluid, a strange and almost hypnotic dream that had him chasing things he couldn't quite see.

The images fled as something cold and wet touched his arm. Disturbed, he pulled his arm away, barely aware of what he was doing, and tried to sink back into the dream.

Moments later, he got a firm jab in the ribs.

Shocked out of sleep, he bolted upright and tried to remember where he was. It was dark. The windows were in the wrong places. He had been lying on a...couch.

Markie's place. But what the hell had poked him?

The poke came again, this time on his knee. Cold and wet. *Kato*.

Something like relief shuddered through him as he made out the dog's dark shape, a shadow among shadows.

"You need a walk, boy?" he asked groggily. Damn, and the couch had been so comfortable.

The shadow backed up a little, and some of the light from the street lamps outside glinted off golden eyes.

"Okay." He rubbed his eyes and rolled his head, trying to loosen his neck.

Hadn't Kato been sleeping with Markie? He'd thought she'd closed her door.

But it was too early in the morning to be solving puzzles, so he pushed himself to his feet and went to get the leash.

But Kato didn't follow. Instead, the quiet click of his claws and the jingle of his collar led toward the kitchen. Maybe Markie let him out back at night.

Willing to do it whichever way, Dec followed.

As he reached the kitchen and breakfast area, he saw Kato clearly silhouetted against the glass doors. The wolf was on his haunches, staring out into the night, clearly on alert.

All of a sudden, the sleepy fog cleared from Dec's brain. He went to stand beside Kato. "What is it, boy?"

The quietest of whimpers escaped the wolf, short and to the point. Dec looked in the direction Kato was staring, trying to figure out what had him disturbed.

At first he could see nothing unusual. The backs of

houses, shadowed strangely by the limited light from the street lamps. Everything looked peaceful.

But Kato whimpered again, then gave a low growl that sounded like the ominous rumble of distant thunder.

The hair on Dec's neck stood on end, and he squinted into the poorly lit area behind the house, trying to see something.

Kato stirred, just a shifting of posture, but it bespoke uneasiness. Dec didn't know dogs as well as Markie did, and he wondered if he was making too much of this behavior.

A soft, almost caressing chill wandered across his shoulders. At that instant, Kato rose to all fours and lowered his head, his attention still fixed outside. The chill came again, stronger.

Dec shivered at the cold trickle of sweat in the small of his back. The caressing chill came and went, came and went, elusive but unmistakable. He was being played with, teased…in the way a cat would tease a mouse. As soon as the thought came he told himself not to go over the edge. There was nothing there.

The wolf growled again, the rumble seeming to be emitted from his entire body.

That was when Dec saw it. It came floating over the houses, slowly, just above the rooftops. A dark, vaporous cloud, not a fog, but something darker. As it passed before streetlights, they dimmed as if partially obscured.

Then it was gone.

He would not sleep this night. Finding Markie's bedroom door open a crack, he shooed Kato in there.

"Watch her, Kato. Keep her safe." He was certain that the command was unnecessary.

Then he pulled a chair from the kitchen and parked himself right outside Markie's door. The chair was uncomfortable, not something he could fall asleep in.

Folding his arms, he stared into the darkness of the house and faced things he'd cast out of his life years ago. Things he was staunchly opposed to.

Things his Irish blood told him were real.

It struck him that he'd become as devout an atheist as he had once been a Catholic. Because both, for better or worse, were beliefs. He'd gotten angry at God and decided that God couldn't exist, because a loving God wouldn't allow such horrors as he had seen all too often.

Which was not exactly a brilliant deduction, Watson, he told himself now. It was a reaction, not a considered position. Somehow he had decided it would be easier to bear the difficulties of life in a vacuum.

Well, it hadn't been. And sitting there in the darkness, he at last admitted that the evil he had seen had been done by men, not by God.

The mere fact that God had not intervened to create a perfect world where everyone lived in harmony, health and abundance didn't mean God didn't exist. It meant only that God had given men free will, and that men abused their ability to choose.

But if he were to admit to the existence of God,

then he had to confront the next logical question. If there was an ultimate good, was there an ultimate evil? For most of his life, he had believed that there was no need for Satan. After all, men seemed to do enough dirty work on their own.

But the question he had never answered was *why* men did such horrible things. Try as he might, he could not refute the notion that there might be an evil presence as surely as there was a God.

And why wouldn't there be? he asked himself. Why not a sort of yin and yang struggling for dominance of the world, just as so many in the past had believed? If a God, why not an antigod?

He sighed and shifted on his chair, wishing he weren't pondering these questions right now, alone, in the dark, with his shirt still clinging to the damp detritus of fear. This was a question he should ponder by day, with calm and dispassionate reason. Not when he was feeling things go bump in the night.

And yet, he had heard Alice Wheatley speak with utter conviction about having seen the ghost of Annie Black. Then, hours later, he had watched her death throes, a marionette being shaken by a brutal hand. He had felt the darkness at the fort. And tonight he had felt it again. More, he had seen it.

Skepticism was a healthy trait and part of his training as a doctor. But so was confronting the cold facts before one's eyes: something was at work on this island. And if that meant believing in God and antigod, well, he had no reasonable alternative.

He listened to the darkness for a while but could

detect nothing unusual. Silly. He ought to know by now that if anything were happening, Kato would be alerting in whatever way the wolf deemed necessary.

Sighing again, he rose from the chair and went to the kitchen, where he stood in the dark and used Markie's phone to call Father Pedro Gutierrez. Pedro was his good golfing buddy and would probably fall into ecstasy when Dec told him what he wanted...even if it *was* three in the morning.

"Father Gutierrez," said a familiar sleepy voice.

"Pedro? It's Dec."

A rustle and a yawn. "The course doesn't open until seven."

Under other circumstances, Dec might have laughed, but there was nothing to laugh about tonight. "Pedro, I need to make my confession."

A long silence this time. A very long one. When Pedro spoke again, his voice was gentle. "I can't do that over the phone, Dec."

"I can't come over there. I'm...watching over a friend."

"Then I'll come to you. Where are you?"

Dec gave him the address.

"Give me twenty minutes. I need to wash the sleep out of my eyes. Do I need to shave?"

"Come in your pajamas if you want. Just come. Please."

"On my way."

When he disconnected, Dec realized his hand was shaking. He'd just taken a frighteningly huge step.

The words of Nietzsche came to mind: *When you look into the abyss, the abyss looks into you.*

Father Pedro arrived as quickly as promised. He wore shorts and a faded, lemon-yellow T-shirt that read *Golf: The perfect combination of exercise and swearing.* A wiry man of moderate height, his blond hair had been bleached almost white by years of tropical sun, and his skin had aged prematurely, making him look a good ten years older than his forty-five. He had a lively manner about him—when he was fully awake—and a smile that could light up a stadium.

Dec put a finger to his lips as he let Pedro into the house and led the way to the kitchen. He was grateful that Kato apparently chose to ignore the intrusion. No sounds emerged from the direction of Markie's room.

The kitchen was still dark; he hadn't turned on any lights. Pedro didn't say a word about it, simply felt his way to a stool at the island.

"What's going on, Dec?"

Dec slid onto the stool beside him and sought words. Thinking these things was difficult enough; voicing them was even harder. Finally he settled on, "Do you believe in Satan?"

"Depends on what you mean by that. If you mean an Enemy in opposition to God, who tries to weaken us and tempt us away, then yes. If you mean a guy in a devil suit with a pitchfork, then no."

"But what exactly is the Enemy?"

"You know, God is so great that we can't even

begin to imagine Him. We use words to describe Him that are true, but our consciousness can't begin to grasp the whole truth behind them. He is a being, a force, utterly beyond our comprehension. As we have been told, His ways are not our ways."

Dec nodded. He'd been brought up with this.

Pedro continued. "Consider, then, that some Enemy opposes him. Some people say human evil is enough to explain bad things. Maybe it is. But that doesn't explain what draws us to do these bad things. And at times, we're *all* drawn to do bad things. And some of these urges are pretty hard to explain. It's my feeling that the Enemy exists, but that he's so far beyond our comprehension, we can't truly discern *His* ways, either. Only that he is in opposition to the light."

"But what about...evil spirits?" Dec had to squeeze the words out. He couldn't believe he was thinking these things, couldn't believe he was actually saying them.

"What kind?" Pedro asked. Then, as Dec hesitated again, he said, "Look, let's not talk about this philosophically. You know the philosophy, probably as well as I do. Why don't you just tell me what's happening that has you asking these questions?"

So Dec told him. *Just the facts, ma'am*, like Joe Friday in *Dragnet*. He chose to leave his feelings and reactions completely out of it. As clinically as he could, he told Pedro about Alice Wheatley, about the fort, about the dogs' behavior, Kato's in particular, and about what he had seen that night.

Pedro's expression was virtually invisible in the dark, for which Dec was grateful. He waited uneasily for the priest to digest what he'd just heard and to assemble some thoughts about it. Pedro was rarely one to shoot from the cuff.

"That," said Pedro finally, "gives me pause, too."

"How so?"

"I'll let you in a secret. I didn't believe in the devil until my bishop asked me to assist in an exorcism."

"No kidding." Dec hadn't been aware such things still happened.

"No kidding. Every diocese has a priest who is trained in the rite of exorcism. But he can't do it alone. We never leave a priest alone to confront a demon, so one or two other priests are designated as assistants. I was designated, given a bit of training, and went merrily on my way, figuring I'd never be called on."

"But you were."

Even in the darkness, he could see Pedro nod.

"I was. An exorcism, you know, isn't really anything mysterious. It's basically a blessing, a prayer. Not much different from the anointing of the sick, in essence. Most of the time it takes an hour or two, and the possession is over. No big deal. Believe me, we don't see a lot of rotating heads and flying pea soup."

Dec chuckled. "I would hope not."

Pedro paused before continuing. "Anyway, one day I got the call. I trotted over there, expecting to spend an hour or two in intense prayer, maybe hear a few shameful secrets about myself, but sure I could withstand the humiliation. I wasn't prepared.''

He sighed. ''All I can say, Dec, is that I have seen the devil. And he's more vile and terrifying than anything you want to imagine. But he's also puny and weak compared with God. If we're strong in our faith, he's helpless. He tries to rattle that faith, to make us doubt and turn away. If we stand firm, he moves on to easier prey.

''Let me tell you, Dec, there's nothing like an encounter with the devil to make you believe in God.''

''So...you don't think I'm crazy?''

''Heck, no. In fact, you have me seriously worried. I've dealt with demons, yes, but I've never dealt with a persistent evil spirit of a dead person.''

There. It was out. Pedro had finally said the very thing Dec had been trying to avoid. ''I don't want to believe that.''

''I don't blame you. And if you think I've got any ideas for how to deal with a disembodied spirit, I'm going to have to disappoint you.''

Dec sighed and drummed his fingers on the counter. ''I think I was hoping you'd tell me such things couldn't exist.''

Pedro gripped his shoulder. ''You're a good observer. And you're too honest a man to lie to yourself. You know what you saw, and you know it wasn't natural. You know what evil feels like, and you felt it. So, do you still want to make your confession?''

Somehow, Dec did. After all these years, he felt the need to reconcile with God, to say he was sorry for being so stubborn. It was time to admit that he'd acted like a child, turning his back on God because God wasn't playing by Dec's rules.

Pedro handled it like a conversation, talking with him quietly, and in the end absolving him and giving him his penance. It was a mild penance for one who'd denied God for so many years, but Dec figured Pedro was just glad to have him back in the flock.

"Read Matthew, chapters five through seven, every day for the next month," Pedro told him.

"I don't think I have a Bible."

"You know where to get one. If you can't find it, let me know. I've got plenty of extras."

Feeling oddly lighthearted, Dec almost laughed.

That was when the kitchen lights snapped on, nearly blinding them both for an instant.

In the doorway, wrapped in a red silk robe, stood Markie, with Kato beside her. "I thought I heard voices," she said sleepily. "What are you two up to?"

20

It was gone. Whatever had driven Gary was gone as surely as if someone had flipped a switch. His face softened into its customary lines. For an instant, he looked confused.

Watching the change, Wendy grew uneasy. This time, when she pulled her robe on, he didn't say anything. In fact, he looked at the steak he was cooking and asked, "Did you want this?"

A shiver passed through Wendy. She dropped abruptly to one of the kitchen chairs. "You started cooking it, Gary."

"I did?"

"I thought you wanted it."

"Odd," he said, looking at the rapidly charring T-bone. "Well, I don't want to waste it."

Gary was always very conscious about not being wasteful. As soon as the steak was ready, he divided it onto two plates and put one in front of Wendy. Her stomach turned over at the sight.

"Do you want anything with it?" he asked.

She shook her head. "I don't think I can eat."

She waited for him to become demanding, the way he had only a few minutes ago, but he let it pass.

"I'm not sure I can, either. Maybe I could save it for sandwiches?"

She didn't know how to answer that. She had the eerie feeling that over the last couple of hours she had been dealing with someone else, someone other than Gary. It was as if he had switched personalities.

"Whatever," she said, feeling cold deep inside. "Throw it away, for all I care. Give it to somebody's dog."

If she'd hoped to make him become stern again, she failed. He took the two plates from the table and sat across from her. She wondered if he even remembered the last couple of hours.

"We've got to find out how those words got on the tape," he said.

So he remembered that much. She wondered about the rest.

"Your automatic writing didn't tell us much."

"No." She remembered the golden eyes and wondered what she had been seeing. Even the memory of them spooked her, and she wasn't easily spooked.

Gary rubbed his eyes. "God, I'm tired. I feel like I just ran up and down the mountain."

She was tired, too, but everything was so suddenly off-kilter that she didn't know if she would be able to sleep.

She wondered what she had been in touch with earlier. Had it been some kind of remote viewing?

Had she been getting something from someone else's mind? If so, she wasn't sure she ever wanted to be in touch with it again. It was powerful, and, in retrospect, it had been evil, although at the time she had noted only power and the exhilaration of using it.

Then something inside her began to collapse, filling her with fatigue and sadness. All of a sudden she just plain didn't care. The adrenaline rush was gone.

Gary touched her shoulder. "Come on, honey. Let's go to bed."

For the first time in a long time, she was grateful for his gentleness.

Markie made coffee, and joined Pedro and Dec at the counter. Kato paced around for a few minutes, then curled up on the rug beneath the breakfast table.

Dec was beginning to feel sheepish. In the bright light, surrounded by friends, he was beginning to wonder if he'd imagined everything, if he'd just pushed the panic button. If, in fact, he'd acted like the superstitious kid he'd once been. A kid with a mother who told him not to open an umbrella in the house because it would bring bad luck, not to step on cracks and to never, ever make an important decision on Friday the thirteenth. To this day, he had to fight an urge to knock on wood.

"Why didn't you wake me?" Markie asked Dec.

Her eyes were ringed from fatigue, and the sight made his heart squeeze. Whatever his late-night fears, she had needed her sleep.

"It was over before I was sure I saw anything."

She nodded. "Okay."

She didn't believe him. That was obvious. But he left it there. The alternative would be to admit to protective feelings that frightened him as much as anything he'd seen in the past week.

Pedro seemed to read her eyes, and Dec's, and said, in his best and most enigmatic clerical tone, "You have a good watchdog, Markie."

Markie smiled, then paused a moment and made her way to the coffeepot. "Can I get you anything, Father? Do you guys want breakfast?"

"How could I say no?" Pedro asked. "Your culinary skills are legendary."

"And here I thought you only cooked for me," Dec said, hoping his voice carried the levity he intended.

"Dr. Cross is a cherished participant in our potluck dinners," Pedro said. "They mob her in the parking lot. She's lucky if she can get a dish into the parish hall before it's empty."

"Now that's a bit over the top, Father," Markie said, blushing.

"Perhaps," he said. "But only a little."

Twenty minutes later, their mugs were filled with steaming coffee, and she had transformed a few eggs and some leftover ham and vegetables into an omelet to die for. In the process, Kato's bowl had been filled with and then emptied of kibble, and he lay contented on the floor as they ate.

"How well do you know Loleen Cathan?" Dec asked as he lifted a fluffy forkful of eggs to his mouth.

Pedro sipped his coffee. "Loleen is one of the most fascinating women I have ever met. If I had half her wisdom, I would think myself blessed."

"But you know about her...other beliefs?" Dec asked.

"Of course," Pedro replied, smiling. He paused, as if to weigh his words carefully before continuing. "I am a priest, Declan. I know the sacred scriptures and church tradition. I can find the dogmatically correct answers in the *Catechism,* in paper encyclicals, in the writings of the saints. I believe in the tangible grace of the sacraments and the intangible truth of the Nicene Creed. I know I can and have found God in the church. Or, more accurately, God finds me there.

"But I also know that God is too vast to be encapsulated, His power too great to be contained within a single building or set of beliefs. God loves us enough to reach down and find us on many paths. And for that reason, I can say this: God finds Loleen in the church, and also in every grace-filled prayer she offers. Her heart is good and pure, purer than many priests I've known. And what she says comes from that pure heart. So I listen, and hope that in the listening I will glean even a fragment of what life has taught her."

"So I should listen to her," Dec said quietly.

Pedro laughed. "Declan Quinn, sometimes you are entirely too Irish for your own good. Maybe it's your cultural legacy, coming from an island where outsiders too seldom brought hope and too often brought tragedy, but you are the most suspicious people I've ever known. That's probably why so many of you become cops.''

"Probably so," Dec agreed. "Skepticism runs deep in our blood.''

"And so does mysticism, Dec. Never forget that. To deny it is to deny part of who you are. And that, my dear doctor, is the worst of folly.'' The mirth had gone from Pedro's eyes. "If Loleen Cathan speaks to you, you listen. And pray that you hear.''

Tim had never before called the group together. Steve and Gary knew of each other, of course, and each had some sense of the other's involvement. But this was the first time he'd met with both of them at the same time. The first time he'd been able to watch their faces and read their eyes as each felt out the other's presence and sphere of influence.

The boat rocked gently with the rising midmorning tide. Gary sometimes seemed to glance at the hatch to the cabin below, as if sensing the lingering presence of his wife. But for the most part, his eyes spoke of a new and clearer focus. A strength that Tim found more than a bit disturbing. Tim had chosen his conspirators with purpose. Men who held useful positions without strong convictions. Men whom he could bend as necessary, without wondering if they would break. Gary now seemed to have more spine than Tim had anticipated. That could become a problem.

Steve's demeanor gave Tim entirely different concerns. He was more than malleable. He had become fragile, growing more cautious, more skittish, with

each new death. He would never have cut it as a crew-
man on one of Tim's boats. The man had no taste for
blood. No taste for true power.

No, Steve still clung to the delusion of power that
came with his political position, when Tim knew for
a fact that the Senate was little more than a legiti-
mizing gloss for his father's own plans and designs.
Steve Chase had no understanding of what power really meant. Like most paper tigers, he quailed at the
prospect of real prey. And that was as dangerous as
Gary's nascent resolve.

"Too many bodies are piling up," Steve was saying. "None of us knows why. I just think it's dangerous to continue until we do. That's all I'm saying.
Pick a time when there isn't quite so bright a light on
everything that happens on the island."

A typical Steve-ism. In another situation, another
context, it might make sense. But Tim was *that* close
to a prize he'd spent months working toward. Years,
even. He was not about to back away because of
"bright lights." In any campaign, there were casu-
alties. How long had he been a casualty of his father's
business campaigns? He knew what it meant to be
collateral damage. That was the price of all success.
A bigger slice of the pie for one meant a smaller slice
for someone else. That was life.

"Oh, we know what's killing these people," Gary
said softly. "One of the advantages of teaching history is that life happens in context. Patterns emerge."

Steve looked at him quizzically.

"In 1969," Gary continued, "a bored army lance

corporal with an interest in folklore started sniffing around the Annie Black legend.''

''And?'' Steve asked.

''And seven soldiers died in a month,'' Tim said. ''After three died in one night, the post commander made a midnight call to the Pentagon. The next morning, the army closed the fort and left.''

Steve's face was turning ashen. He turned to Gary. ''This is true?''

Gary nodded. ''Yes.''

''My God! Why hasn't anyone heard about this? I've lived here…twenty years. How did you…when did you know?''

''As I said, there are advantages to teaching history. The army kept it quiet. No one else on the island has been affected. A small team from USAMRIID came in afterward and went over the fort with a fine-tooth comb. They found nothing. It was written off as a fluke.''

''But…seven soldiers!'' Steve said.

''It was 1969,'' Tim answered. ''The height of Vietnam. Seven dead soldiers were a blip on the radar.''

Steve nodded. He looked over at Gary. ''Okay, so how *did* you find out about this?''

Gary laughed. It was a hard laugh with a razor edge. ''It was in the turd file.''

''Turd file?'' Steve asked.

''Odd as it may seem,'' Gary replied, ''even history professors have a sense of humor. Every once in a while, some student turns in a paper that is truly outstanding. The kind of paper the professor wishes he'd written when he was in college. The kind that makes him think maybe he's accomplishing something more than bouncing words off the classroom walls. We save them, in the department. We call it the Greatest Hits file. So that if someone wins a Nobel Prize someday, we can pull out the paper and say 'I knew him when...'"

"And this paper was in that file?" Steve asked.

Gary smiled. "Hardly. But we also keep another file. There are papers we read and just can't stop shaking our heads. If their authors own a dictionary or a spell checker, they'll be able to return it when they graduate, still in its original packaging. They think the MLA is a government agency and a source is someone to buy drugs from. Their papers, the worst of the worst, go in the turd file...to amuse and bemuse bored professors long after the students have gone on to careers in politics."

Tim chuckled at that remark. Steve cast a warning glance, but Gary ignored it and continued.

"A year ago, I got one of those papers. A dreadful pile of verbal diarrhea that advanced the stunningly original hypothesis that the twentieth century saw the rise of capitalism as the only viable economic system." Sarcasm dripped from every word. "It could have been a mildly interesting if shopworn argument if the student hadn't based it on Internet chat logs. Complete with emoticons and flame wars. Hardly what I'd call scholarship."

"And your point is?" Steve asked, clearly growing impatient with Gary's pedantry.

If Gary noticed, he gave no indication. "I felt that paper was deserving of inclusion in the turd file. And as I often do when I tuck a paper in there, I thumbed through the other exhibits in our little hall of shame. And that's when I tumbled across a student's paper from the autumn of 1969. There were no verifiable sources, only overheard snippets of conversations between soldiers in bars. To the professor, it seemed ridiculous. As it turns out, it was surprisingly accurate. You might say it proved the adage that even a blind squirrel finds an acorn now and then."

"Gary and I had talked about Annie Black and her treasure," Tim said. "He brought the paper to me. It was…something we factored into our plans from the start."

Steve's mouth fell open. "You…you *knew* people could die? And you went on with this anyway?"

Such a wimp, Tim thought, though he kept his face neutral. "It was a possibility, Steve. Death happens."

It helped, of course, that there was even a sliver of evidence suggesting that Annie Black's treasure might lie beneath Carter Shippey's house. Carter had long been a thorn in Tim's side, a competitor who more than once had reported Tim's crews for ignoring catch limits. Siccing Annie on the old man had been a test of her potency. That it had also removed a barnacle-crusted pain in the ass was icing on the cake.

Tim hadn't foreseen that Annie would kill Carter's wife, of course. He hadn't realized she was *that* vicious. But if you happened to snag a sea turtle while dragging for shrimp, hey, things happen. As for Alice Wheatley, well, Annie had done that on her own. Alice had *seen* her, for crying out loud. Annie was just acting in self-defense.

"I can't be a part of this anymore," Steve said. "I won't. Treasure is one thing, but human life…"

Tim caught Gary's eye and saw his own thoughts reflected with chilling clarity.

Yes. *Death happens.*

Kato stretched languidly as he watched Declan napping. Markie was working on a sick cat, and Declan had come to work with her, hovering protectively for a while, before his body finally gave in to exhaustion.

Humans were strange creatures. They seemed to take pride in denying themselves that most basic of pleasures, sleep. Kato knew better. There was a time to hunt, a time to play, a time to train pups, a time to reinforce roles in the pack. All of that was important. But sleep…sleep was where life really happened. Sleep was where he could curl up in the souls of his pack mates, share minds, roam far and wide over pristine meadows and dense woods, noses in the breeze, scenting leaf and loam and the essence of life itself. In awake times, he lived mostly within himself, save for those all-too-rare times when Markie opened herself to him. But in sleep, he was whole.

He wondered if humans experienced this wholeness in their sleep, or if they simply frittered away their dreams still isolated within their own thoughts and fears. They certainly didn't seem to emerge from sleep with the sense of connectedness that he felt. Perhaps that was why Declan hadn't slept with Markie last night. Perhaps humans didn't understand or experience the dreams that a pack shared when its members curled up as one. He felt Markie's dreams, sometimes, when they lay together in the bed, her feet tucked beneath his neck, her toes occasionally wiggling in his fur. But Markie was special. Or maybe she just shared that with him. Maybe humans couldn't share that together.

Regardless, it seemed absurd that Declan hadn't slept with Markie. They were pack mates. That much was obvious, to him if not to them. And pack mates slept together. He would have to work on that.

The cat sagged on the table, and Markie's face collapsed. She had lost. He had seen this before, and it hurt every time. He padded silently into the room and sat with his flank against her leg. It was all he could do.

"I'm sorry, Kato," she whispered.

She always said that. As if she had let him down by the death of the patient. As if anything she could do with her needles and pills and instruments could stand in the way of the eternal cycle. Kato had known the cat was dying from the moment he'd scented it as it was brought in. Its soul was struggling to escape, to fly forever into the land of dreams. Its pain stung his nostrils, and that was why he'd gone in to check on Declan. But he'd known. There was nothing Markie could have done.

And in truth, nothing she *should* have done. It was time for that soul to leave. Time to be free. Time to be connected with all of the other souls, forever. While he ached for Markie's pain, he also celebrated the liberation of a tired soul. A soul exhausted from the isolation of living in a body. A soul needing to breathe.

The cat's owner came in. Markie spoke a few words, although words didn't matter. There were times when even humans let go of words and simply experienced. The woman broke into tears, sagging against a wall. Markie reached out to touch her, just a hand on a shoulder, but Kato knew with utter clarity how much more that said than all the words humans could ever speak. The woman fought to compose herself, finally managing a brief nod that lied about a strength she would not feel for days or weeks. She bent over and kissed the cat's body.

If only she could have kissed the soul.

Kato saw the soul hovering and opened himself to it. *She loves you.*

I know, the soul answered.

The air in the room went cold, and the soul fled. Kato smelled it an instant before he saw it.

Staring at Markie.

Smiling an evil smile.

The growl rose in his throat, and he leapt.

21

Markie fell to the floor as Kato jumped on her. A chill swept above her as she fell, and she looked up as, for an instant, Caroline Fletcher shuddered. Kato's low growl was directed upward, but his weight kept Markie pinned to the floor. Then the chill passed.

"What the hell?" Caroline asked.

"I'm sorry," Markie answered, trying to roll out from under eighty pounds of wolf. "He's not usually like this."

But Caroline wasn't looking at Kato. Instead, she raised a finger to her lip. It came away red and wet. Her nose was bleeding.

"I'll get you a tissue," Markie said. "Sit down and tip your head back. Kato, get *off!*"

The dog moved away reluctantly, and Markie grabbed a handful of sterile gauze pads. Caroline had sunk into a chair and was now looking up at the ceiling. Markie pressed the gauze against her upper lip, both to catch the blood and to compress the blood vessel, slowing the flow.

"Did Kato hit you?" she asked.

"No," Caroline answered. "I don't think so. I don't know what it was. It was like...a punch from inside."

"I'm so sorry," Markie said. "Just sit for a moment. I'll get some ice."

"No. No. I'm okay. It's just a nosebleed."

Kato had left the room and now returned with Declan. A thought flitted through Markie's concentration on Caroline like a snake in the grass: *Kato and Declan have learned how to read each other remarkably well.* She shoved the thought and what it meant aside, and focused on the task at hand.

"Kato knocked me down," she said. "I might have bumped her, or he might have. I don't know."

"Let me take a look," he said, turning to Caroline. His face softened into a bedside manner smile. "I'm Dr. Quinn. I do humans."

"It's just a nosebleed," Caroline repeated.

"That's what it looks like," Declan agreed. "But just in case."

He pressed gently at her sinuses, his face betraying nothing as she groaned. When he touched the bridge of her nose, the groan intensified into a short, sharp cry.

"You have a broken nose," he said. "You'll have a couple of black eyes by tonight. Are you sure Dr. Cross or the dog didn't bump you?"

"Yes," she replied. "They were...I mean...no, they didn't touch me. I told her. It felt like I got punched from the inside. Damn, it hurts."

"I'm sorry," Declan said, still gently probing the nasal ridge. "Yes, I'm afraid it's broken. You'll need to get over to the hospital and have it set. They'll pack and tape it, and drain the septum so your nose will stay thin and pretty. But you should be fine."

"Dr. Evans is a good ENT," Markie said. "I'll call him and let him know you're coming."

"So much fuss," Caroline said. "It's just a nose-bleed. Really. I'll be fine."

"Just in case," Declan said.

Markie knew what he was thinking. Liability. It was an ugly thought intruding on a treatment procedure, but it was there nonetheless. She would be paying for Caroline's treatment. That was a given. But if she treated the woman with caring, concern and professionalism, perhaps she wouldn't find herself in court over a broken nose.

She spent the next fifteen minutes making phone calls, walking Caroline to Declan's car, convincing her that it wasn't safe for her to drive, then finally instructing the staff to dispose of the cat's remains. Declan returned in time for lunch.

"Is she okay?" Markie asked.

He nodded. "Rick Evans is good. She's stable. She'll be fine."

"I must have bumped her when Kato knocked me down. That's all I can imagine."

"I don't think that was it," Dec said.

"No?"

"No."

"What do you mean?" she asked.

His voice was quiet. "She'll need cosmetic surgery. The cartilage in her nose was all but gone."

Eyes.

Wendy looked at the drawing again, picked up another colored pencil and added a few strokes, changed pencils and added a few more. Finally she put the pencils down.

Golden eyes.

The ringing of the phone disturbed her concentration. She picked it up.

"Darling."

It was Tim. For some reason, his voice no longer sent a chill through her. But a tiny voice whispered that there was no reason he should know that...yet.

"Hello, love," she said.

"Are we getting together tonight?" he asked.

"Hmmmmmm," she purred, knowing he wouldn't detect the falsity. "It's possible."

"I'd like that."

His voice had the eager tenor of pleasure imagined. The thought struck her that he was, in many ways, a child. Promise him some sex and he would walk right into the mouth of a volcano. To think she had imagined him a man.

"By the way, is Gary home?"

"No, he's not. He said he was going to pick up a few things on the way home."

The undertone in Gary's voice when he'd called had made her sex throb. She still wondered what he had in mind. The possibilities were...endless.

"Give him a message for me," Tim said. "Tell him there's been another...incident. We need to talk."

Such a boy, she thought. Trying to talk in little boys' codes. As if women wouldn't know or want to know such things.

"Yes," she said. "I'll tell him."

A faint click flitted down the line. The question answered itself almost immediately. *You've been caught, little boy!*

"Thanks," Tim said, hesitation in his voice. He'd heard it, too. "Tell him to call me, okay?"

"I'll give him the message," she answered.

As she hung up the phone, a dark smile emerged on her face. Tim would have an interesting day. She doubted she would even have to come up with a reason to avoid their meeting tonight. Dawn would probably take care of that. Yet another of Tim's lies. It served him right.

Just then the door opened and Gary entered. She turned to catch his eyes, to see if they held the same dark pleasure that had thrilled her so thoroughly last night and teased her so casually when he'd called. They did. Without even thinking, she found herself on her knees, holding the drawing out to him.

"Golden eyes," she whispered.

Tim stormed into the sunroom, which Dawn had turned into an office for her charity projects. She was sitting at her desk, pencil poised over a checklist of some sort.

"You were listening to my phone call," he said.

She turned to face him, her face eerily calm. "Excuse me?"

"*Excuse me?*" he said, mimicking her. "You were on the goddamn extension! I heard the click!"

"So you called your girlfriend," she said. "Big deal. I reached for the phone to call a sponsor and heard you were on the phone. I hung up. I don't see why you're getting so bent about it."

He wanted to wring her delicate neck, right then and there. It would be so easy. He was bigger and stronger and had a workingman's strength. She was soft, despite her twice-weekly tennis lessons. He could almost hear the *crack* of vertebrae separating. Five seconds, ten at most, and it would be over. He would be rid of this infuriatingly cool, calm excuse for a woman.

But not yet. There were others ahead of her on the list. And having Annie do it would be infinitely more satisfying. He'd heard the rumors of how she worked, what she did. The idea of Dawn shuddering in agony while Annie tore her apart from the inside made his loins twitch. It would be so perfect.

"Don't listen to any more of my calls, bitch," he said, before slamming the door of her office.

Oh, yes. Annie would do it so well.

Declan called his office first and heard what he'd expected to hear. Yes, his afternoon patients had called to cancel. He wasn't surprised. They'd been routine appointments, follow-ups on previous treatments, annual physicals and the like. Things people wanted to put off until someone had an answer for what was happening on Santz Martina. He gave his nurse instructions to call in refills for a couple of routine prescriptions and hung up the phone.

"So what now?" Markie asked.

She, too, was closing her office for the afternoon, double-checking the animals in the kennel, catching up on treatment notes from the morning clients.

"Now we pay a visit to Loleen," he said, once again dialing his cell phone. He put the instrument to his ear and listened to the ringing. *Be there, Jolly,* he thought, hoping against all logic that the undertaker hadn't closed up shop. He probably had. There was no reason not to.

"Hello?"

A surge of relief passed through Dec. "Jolly?"

"Yes. Dr. Quinn?"

"Yes. Jolly, this is going to sound strange, but…I need to find your grandmother."

"Loleen? Nothing strange about that, Doc. She told me to wait for your call."

Doesn't that just figure? Dec thought. "I should say I'm surprised, but…"

"You're learning, Doc. Learning to see from the inside. As Grandmother would say, 'Praise de Lord, it about time.'"

"Where can I find her, Jolly?"

"She's waiting for you at the ruins. You know where they are?"

He knew. It was on the real estate welcome tour,

part of the patter he'd been given when he'd been thinking of buying a house. Own a piece of a mysterious Caribbean island, only ten percent down, low interest rates, great climate, excellent schools.

"Thanks, Jolly."

"No, Doc." The cheery island lilt was gone from his voice. "Thank *you*."

Markie and Kato piled into his car, and he headed up the winding road that climbed the knobby ridge overlooking Martina Town. In the rearview mirror, he watched Kato sniff the air. There was none of the grinning, eyes-half-closed, ears-flopping, tongue-lolling, happy-dog-in-a-car mannerisms about him. He was scenting with deadly earnest.

Markie's face was drawn and pale. Her hands fidgeted in her lap. Her eyes held a dark, haunted look. "She came for me, Dec."

There it was, out in the open at last. The unspeakable, the unthinkable, they had both been avoiding. He made one more push to deny it, vain though it was.

"We don't know that," he said.

"Kato knew. That's why he jumped on me. He kept me out of the way." She paused and turned those haunted eyes to him. "She wants *me*, Dec!"

He couldn't pretend anymore. He would only be lying to himself. "I won't let her take you. Kato won't let her. Somehow, I don't know how, we'll keep you safe."

It was, he thought, an empty promise. A statement of intention with no firm idea of the method to back it up. And she probably knew it. Hell, there was no *probably* to it. She had to know. The look in her eyes said so.

Once again, here he was, the doctor. One step removed from God. Making promises he could only hope to keep. So many times he'd done that. So many times he'd said, "We'll take care of you, you'll be fine," when he knew there was little or nothing he could do. So many times he'd seen patients look up at him, eyes full of betrayal, as their lives ebbed away. Too soon. Too often. Too many. And he was doing it again.

But he would be damned if he would just stand by and let it happen now. Yes, he'd had his failures. Times when not all the training, experience, skill and equipment in the world could change the inevitable course of a body's losing battle with injury or illness. In med school they'd called them "negative outcomes." In the trauma surgery suite, he'd tried to use that same, dispassionate language. In the family lounge—in the eyes of mothers, fathers, wives, husbands and children—he'd seen it for what it was: a cruel euphemism. He'd ridden that roller coaster, and it had taken him down into the depths of his soul.

Okay. That was then. This was now.

"We'll keep you safe," he repeated.

He needed to believe that.

Wendy smiled as Gary looked at the drawing and nodded.

"Wolf's eyes," he said.

"Yes. Wolf's eyes."

He reached out and cupped her chin. "You did well, my pet."

She lowered her eyes, feeling the steady pulse in her loins. Her voice was a grateful whisper. "Thank you."

"You know what the wolf eyes mean?" he asked.

"No, sir."

"It means we've found it. We've found Annie's treasure."

She looked up, smiling. "You're sure?"

"It all fits. The vet has a wolf. Everyone knows that. Annie must have been looking around." He paused. "Of course..."

His voice trailed away, and she studied his eyes.

"Yes?"

He dragged a finger across his chin. "This means the wolf can see her. Is that possible?"

"Dog owners have long imagined that their pets have some extrasensory capacity," she said. "There's some recent research to support that. Some dogs will wait at a window when their owner leaves work and heads for home, even if the owner leaves at an unexpected time, as if the dog can sense that he's coming home. And a wolf hybrid is, well, one step closer to its wild roots. So yes, I'd guess it's possible that the wolf can see her."

It felt good that, even as servile as she felt—and that was *exactly* how she felt, how she now realized she'd longed for years to feel—he still respected her education and insight. It was, she thought, the perfect combination: love, respect and a firm, dominant hand that made her feel sheltered, cherished and owned. Why hadn't she found this with him long ago? Why had she wasted so many years with lonely fantasies and so many months with a man whose eyes had never really said *I love you?*

Those were questions she would ponder in idle moments for years to come. But the answers really didn't matter. She had found her happiness now.

"You've been a good girl," Gary said.

The words hit her like a live wire. She shivered and smiled silently. She didn't need to say it. She knew he could see it. But she said it anyway.

"Thank you, Gary."

His fingers trailed over her face. "And now, my pet, I have a surprise for you."

His other hand reached into the plastic bag at his side. She saw the gleaming black leather as he withdrew his hand.

Yesssssss.

Loleen was sitting on a pile of rubble as Dec pulled up to the ruins. Her eyes were closed, the rattle shaking almost soundlessly in her hand. Her lips murmured a prayer he could not understand.

"Loleen?"

Her eyes slowly opened, and he gasped.

Her irises were an icy white. Tiny black pupils, contracted in the afternoon light, seemed to bore through him.

"The doctor comes," she said.

"Yes, Loleen. We're here."

She nodded. "And the woman and her wolf, who share their minds."

Now it was Markie's turn to gasp. "How did you…?"

Loleen smiled. "It's what we see, child. It's what we've always seen. That's why my Jolly brought you the pouch. It wouldn't have worked for anyone else. You will need it now."

"It's…gone," Markie said. "The humidity. The leather was rotting."

Loleen's eyes widened. "Not good. Dat's not good, no. You need protection. De bad wam come."

"Excuse me?" Dec asked. He'd picked up a smidgen of island Creole, but not enough. "I don't understand."

"Annie come," she said quietly. "Someone stir her up bad. Bring her out. Send her for you."

"What do you mean, *send* her?"

Loleen shook the rattle softly as she talked. "Annie hate. All her life she hate. Hate her father. Hate her brothers. Hate her husbands. Hate her slaves. Her black heart full of hate then. An' full of hate now. Only she don' know no one now. She linger in de earth, like dust in de corners. You look and see, it just a little dust here. A little dere. But you gather it all up an' blow…it fill de air. You choke on it. Someone gather her all up an' blow."

Her eyes fixed on Markie. "An' blow on you, child."

Markie shook her head. "But I thought her body

was burned to ash. The ashes spread all over the island. So she would never again be, how did you say, gathered up.''

''Yes,'' Loleen said, nodding. ''Dey do all dat. But her gold. Dey took away her gold and bur' it in de ground. Her body, dey burned, 'cept da bones. But her black heart always in her gold. She wan' it back. She wan' it all back. Dey fin' her, dey promise her dat, and she come and do what dey wan'.'' She paused for a moment, shaking her head, mouthing a silent prayer. ''Den she do what *she* wan'.''

Slowly, Dec nodded. ''So what do we do?''

Loleen offered a faint smile. ''You fin' who stir her up. You fin' dem by her black heart in dem. You fin' dem and take away dat black heart. Den you fin' her gold an' you destroy it. You t'row it in de mountain and burn it up. Dat's how you stop her. De only way.''

''But how will we know who they are?'' Markie asked.

Now Loleen looked at Kato.

''You already know, child. De wolf know. De wolf see her. You follow de wolf. You fin' dem.''

''And then?'' Dec asked.

''And den,'' Loleen said, her eyes once again boring into him, ''den you gon' know ta do, Doc. You gon' know when it be time to know.''

Her voice became a hoarse whisper. ''Den you have to fin' de heart ta do it.''

22

Dawn told herself she hadn't known. She told herself she'd been too busy with her projects, with Brindle, with the conscious effort of ignoring Tim's infidelity, acting as if nothing were wrong. But she knew that wasn't true.

She'd known.

Tim refused to hire a maid service. Too ostentatious, too much like his father, he'd said. Not that it mattered, really. He wasn't around all that much, and it took little effort to keep up after herself and the dogs. So of course she dusted his office from time to time. She'd glanced at the maps and notes, even if she told herself she hadn't. She'd known.

Now Tim was gone again, to who knew where, probably to his boat to meet with Wendy Morgan. Although, in truth, the woman hadn't sounded thrilled at the prospect of meeting him. Maybe she'd finally figured out that Tim didn't love her, not in any meaningful sense of that word. Maybe Dawn was figuring that out, too.

So she'd gone into Tim's office and taken a closer look at his papers. One of them was a photocopy of an old college term paper. She'd read it. And the feelings she'd kept pent up for so long came bursting out. First shock. Then horror.

Then anger.

She considered calling Abel, then decided against it. Running to Tim's father seemed childish, and besides, she didn't know if she had time. Instead, she called Markie Cross. The phone rang. Rang again. And again. Then Markie's answering machine kicked on.

At least she could leave a message.

"Markie, it's Dawn Roth. If you're there, get out. When you get this message, get out. Get away. And stay away—"

The connection was cut off.

She toggled the receiver. No dial tone.

A moment later, she heard Brindle howl.

Wendy stood in front of the mirror and looked at the faint welts on her bottom. Some part of her said she ought to feel anger or hurt. Instead, she felt pride. She ran her fingertips over the raised skin and felt the warm tingle.

Arms slipped around her, and she glanced up at Gary's reflection in the mirror. His eyes were kind and soft.

"You like?" he asked.

"*Mmmmmmmm*…yes," she said. "It felt so good."

He trailed tender kisses over her shoulder. "I think I like this, Wendy."

She turned into his arms and met his eyes. "I *know* I like it, darling."

Tears brimmed in his eyes. "Welcome back, love."

She slid her arms beneath his and gently dug her nails into his back, clinging to him. "Oh, Gary..."

The words died away as she felt the presence again. The chill swept over them, and they clung tighter.

"Not again...." Gary whispered, before his eyes began to harden.

Wendy felt the tug within her chest. Was it Gary she had rediscovered, or Annie within him? And if she clung too hard to Gary, would Annie's jealous rages turn on her? She wanted the hard Gary, the Gary who took her, claimed her, made her his. But she didn't want to share him with the savage ghost of a homicidal psychopath.

"Bitch," he said, his eyes fixed on her.

In part the word thrilled her. But she also felt the dismay, knowing that was only partly Gary. Only partly the man she loved. She would have to deal with that later. First, though, she had to deal with the present.

"Yes," she whispered.

"It's time to work," he said. "Get in the study."

She scurried into the room, knelt on the floor and picked up her drawing pad.

"Find the old witch," he said. "Find her now."

"I...don't understand."

Now he spoke with a voice that was not his own. It was the wavering, icy-cold voice from the tape. "Find the old witch *now!*"

This wasn't how it worked. Hadn't she been looking through Annie's eyes last night? She could have sworn she was. This was different. Annie—and she had no doubt whose voice that was—Annie wanted *her* to find someone.

Which meant…she hadn't been seeing through Annie's eyes after all. But whose, then?

"I need a cigarette," she said, softly. "Please."

"You may," Gary replied. That was Gary's voice. Her husband's voice. Her lover's voice. A voice she could trust.

She lit a cigarette and watched the smoke rise from the tip, letting her consciousness drift on its streams and eddies. She cast aside the certain knowledge of what Annie would do to Loleen. She couldn't think about that now. If she did, she would hesitate.

And Annie's wrath would come to her.

Blue smoke rising in the near darkness. Curling in on itself. Twisting in the stir of air. Rising toward the desk lamp. Rising into the light…

Markie had no idea where to start looking. Loleen had closed her eyes in prayer, murmuring quietly, the rattle all but still in her hands. When she finished and opened her eyes, their bottomless brown color had returned.

"Best be gettin' on," she said to them.

"But…" Markie wanted to argue, wanted to plead

for more information. But Loleen turned her head away, dismissing them.

Looking at Dec, Markie saw the same urge to question on his face.

"Loleen," he said.

"It's time you go," was her answer, spoken in a voice as old and crackly as dead leaves. "Go see Jolly."

Kato sniffed around the feet of the old woman. She had the smell of age about her, and something more. Curious, he looked up and for an instant met her dark gaze.

It was time for her soul to fly. She knew that, and she was trying to pass something on to him. He felt it as a brush deep within his mind, a touch of something bright. Then he felt her stiffen herself, getting ready.

Oh, no. Not her, too. He scented it in the distance, cold and black rotten, like meat that had gone rancid in a cold box. He knew she knew, in the way she turned her head and looked into the distance. Then he felt its icy breath, still a long way away.

He knew what he had to do. He gripped Markie's slacks with his teeth and pulled at her. *The car. Go. Now!*

The old woman spoke, a word that Kato understood.

"Go," she said.

And in his mind he felt the stern command: *Now!*

He tugged again, a whine emerging from his throat.

Dec understood and took Markie's hand. He pulled her toward the car with a force that left no time or place for argument.

Moments later they were driving away from the bad place. Kato stared out the back window of the car and saw the black, rotten shadow waft toward the old woman.

And in his mind he heard her say to the shadow, "It's time."

The contact was severed. Later he felt the old woman's soul fly free and joyously. He looked up and whimpered, at once happy for her and mournful, for her liberation had not been an easy one.

"Well, hell," Dec said as he slowed through a hairpin curve. "Jolly sends us to her, and she sends us to him."

"I know." Markie's voice was subdued. "It was so…vague."

"Maybe vague is all she knows. Maybe Jolly knows something more. Unless you object, I'm going to hunt him up."

"Why would I object? Lord, I feel like I've dropped through the rabbit hole. I still can't believe that I'm thinking what I'm thinking."

"About…*her?*" He didn't want to say Annie's name. It was an old superstition that a name could hold power, but it was a superstition he didn't want to test right now.

"Yes. *Her.*"

"Me, too. But…last night outside your house…I

didn't want to tell you, because I felt so stupid about it. I saw a dark shadow pass by. It dimmed the street-lights."

She drew a sharp breath. "Did Kato alert?"

"He was the reason I went to look. And that shadow was the reason I called Pedro. I think I'm beginning to find religion again."

She gave a hollow laugh. "I've already got it, but it doesn't seem to be helping."

He reached out a hand and gripped hers. "It will. It's all got to be part and parcel of the same thing. Two sides of the same supernatural coin."

"You think?"

"It's the only way I can explain what I'm experiencing. I may feel like a jackass when this is over, but right now...right now I need faith. It's all I've got."

She squeezed his hand. Fingers linked, they drove in silence the rest of the way.

Jolly's mortuary was closed for the night, but the side light was on, illuminating the path to the stairs that led up to his apartment above the business. Markie and Dec climbed them together, Kato on their heels. It was plain to both of them that Kato wasn't going to let either of them out of his sight, and, for the moment at least, Markie was in full agreement.

As she had told Dec, "He's the only early warning system we have."

Jolly answered the door himself, and a smile of welcome creased his dark face. "You saw Loleen?"

Dec nodded. "She sent us to you."

Jolly chuckled. "And you're wondering why you're getting the runaround. Come in, come in. Sorry to say I'm all alone. Bettina took the children to the States to see her mother, and now they won't let her come home."

"Maybe," Dec answered, "we'll get lucky and settle this trouble soon."

"I hope." Jolly led them into a comfortable living room furnished in wicker and rattan in the popular island colors of pink and turquoise. It was a light and airy place, even at night. "Coffee or tea?" he asked.

"I'd love some coffee," Markie admitted. "I don't think I ever want to sleep again."

Jolly returned moments later with cups of coffee for everyone and sank into a chair that creaked beneath his bulk. Markie and Dec sat side by side on a rattan couch.

"What did Gram tell you?" he asked.

"That…" Dec hesitated and looked at Markie.

She spoke, a tremor in her voice. "That someone stirred up Annie. That she wants her gold. That we have to find the people who stirred her up and take her heart out of them somehow. That Dec would know what to do. It's so…confused."

"Not confused," Jolly corrected her. "Difficult to express. English doesn't have a vocabulary for this sort of thing."

"That's true." Markie looked at Kato, who was sitting alertly at her feet. "She said we have to follow my dog. That he would find them. And that it's a shame the pouches you gave me rotted because I needed them.''

Jolly nodded. ''Indeed. It is. You do.''

Markie lifted her eyebrows.

Jolly chuckled. ''I'm a good Christian, Markie, but I'm also a shaman in the old ways. I can give you some protection of that kind. A little extra never hurts.''

''No, of course not.'' Markie didn't want to offend him, though she had her doubts. If anything should protect her, it was the crucifix around her neck.

''I'll take one, too,'' Dec said. ''And Kato might like one.''

Jolly looked down at the wolf and held out his hand. Kato sniffed it cautiously, then licked his fingers. ''This wolf,'' Jolly said, ''has got all the power he needs. See, he isn't constrained by language. What he experiences, he experiences. What is simply…is. He's better prepared for this than any of us.''

''Well, short of having a stroke and losing my faculty for language, what then?'' Dec asked. ''We're supposed to find the people who are stirring up the problem, but what about the folks they might hurt along the way?''

''Like Alice,'' Markie said, her throat tightening. ''And the Shippeys.''

Jolly waved a hand, as if making a sign in the air. ''Anyone who sees her had best look out for themselves.''

They left Jolly an hour later, both of them wearing leather pouches around their necks. Neither Markie nor Dec had the least curiosity about what might be in them. Some things were better left alone.

"I'm tired," Markie said.

"It's been a long day."

"I need to go back to my place. Shower. Change."

"You're not staying there, though." He faced her, his features stern. "I saw that shadow. You're coming to my place."

"We'll see."

Dec opened the car's passenger door. Kato jumped in and over to the back seat. Markie slid in, feeling wearier than she could remember feeling in her entire life. Wearier than a day at the clinic and a trip to the ruins should have left her.

Knowing she was going to be a lot wearier before this was over.

Then Dec said, "Before we go to your place, I want to go to the hospital."

She looked at him. "Why?"

"To talk to Gardner and his guys. Maybe they found something."

She felt a surge of sympathy. "You're still hoping they'll find a bug. Something rational."

He glanced at her, the whites of his eyes glistening in the reflection of the streetlights. "Aren't you?"

Markie hesitated before answering, taking a serious check of her hopes and thoughts. Somehow it seemed important to be absolutely honest. "I was," she admitted. "It would be…easier. But now…now it feels too late."

* * *

The swirls of smoke still rose into the lamp, silvery gray, misty. Wendy felt as if she were twining with them, lifting with them, becoming one with them. The mist began to feel cold and wet, and it shrouded her mind like the foggiest day.

It was Annie. Annie's kindest touch, really, one that would take time to freeze her. Wendy didn't want to welcome it, but she had no choice. She needed to do it for Gary, and she needed to protect herself. To do anything else would enrage Annie.

Into the mist came the golden eyes again. Eerie eyes, at first not clear, as if a veil separated them from her. These eyes were important. The urge to strike out at them filled her, and she wanted to raise her cigarette toward them again.

But then she sensed something beyond Annie's rage. Something…frightened. She couldn't tell where the fear was coming from, but it held her rapt, trying to learn more about it.

At some level, she thought she sensed freedom.

As a child on Long Island, she had figured out how to stop her parents' incessant, trivial arguments. It had been so easy, in retrospect. She would simply go out onto the screened porch, leaving open the family room door. They would feel the breath of fresh air in a moment or two and realize that every word they said could be heard by the neighbors. Embarrassed, they would hush. When they asked her why she left the door open, she simply smiled and said that she'd gone outside to get away and left the door open to air out the house.

Fear of being overheard, of losing face with their neighbors, had quelled their fights. Fear of exposure. And that, she realized, was the key.

Annie had grown up in a coal-blackened world where no one cared what was done to her and had lived her adult life in a world of privilege where no one looked too deeply into what she did. Now she inhabited a netherworld where no one saw her, where few even dared to utter her name. All her life, and into her afterlife, she'd been…invisible.

But those golden eyes could see her.

And in that would lie Wendy's salvation.

23

The hospital parking lot was nearly empty, as was usual this late at night. However, even the emergency room appeared to be as empty, and that *wasn't* usual. Apparently people were staying so safely at home that the common accidents weren't even happening.

Behind the hospital, screened as much as possible from public view, were the CDC trailers, airtight constructions that looked much the same as the trailers on semis. There were two of them, one a lab and one for sleeping quarters. As far as Dec had been able to tell, even CDC had given up fear of airborne contagion a while ago. Tonight they were sitting outside their trailers on folding chairs, sipping beers and coffee and shooting the bull.

As Dec, Markie and Kato approached, however, their conversation fell silent. Joe Gardner stood up and looked at Markie and her dog. "That dog is supposed to be quarantined."

"That dog isn't sick," Dec said flatly. "Did you check out Carolyn Fletcher's tissue samples?"

"Should we have? Who's she? Another stiff?"

Markie scowled but kept her mouth shut.

"Actually, she was the victim of an attack, and she survived."

Joe cocked his head. "What kind of attack?"

"Her nose was melting when I took her to the hospital. Dammit, Joe, I left a message for you to take a look."

Joe flung the coffee from his cup, and dropped the mug on his chair. "I'll get my bag. We'll look into it right now."

Markie's jaw had dropped, and as Joe walked away, she faced Dec, her hands on her hips, her head tipped belligerently. "What do you mean, her nose was melting? All you said was that it was broken. Why did you lie to me?"

"I didn't lie to *you*," he reminded her. "I didn't want the woman freaking out. I lied to *her*. And I was hoping by now that Gardner could tell me what the hell happened. It really *was* like the cartilage in her nose had melted. She's going to need some serious plastic surgery."

"Oh, lord." Markie bowed her head and said a silent prayer.

Joe joined them a minute later with a small black case. "Let's go."

"If we're lucky," Dec said as they strode across the grass to one of the back entrances, "somebody's already taken samples and sent them to Pathology. But I'm concerned you didn't get my message."

"Me, too," Joe agreed. "You're not taking that dog inside?"

"Yes," said Dec, "I am. We're going straight to Path to see if I have any samples." Samples that should have been in Joe Gardner's hands hours ago. He hoped nobody had fucked them up. He would hate to have to disturb Carolyn Fletcher to get more.

The corridors were quiet, this end of the hospital closed for the night. Only one orderly passed them by, leaving the odor of cigarette smoke in his wake. He must have been outside in the lot, smoking. It always amazed Dec how many doctors, nurses and orderlies smoked, the same people who would cheerfully lecture their patients about the habit.

His office was dark, the sign over the door looking odd this evening, as if the colors had somehow been altered. He flipped on light switches, then signaled Markie and Kato to remain in the anteroom. He and Joe entered the main lab, flipped on more unforgiving fluorescent lights, and Dec opened the refrigerator.

"Well, what do you know?" he said. He pulled out a paper bag, stapled shut, with Carolyn Fletcher's name and patient number on it. "Somebody was awake in E.R."

"Are you used to people missing things like this?" Joe asked.

"We see so little on this island that's unusual that it can be easy to fall asleep at the wheel," Dec said frankly. "Most don't, but sometimes one of us does."

From the anteroom, Markie watched as the two men donned Tyvek gowns with the ties at the back and two layers of rubber gloves. Then they prepped a few slides from the samples contained in several vials.

Kato stood on his hind legs beside her, resting his paws on the window ledge, and watched, too. The minutes seemed nerve-stretchingly long.

"No unrecognizable organisms," Joe Gardner remarked finally.

"No," Dec agreed. "Everything looks normal. Except for one thing. Did you notice? Every single cell wall was ruptured."

Joe swore and straightened, looking at Dec. "Talk about missing the obvious! Damn, we've been looking for prions and viruses...."

"I did the same thing," Dec said. "It didn't occur to me before to look at something this large."

Joe began stripping his gloves. "I want to see the patient. Then I want to check the samples we have from the DOAs."

"I'm with you."

Markie sat down on the bench, and Kato dropped down beside her. Every cell wall ruptured? Her stomach turned over as she tried to imagine what could have committed such violence so swiftly.

As if he sensed her need, Kato leaned into her, hugging her as best he could.

Two hours later, the two men sat on the steps outside the CDC trailers, cups of coffee quivering slightly in fatigued and nervous hands.

"Shit," Joe Gardner said succinctly.

"Exactly," Dec agreed.

Cells were remarkably resilient, Dec knew. He'd once marveled as he watched on a microscope as an ultrafine needle was inserted through a cell wall. Even with the tip of the needle only a few microns thick, the cell wall bent inward before it slowly, reluctantly gave way. Banging a shin on a coffee table would burst capillary walls to leave a bruise, but the cells themselves would be intact. The kind of force that could crush cell walls *en masse,* well, that was the stuff of gunshot wounds or pile drivers. It simply didn't happen in the ordinary course of things. And certainly not throughout an entire body.

Yet that was what they'd seen in slide after slide from the Shippeys and from Alice Wheatley. Bones, tendons, cartilage, internal organs...all ruptured and crushed at the cellular level. But not the skin. And, most horrifying of all, not nerve cells. Whatever— *whoever,* he knew, in his heart of hearts—had done this, it had kept the nerves intact. So the victims could experience every second of the agony of their bodies being shattered.

Nature, he was sure, could never devise so utterly sadistic an organism. No, this was the work of pure evil.

"I don't know anything that would do this," Joe Gardner said.

"No, you don't," Dec replied. "None of us does. We train for something else entirely. We're trained for the ordinary detritus of life on planet Earth. Illness. Injury. Even primitive violence. We're trained to do battle with the basic forces of Darwinian selection. But we're not trained for...this.''

"You sound like you have an idea," Joe said.

Dec nodded. "And if I told you, you'd laugh. Or suggest I see a psychologist. Or a priest, but I've already done that. I only hope it will help."

Joe's face had taken on a pallor as he'd stared into the microscope at one sample after another. The pallor hadn't gone away. "Whatever it is, Dr. Quinn, my team...we can't help. I just...can't help."

Dec could see it in the man's eyes. A look he was sure had been in his own eyes far too many times. But perhaps, for this young man, this was the first time. The first time he'd realized the limitations of the title "medical doctor." It was a moment that would haunt Joe Gardner for years to come, in the quiet of night, when the only sound was the beating of his own heart. It was a moment he would have to transcend, if he wanted to be an effective physician. Transcend, but never forget.

Dec had never forgotten. He hoped, maybe, that he had, that he *could,* transcend it.

Thomas Jefferson had once said there are times when doing one's best is not enough, times when one must do what needs be done. It was a noble statement, born of the hubris of the Enlightenment, when man began to believe that he was bigger than the world around him, more powerful than the forces of nature, wiser than his creator. Jefferson might have been a brilliant statesman and politician, but as a philosopher, he suffered from the blindness of his age.

There were times when one could not do what needed to be done, times when one could only do one's best. Dec had had to learn that. And Joe Gardner would have to learn that, too. In his own way. In his own time.

Dec rose and extended a hand. "You should be proud of your team, Joe."

Joe took the hand, but without any energy. "Why? We didn't track down the bug. We lost."

"No," Dec said. "Carter and Marilyn Shippey, Alice Wheatley, Caroline Fletcher…they lost. And your heart should grieve for them. But not for yourself, Joe. One of the hardest things to learn about this profession, what they can't teach you in med school, is this: it's not about you. It's never about you. It's about the patient. And you can't let it be about you, or you're no good to the patient. Or to yourself."

Joe seemed about to reply, anger in his eyes.

"Your team did great work, Joe. But this wasn't one you could have solved. I'm sorry. I've been there. And it's not fun. But it's part of being a doctor."

Joe finally nodded. "You're right, of course. But I don't have to like it."

"No, you don't. But you have to find a way to live with it. Or it will eat you alive."

"Words of experience?" Joe asked.

Dec simply looked at him. "I have to do some things. You won't need me here."

"No, I don't guess we will." Joe's back stiffened a bit, and his eyes held a fraction more resolve.

"Good luck, Dr. Quinn. Maybe I'll read about it in a journal someday."

"That," Dec said with a crooked smile, "would be a greater miracle than what I'm going to try to do."

"So there's no doubt?" Markie asked as they drove back into town.

"Not in my mind," Dec said. "No pathogen did that. No pathogen could have done that."

Markie let out a quiet shudder. "I can't believe it...she...leaves the nerves alone. I can't even imagine what...you know..."

"Neither can I," Dec said. "It must be terrible beyond words."

Markie thought back to what Jolly had said, about English having no vocabulary for some things. Dec had just encapsulated this entire series of events. Terrible beyond words. And somehow, that was where he would have to go, if Loleen were to be believed. Beyond words. Into something even he did not understand.

The thought made her quail inside. Yes, she had a job, too. But she would rely on Kato. And that, she realized, was a comfort she too often took for granted. She relied on Kato in a hundred little ways every day. She knew she could trust the dog, and that, at an intuitive level, she trusted him beyond the ordinary give and take of life. Looking back, she could remember times when a quick nudge had broken her concentration on a book in time to get into the kitchen and rescue a meal that was about to burn, or a pull on the leash had made her sidestep a hole in a grassy field. Yes, she could rely on Kato.

But Dec had no such safety net. Neither of them knew exactly what he would have to do. Or what risks it might entail. Annie Black had been as evil a human being as had ever walked the earth. Apparently her residue, her spirit, was no less evil. She went after what she wanted, and if someone had to die along the way, well, so much the better. Not "them's the breaks" but "them's the perks." Markie couldn't imagine such a mindset. But that was the kind of spirit that, according to Loleen, controlled the hearts of those who had stirred her up. And that was the kind of spirit Dec would have to battle.

She didn't fear for herself. Nor, really, for Kato. Behind those golden eyes lay an intelligence she could only barely fathom. Kato would be fine. And he would take care of her. But Dec…she feared for Dec. The thought of losing him, when she had only just found him, was almost too awful to bear. As a child, she had, like most girls, fashioned a mental list of attributes for her dream man. Her fiancé had most of those qualities, and he had turned out to be a blight on her soul. She'd thrown away the mental list. It was the stuff of adolescent fantasies. And with it, she'd thrown away a dream.

But now a dream had walked into her life.

And she might lose him.

And that hurt.

* * *

Kato bounded out of the car and up to the door, drawing in quick sniffs, testing, examining. Markie and Dec had followed, but he turned and looked at them. *Not yet.* First he wanted to walk around the house. His body needed the walk, although he discounted that need. His pack needed to know something. And he was the only one who could find out.

The tangy-sweet scent of blooming azaleas and the rich, musky taste of freshly cut grass were normally warm and welcome beacons in his world. His own scents wafted on the rising evening air, a scrapbook of days gone by. Too many of those scents held worry and strain. Each brought back crystalline images. Images he would rather forget. Images that did not belong in this world.

The back of the house seemed normal, and he circled around to meet Markie and Dec, who had shown the good sense to wait for him at the sidewalk. He walked up to the front door and nosed it. *It's okay.*

Markie opened the door for him, and again they waited at the entrance while he toured the house. Everything was as it should be. That fact troubled him, but he could fix no target for his concern. He let them enter and trotted ahead of them to the kitchen, where he allowed himself a drink of cool, fresh water. Food and his other needs could wait until he was sure they were safe.

Markie walked over to the box she always went to when she got home. The box from which tinny, disembodied voices came. Dec had gone to the refrigerator and taken out a bottle of water while she pushed the button.

"Markie, it's Dawn Roth. If you're there, get out. When you get this message, get out. Get away. And stay away—"

Dec froze in midstride. Markie's face went pale.

Kato understood the message, if not the words.

Get out!

The black shadow loomed, invisible in the darkness over the ruins. The old woman's body, gone cold and flat long since, no longer interested it. It was still in the process of getting used to its regenerated existence, to the fact that it was existing apart from the body of Annie Black, apart from all that confinement of old. Yes, Annie was still part of it, but it was now so much greater.

The brief freedom it had enjoyed long ago at the old fort paled by comparison with the freedom and strength it had now. Those who had summoned it had also fed it with their own strength and will.

It flexed, stretching, learning its new parameters. No longer driven only by the need for self-protection, it had begun to think. It was no longer so ready to be ordered about by those who had freed it.

In fact, it had begun to fear them. For they had freed it and might be able to imprison it once again.

So it floated over the ruins, a mere inkblot in the black of night, so well camouflaged that only the most attentive eye would notice that it dimmed the stars behind it.

It floated and thought. The gold, yes. That drive of Annie's still goaded it. It must keep itself safe. But more importantly, it must keep itself safe from those who knew of it.

Those who had seen it must die. But also those who had called it, for they held the most power to harm it.

Swaying gently, unaware of its own hideous beauty, feeling safe in the night's concealment, it probed the minds of the summoners.

The woman...she was a mere pawn. Her mate...he thought he was so smart, but he could be used at will. But there was the man who had seen it at his office, and the man who had started the whole thing.

Consciously, deliberately, it pulled back from all the humans who knew it, with whom it had come in touch. It departed them all and hovered alone, out of reach, debating what to do next.

For it had decided that *it* was in charge.

24

Steve Chase would no longer stay at his office alone. When his secretary left, he left, too, his briefcase stuffed with work.

It was late, he was tired, but he labored on at home, never so aware as he was that night that he was a lonely man. His wife had left him years ago for what she described as "a cab driver with a spinal cord." His 9,500-square-foot home, the embodiment of his architectural dreams, seemed cold and empty.

Finally he let his hands fall from the computer keyboard and turned to look out the wall of windows beside him. The view, as always, was spectacular. He had chosen the site well and had built well on it. There wasn't a room in this house that didn't offer a breathtaking view down the north slope of the island to the crescent beach below and the private marina.

From this dizzying height, the marina was small, hardly interfering with nature. And his neighbors' homes were spread far enough apart by design that only an occasional light blotted the night's beauty. It was a perfect location for a life that should have been perfect but had never quite achieved that exalted state. Oh, hell, who was he kidding? He was one of life's major screwups.

He hadn't inherited his father's business acumen, so he'd had to leave the running of the family oil and gas empire to cousins. He wasn't proud of that, and he was sure that the only reason they even called to "consult" him was that his father had left him a majority ownership.

It was small comfort to a man who had been bred to believe he would be more important than most heads of state. Instead of stepping into the shoes prepared for him by generations past, he'd had to step aside and come to hide on this small tropical isle.

Not that it was so awful. But it was a sign of his failure. Abel Roth, whose equal he should have been, had chosen to be here, to sit amidst his electronic web and control the futures of nations by the simple expedient of deciding whether to lend them money. Abel was here because it allowed him the privacy to conduct his schemes.

Steve was here because he couldn't do anything else.

His law practice was okay. But only okay. With Abel's tight grip on this island, there wasn't a lot of call for litigation. Architecture was his first love, but Abel's vision for this island did not include a stunning, Steve Chase-designed skyline. Instead, he had designed tract homes for the handful of subdivisions Abel had deigned to allow, in deference to the island's growing economy, and the occasional vacation villa for someone Abel had decided to invite to share the northern enclave.

Sitting in his aerie now, recounting the events of the past weeks, Steve admitted that he'd screwed up yet again. He'd let Tim Roth make him feel important. Essential. So he'd fallen in with the conspiracy to find Annie Black's treasure. It had seemed like an adventure, a chance to prove that he and Tim could do something astonishing.

But then the deaths had begun, and Steve was smart enough to realize they were connected to the treasure hunt. Nobody had been supposed to die, and certainly not by such awful means. Tim, fool that he was, thought he was controlling Annie. That she was going to show them where the treasure was buried, that every death merely meant they were looking in the wrong place. Annie, Tim insisted, wanted her gold found. If that were the case, then why did Steve feel they'd let a horrible genie out of a bottle and that Tim's control was purely an illusion?

He'd seen that shadow in his office. He'd felt its chill breath. There was no reason it should have been anywhere near *him*. But it had been.

Suddenly he leaned forward, wondering what had moved out there. The night was too dark to see much, and the reflection of his own image in the glass was probably what had startled him.

Nevertheless, he reached for the switch that cast his office into darkness and closed the lid on his laptop. Then, when everything was as dark inside as out, he slowly, carefully, eased open a desk drawer and pulled out a pistol.

Break-ins were almost unheard of, but they did happen from time to time. If someone was lurking out there in the garden...

Then he felt an icy breath blow across his nape.

It didn't take long at all for Markie to grab a few things for the next couple of days while Dec carted Kato's bag of kibble and dog bowls to the car. She shoved the bare minimum into a duffel, locked the door behind her and Kato and headed to the curb.

"We need to call Dawn," she said. "She knows something."

"Obviously. But we'll call from my house...unless we get a message telling us to leave *it,* too."

There was a grim set to his face, a tension that bespoke more than concern because of the phone call.

Not that Markie could blame him. There had been too many horrors in this day already. He gripped her hand tightly all the way to his house, then carried everything inside for her.

"I've only got one bedroom," he said flatly. "And I'm not letting you out of my sight. So you've got a choice. You can sleep on the couch and I'll doze in a chair, or..."

"We'll share your bed," she said. She'd gone past all the normal cautions of life, things that might have held her back. There was one place and one place only that she wanted to be, and that was in Dec's arms. Whatever safety the world held, she was sure she would find it there.

Wordlessly, he reached out for her and hugged her close and tight, as if he needed her in his arms as much as she needed to be there.

"God, Markie," he whispered, his breath stirring her hair. "God."

There didn't seem to be another thing to say, only the need that was drawing them so tightly together that their bodies seemed to want to fuse.

"If anything happens to you..." It was a ragged whisper, and he didn't finish the thought. It hung there, a promise and a plea.

It was as if a dam opened inside her, letting out all the feelings she'd been trying so hard to hold at bay, from grief to terror to love. They overflowed, filling her eyes with tears and her muscles with strength as she hugged him even tighter.

All she wanted, she thought with hazy desperation, was this one night with Dec. Just this one night. Before it was too late.

For an instant she teetered, almost as terrified of herself as of the terror that stalked the night.

Then she gave way. Her mouth lifted to his, her body shaped to his, and hunger for life and love possessed her with its undeniable power.

Hungry hands tore at clothes; naked bodies fell to the floor. Kato huffed and turned his back, but neither of the humans noticed.

For instants, precious, beautiful instants, everything else fled before the force of longing. Hands touched, caressed. Bodies slickened. Moans escaped from places so deep they had never been plumbed.

Bodies melding into one...hearts beating as one...driving higher on an aching promise of fulfillment...

He was in her, on her, all around her, and for a wild moment Markie opened her eyes and stared blindly upward, feeling safe...safe....

And oh, so hungry and needy. Thrust for thrust, she met him. Touch for touch, wanting him as maddened as she was...

She teetered on the brink...aching so badly she hurt...afraid she wouldn't topple....

Then she fell into an abyss of pleasure, his groan following hers into the little death of joy.

For a little while they pretended everything was okay. They cuddled and kissed and finally rested, Markie's head on Dec's shoulder. They exchanged the soft words of lovers, even a little laugh or two as their eyes met, finally empty of all barriers. Vulnerable and safe all at once with each other. It was heaven.

Then Kato grew impatient. He padded over and started licking both their faces. Markie laughed, Dec chuckled, but Kato huffed.

That huff was as effective as a cold dousing. Reality intruded with its icy thorns, reminding them.

Reluctantly, all of a sudden faintly embarrassed, as if they'd just been thrown out of Eden, they reached for clothes. Dec gave Markie his T-shirt. She slipped it on, loving the scent of him even as she felt guilty for it. How could they have forgotten?

He stood, pulled on his shorts. "I'll call Dawn," he said.

Then he paused and squatted down beside her. He caught her chin in his hand and kissed her soundly. "We're going to survive this," he promised. "And then we're going to have a lot of living to do."

She liked the way he said it and gave him a smile. Something warm seemed to curl up inside her and purr.

But then he sat on the end of the couch and reached for the phone. Instinctively Markie wrapped her arm around Kato, burying her fingers in his fur. He didn't usually tolerate such confinement, but this time all he did was lean into her and give her a quick sniff, testing her emotional state.

Dec dialed, waited a few seconds. Markie saw the concern in his eyes an instant before his lips curled down into a frown.

"What is it?" she asked.

He held the receiver out to her, and she put it to her ear. *The number you have dialed is out of service....*

Dawn knelt on the floor, holding the dying pup as Brindle licked it and whimpered softly. Sobs shook her. She looked up at her husband.

"You bastard!" she whispered.

Tim gave her a cold stare. "You should have learned by now, Dawn. Never, *ever* fuck with me."

She'd come in to find him standing in the garage, a phone cord ripped from the wall in his hand, wrapped around the throat of the puppy she had named Sparkle. Brindle had been lying on the floor, whining, oozing blood from between her legs. The specks on Tim's shoe told the rest of the story. He'd kicked her in the one place that would keep her from protecting her litter. Then he'd gone after the pup that Dawn had grown most attached to. With a savage twist, he'd snapped the phone cord tight around the pup's tender neck.

Its yelp had propelled Dawn into action. Manicured nails had slashed into facial skin until he finally dropped the pup to the concrete floor with a sickening thud. She'd raked her nails across his cheek one more time for good measure, leaving parallel trails of bright, oozing red, then knelt to lift Sparkle into her hands.

The puppy's tongue eased out at Brindle's touch, though it was still too young to open its eyes. Its legs were limp, its tender neck almost surely broken. The end was only a matter of time, and Dawn felt the tearing in her heart at the final betrayal.

"I will fucking kill you," she said, her voice a low hiss.

Tim wiped blood from his face and spat on her. "You are too soft to kill anything. You are too weak to live."

Brindle let out a low, mournful wail as Sparkle went totally still. Her deep brown eyes locked with Dawn's. In any other situation, her nearly two-hundred pounds of bulk would be sufficient to wreak her own vengeance on the man who had killed her child. But she was still weak from birth, and the normal pains of the whelping process had been exacerbated by Tim's vicious kick. She herself might not make it.

But neither would Tim.

Dawn laid the puppy in the curve beneath Brindle's chin, then rose slowly. Tim's toolbox was on the floor of the garage, against the wall. Atop it lay a fourteen-inch screwdriver. He'd never been good about putting away his tools, Dawn thought. Too bad for him.

Their eyes met in a deadly stare, and for the first time, Dawn sensed real fear in her husband. It was about time. He had reason to be afraid. She took a step toward him, and he drew back his fist. It was what she'd been waiting for. What she'd counted on.

He launched the punch, and she ducked, in a smooth, graceful movement born of years of tennis and aerobics and the adrenaline rush of sheer rage. Her hand flashed out and grasped the handle of the screwdriver.

He had already regained his balance from the punch and went to kick her while she was bent over. She drove hard off her right foot, the screwdriver now an extension of her hand, and took the kick on her shoulder as she plunged the blade deep into the inside of his thigh. With a savagery she would never have imagined in herself, she kept driving as he went down, sawing the handle back and forth, knowing the blade was clawing away inside his flesh.

He screamed and fell to the floor just as the first spurt of bright red blood gushed out as if from a garden hose and sprayed the wall.

Dawn yanked out the screwdriver and looked at him with cold, clinical satisfaction.

Markie, Dec and Kato had piled into the car almost at a run. The scent of their lovemaking still wafted strongly around them, comforting, until the wind blew away the last of it.

Kato whined and leaned forward, putting his head on Markie's shoulder. She reached up and scratched his cheek, enjoying the weight of his head against her, the softness of his fur against her own cheek.

"Is he trying to tell us something?" Dec asked. He was long since past thinking of Kato as anything except an extraordinarily smart being who simply lacked the capacity to speak English.

"I don't know. He's uneasy."

"Hell, so are we all."

The car leaned, and Markie grabbed at the door for balance as Dec made the hard left turn onto La Media. Moments later, before she had fully recovered, he slewed the car again, to the right, and she thudded against the door frame.

"Dec..."

"Kato's right," he said simply.

An oncoming car veered to the curb, the driver honking, as Dec sped down the narrow side street before screeching to a stop.

"I think this is the address," he said.

The lights were on in the living room, but there was no sign of anyone through the window. Nor any answer when he knocked. Kato, however, had gone to the garage at a dead run and was now clawing frantically at the door.

"We have to call the cops," Markie said.

"We don't have time," Dec replied.

At his heavy kick, the front door crashed open.

"Dawn?" Markie called out.

Kato dashed around and through the door, almost taking Dec's legs out from under him, then made a beeline through the kitchen to the garage door. Markie and Dec were a half step behind him as he froze in the door, letting out a savage growl.

Dec stopped a half second before tumbling over the wolf and took in the scene. It was something out of his worst nightmares, the kind of scene he'd witnessed all too often in the E.R. Dawn sat on the floor, staring blankly, watching the blood pulse from her husband's thigh in rapid, weakening spurts.

"He killed my puppy," Dawn said, her voice devoid of emotion. "He shouldn't have killed my puppy."

"Femoral artery," Markie whispered.

"Yep," Dec agreed.

The trained doctor knew there was little chance. The human being thought Tim had probably gotten exactly what he deserved. The physician knew he had to try anyway.

"Find some scissors," he said, his voice crisp and

clear. "And dry towels. A lot of them. And a pair of pliers. Vice grips would be better."

"I'm on it," Markie said, already knowing what he needed, already in motion.

"He shouldn't have killed my puppy," Dawn repeated.

"No," Dec said. "He shouldn't have."

Tim's face had gone nearly white. Dec knew he didn't have much time. The average human body held about six quarts of blood. A severed femoral artery could expel that in minutes.

Markie returned with scissors and a handful of towels. Dec cut away Tim's khaki shorts, already knowing what he would find, already reaching with a towel to clamp down on the wound. It was high on the thigh, less than six inches from his crotch. Pressure wouldn't be enough. Not nearly enough.

"Let's get some towels under his hips," Dec said. "We have to elevate."

Markie nodded. Dec grabbed Tim's knees and rose, wincing at the man's agonized groan, knowing he had no choice but to try to get the wound over the heart, keep the head down, and hope gravity would keep enough blood flowing to his brain to keep him alive. Markie had stuffed the towels under Tim's hips, and Dec let his body settle.

"I need a knife," Dec said. "A sharp one."

"He has a box cutter in the toolbox," Dawn said, her eyes slowly clearing.

"It'll have to do," Dec answered. "Dawn, call an ambulance."

Markie tore open the toolbox and handed him the box knife. "He has vice clamps, too," she said.

"Let's hope I can find the artery," Dec answered.

With a smooth, practiced motion, he sliced through skin and subcutaneous fat and muscle, enlarging the wound enough that he could reach his hand inside.

"I need hard pressure on the pelvis," Dec said quickly. "Stand on him if you have to."

Markie pressed her foot firmly above his groin and kept adding weight until Dec nodded. His hand was inside the wound now, feeling for the wet pulse, reaching up the arterial canal between the thigh muscles.

"Shit," he said. "It's retracted."

He took a breath, gathered himself, and rammed his hand up through the wound, burying his arm almost to the elbow, until he felt a rubbery fluttering against his fingers. The artery.

He ignored Tim's screams and grabbed the artery, rolling it between his fingers, trying to grasp slick flesh in a sea of blood. Finally, convinced that he had as good a grip as he was going to get, he began to slowly pull, until his hand emerged with a bulging red ribbon.

"Clamp it," he said. "Fast."

Markie positioned the vice clamps above his fingers and squeezed them closed, sealing the end of the artery.

"I think it's tearing," she said.

"That's as far as it's going to stretch," he answered. "If it tears…"

He didn't have to finish the sentence. If it tore, whatever slim chance they had was gone.

Tim's hands began to shake, his eyes rolling up.

"He's taching," Dec said, feeling the skittery pulse in his fingertips.

Tim was slipping into tachycardia. He'd lost too much blood, and his heart was fluttering, trying to pump faster to make up for the lost volume. It was the body's last line of defense in a losing battle. There was only one card left to play. And it clashed squarely with the oath Dec had taken years ago.

First, do no harm.

Tim's other leg was undamaged. His hypothalamus was in full fight-or-flight mode, an autonomic response to extreme stress, part of which involved preserving the blood flow into the large muscles of the legs. The human species had not evolved a secondary impulse to save whatever blood remained for the brain. It had had no reason to. For tens of thousands of years, the only hope in such moments had been to flee. And for that, the leg muscles needed oxygen. That marvelous evolutionary adaptation, honed for survival on the African plain, was now killing Tim Roth.

Dec had only one option: to wrap a tourniquet around the good leg. That might well kill the leg. But it was the only way to save the body. He ripped off his belt and wrapped it around the good leg at the crotch, pulling it as tight as possible, then reached for the nearest hard straight tool he could find.

It was a fourteen-inch screwdriver, already smeared with blood.

Dec heard Dawn gasp as he grabbed it and knew, with utter certainty, what had happened. He ignored the gasp and slipped the screwdriver beneath the belt, then twisted it hard. Tim screamed in pain. Dec gave the screwdriver one more hard turn, then wedged the tip into the fabric of Tim's shorts.

Tim passed out just as Dec heard the wail of an approaching siren.

25

Wendy lay limp at Gary's feet, exhausted and heart-sick from the ordeal of watching the old woman die. For a brief instant, she had considered trying to intervene. Only the certainty that she could do nothing to stop it had held her back. Now she lay on the floor, tears welling in her eyes, as he looked down at her.

"I'm sorry," he said softly.

"It was awful," she whispered.

He sat beside her and stroked her hair. "I'm so sorry, darling."

His soft touch brought out the sobs she had tried to keep within, tried to hold back so as not to frighten away the man he had learned to be, the lover she needed. But at this moment, she realized, she would also need the kindness, the tenderness, the quiet, soft soul, that had first drawn her attention those many years ago.

A part of her would never again be satisfied with only that tenderness. She needed the firmness, the harshness, the opportunity to give up everything that was herself and surrender totally into his loving will. But on this night, at this moment, she needed that quiet, soothing touch.

"I was so stupid," he said sadly, his hand still grazing over her hair. "I went where man is not meant to go. And I made you go there with me."

"No," she whispered. It was a word she would rarely utter to him again, if she could help it. A word she did not feel comfortable speaking to him. This time, however, it was the right word. "No, darling. Please don't. We went there together. Made our mistakes together. We'll pay for them together. But please, darling, please don't shut me out of it. I love you by choice. I serve you by choice."

He nodded and sank down to hug her. She melted into his arms, their shared tears watering the dream they had found and lost and found again.

"What happened?" Markie asked as she examined Brindle's womb.

Around them, Dec and the EMTs worked on Tim in a quiet, controlled flurry, starting plasma IVs, taking vital signs, replacing the tourniquet with an inflatable pressure bandage.

"He kicked her," Dawn said quietly. Her eyes were haunted by memories she would never be free of. "Then he strangled the pup."

"I am so sorry," Markie said.

The dog's massive torso rose and fell in slow, tentative breaths. She was hemorrhaging. She would need surgery to repair the tears. But she was strong and healthy.

"I need to take her to the clinic," Markie said.

Dawn's face collapsed, and Markie reached out to touch her. "She's a tough mom, Dawn. She can make it. We need to take care of her now, though."

Finally Dawn nodded. "Please, God, please not her, too."

Markie turned to Dec. "I'll need your help."

"I…"

"Dec, I can't lift her. Tim has the EMTs and there are other doctors at the hospital." She paused, searching in his eyes. "I need you."

Kato padded over silently and tugged at his cuff. Dec looked into the wolf's golden eyes, then nodded. He turned to the EMTs. "He's all yours."

"We've got him," the senior technician said. "You did a hell of a job, Doc. But he's ours now."

"I'll take her hips," Markie said. "Dec, you take her torso. Dawn, I want you with her head and shoulders. It's going to hurt, and she needs to see your face."

Dawn nodded, and they positioned themselves to lift the dog. Brindle gave a distressed whimper, as if she knew what was coming and how it would feel. Kato put his face to hers, nose to nose, then licked her eyes. With that, the huge dog's body relaxed.

"On three," Markie said, slipping her hands beneath the dog's massive hips, setting her feet shoulder width apart, hips close. "One. Two. Three."

Brindle let out a howl as they rose, but she didn't

fight. Her body was limp in their arms, and the howl sank to a low, quiet whimper. Markie felt a quick tug at her neck, but she didn't have time to worry about such things.

"I'm sorry, darling," Dawn said, kissing the dog's huge forehead. "I'm so sorry, but we have to."

As if in reply, the dog slowly returned the kiss.

"Let's take my Jeep," Dawn said. "She'll be more comfortable in the back. It's unlocked."

"Can you give us a hand for a second?" Dec called to the EMTs. "Pop the back hatch on the Jeep."

One of them nodded and opened the hatch, then returned to Tim's side. He was almost white, his lips a frightening shade of blue. Dec knew that his efforts had probably been for naught. Still, he'd done what he could. A year ago, he would have agonized over what he couldn't do. Now he could see the simple truth. He'd done what he could. God and the inherent resilience of the human body would have to handle the rest. Or not. It was beyond his control.

They gently placed the dog into the back of the Jeep. Markie climbed in beside her. "Are you okay to drive?" she asked Dawn.

Dawn paused for a moment, then nodded. "For her, I am."

"I'll meet you at the clinic," Dec said. He turned to the wolf. "C'mon, Kato. You ride with me."

Kato looked at Markie, brows knitted.

She nodded. "It's okay, boy. There's no more room here."

He turned and followed Dec as Dawn drove away.

* * *

If there was one thing it had always had a keen sense of, it was betrayal. Years of hard experience had honed that instinct to a razor edge. The woman had thought about betraying it. That was simply unacceptable.

It stretched its spirit, full and strong now. It no longer needed to draw on the will of these puny beings. It had endured far worse than they could ever imagine for far longer than they could even conceive. It had seen death, up close, touched that black specter and shaken its grip. Hell itself could not contain it. So why did these humans think they had any chance?

It would have its gold. Its soul. It would have its life again. It would take a body. Not to kill, this time, but to claim. To inhabit. To live again. To feel the surging in its loins as a man's member plunged inside. To taste rare meat, barely seared. To feel satin against skin and look through eyes bright with pleasure as he begged for the last moments of life.

The woman who thought she could control it was one possibility. But her pathetic body was no fit host for such a soul. No…there was another. Another who would be ideal. One the wolf trusted. It would be such a joy to wrench the wolf's neck until it heard the *crack* of bone shattering.

Oh, it would have its gold. And a body. And its life. And it would teach them all.

This would be a night to remember forever.

It would be a fine night to be alive.

* * *

"I don't understand what came over me," Dawn said quietly, as Markie pulled instruments from trays. "I...I tried to kill my husband. But it was like..."

"Like it wasn't you," Dec said.

"Yes," she nodded.

Markie returned to the exam table, where Brindle lay beneath the harsh white lights. She looked Dawn squarely in the eye. "You did what any mother wolf would have done. You protected your pack."

"I'm not an animal," Dawn said, lowering her face.

"Yes, you are. At our most basic level, we all are." Markie reached out and lifted the woman's chin. "We are a pack species, Dawn. That's why wolves accepted us and we them. We protect each other. That's how we've survived. Tim was going to kill you. You did what you had to do, to protect yourself and your pack."

"It will be a long time before I can accept that," Dawn said simply.

"Be grateful you'll have the time," Markie replied. "Now let's make sure you can share it with Brindle."

She turned her attention to the dog, lying almost motionless under the sedative. Under ordinary circumstances, a kick to the groin might have caused bruising. But Brindle had just whelped a litter of puppies, and her birth canal was already lacerated. The kick turned those small tears into gaping, ragged holes. It was a mess.

"I'll have to spay her," Markie said regretfully.

The dog would be fine, but Dawn's breeding business was about to take it on the chin. "It's the only way."

Dawn didn't hesitate. "Whatever it takes, Markie. Save her. Please."

An hour later, the procedure completed, Markie sank into one of the chairs in her waiting room, where Dec had been keeping Dawn company. Dawn looked up at her.

"She's going to make it," Markie said. "She'll be fine. You'll have to bottle-feed the other pups, though. I doubt she'll keep lactating. Not enough to nurse."

Dawn shook her head slowly. "So much death. For what? For gold."

"What gold?" Dec asked.

"Annie Black's gold. That's what Tim was after. I found his papers, in his office, after I overheard him on the phone. They're looking for Annie Black's gold."

"Who?" Markie asked.

"Tim. Gary Morgan. I think Steve Chase is involved, too. They…they think…"

Markie leaned forward.

"They think it's buried in your yard. That's why I called you, to warn you. He must have been listening on the garage extension. And then he…"

Her face sank, shame and loss filling her eyes.

"You did what you had to do," Markie insisted.

Dawn's face firmed with something like resolve. "There's more. They're…they *think* they're working with Annie Black's ghost. Tim had some incantation written down and some stuff about finding her dust. He apparently got the idea from some diary in the library.''

Markie felt a shiver trickle down her spine. "Working with her?''

Dawn shook her head. ''Markie, I don't know. The stuff was sketchy. But there was mention of the Shippeys and Alice Wheatley and their deaths, and then some kind rambling about what if they couldn't control her. It was like stream of consciousness, and it didn't make much sense. I didn't get much out of it. Except that…except that Tim felt she was taking him over sometimes, and he liked it.''

She pressed the heels of her palms to her eyes. ''I think…I think it wasn't really Tim who strangled my pup.'' She dropped her hands and looked at the two of them.

''What if that woman's ghost takes over someone's body permanently?''

Dec stood up.

''And now I have to do what I have to do.''

Markie looked up at him. ''Dec…''

He put a finger to her lips. ''I'm the only one who can. You take Kato. He knows what to do. And, I think, so do I.''

''Be careful,'' she said. It sounded lame, even to her. Yet she could think of nothing else to say.

''I'll come back to you, Markie. I promise.''

With that, he strode out the door. And Markie turned to Dawn, grief and fear comforting grief and fear. Markie mouthed a silent prayer.

Please, not him, too.

* * *

For Dec, the first stop was the hospital library and its online links to medical resources. It was not a random search. He knew exactly what he was looking for. The only question was whether the information was there to be had.

The most dangerous inhabitants of the Caribbean Sea were not pirates or drug runners or sharks. Instead, they were the family of fish known as *Tetraodontidae*, the fugu, blowfish or puffer fish. While relatively small, those carnivores contained one of the most deadly poisons on earth: tetradotoxin.

Dec had first tripped over that information while he was in medical school, taking a break from serious study by idly thumbing through his anthropology-major roommate's books. He'd found a work by Harvard ethnobiologist Wade Davis, based on field research on the phenomenon of zombies in Haiti. Davis advanced the theory that tetradotoxin was the prime active ingredient in a poison used by voodoo sorcerers to induce a deathlike state. The effects, Davis argued, were so convincing that even trained medical doctors would declare a patient dead. The grieving family would bury the person, not knowing he was alive and aware. The sorcerer would dig up the grave, revive the victim and claim the new member of the walking dead—the zombie—for slave labor.

Since moving to Santz Martina, where every so often someone would step on a spiny pufferfish, Dec had learned more about the effects of tetradotoxin.

Now he needed to know more. A lot more. And he needed it fast.

His fingers danced over the keys as he flashed through article after article, narrowing his search

If even a small amount could kill, how much would he have to reduce the poison to induce a deathlike coma?

The idea had clicked when he'd heard Dawn describe how she'd felt when she'd attacked Tim. Not herself. And her comments about how Tim seemed to be possessed. Coupled with Loleen's vague warning that Annie was looking to claim a soul, the pieces had fallen into place. Annie Black was not satisfied with the horrors she could wreak in a ghostly existence. She wanted a physical form. A body to inhabit. Another chance at life.

Dec had a pretty good idea whose body that would be. *Someone gather her all up an' blow,* Loleen had said. Yes, he had a good idea where Annie would go. And the only way to stop her from claiming that body was to make her think Wendy Chase was already dead.

He closed the search, convinced that he had found as much information as he was likely to get. The rest would be up to him, his training as a doctor, his understanding of the human body and how it worked.

The next stop was the hospital pharmacy, where he gathered the necessary chemicals to create the poison artificially, and then to the lab. The potentially lethal injection would have to be precise. And he was working with grossly imprecise information. He also needed to make an antidote based on sketchy, anecdotal evidence of how voodoo priests reawakened their victims.

He made the sign of the cross and whispered a silent prayer, then went to work with an eerily calm confidence. He would do the best he could do and trust God for the rest.

Satisfied, he poured the blends into two small, marked glass bottles, then crimped on rubber-topped metal caps. Grabbing a handful of empty hypodermic syringes, he headed for the door...and ran almost headlong into Joe Gardner.

"Hey!" they exclaimed in stereophonic surprise.

"Sorry," Dec said. "My fault. I wasn't looking."

"No problem," Joe said. "By the way, you did one hell of a job on that stabbing victim. The paramedics are still down there talking about it. Looks like the guy's going to make it. That was some gutsy work, Doctor."

Dec didn't have time for conversation, nor even to savor the satisfaction. He shrugged. "I didn't have time to think, Joe. If I had, I probably wouldn't have done it. I just...reacted."

"Well, if I'm ever hurt," Joe said, a genuine smile on his face, "I want you around to...react."

"Thanks," Dec answered. "Look, I have to run."

Markie had shown Dawn to the cot in the clinic and set up a recovery kennel nearby. Together, straining, they had hefted the huge mastiff into the kennel.

"She's going to be groggy when she wakes up,"

Markie said. "Just talk to her. I'll be back as soon as I can."

Dawn offered a weak smile. "Thank you."

Markie took out a business card, wrote on the back and handed it to Dawn. "That's my cell phone number. If there's a problem, call me. I'll be here in ten minutes."

"She'll be okay," Dawn said. "I can feel it."

"Yes," Markie agreed. "She will."

Dawn took a moment to gather a deep breath. "Go. Do what you have to do. I'll take care of her. She's all I have left."

Markie and Kato ran the two blocks to her home. She didn't even pause to go inside but instead led Kato around to the back. She knelt on the grass and looked into his golden eyes. Her heart was hammering so hard, it felt as if it would burst from her chest.

"I need you to find it, Kato. You know what I mean, don't you?"

The wolf's eyes were unblinking. *Yes.*

"Good. Find it, boy. I'll grab a shovel."

26

The wind whipped Dec's hair as he sped along the coast road, the motorcycle's throaty roar shattering the night's silence. He'd gone home and traded his car for the bike, which was faster and more maneuverable on the winding road.

Time, he knew, was not his ally. Minutes stretched like hours as he whipped past the black ocean to his right, circling the volcano to his left. High overhead, almost directly in front of him, the North Star shimmered as a beacon to mariners and navigators throughout the ages.

Dec had no need to navigate by the stars. He had a road and an address and an urgency that left him all but blind to the pinpoints of light in the velvety black sky overhead, the diamondlike shimmer of moonlight on the water or the mountain's dark mass. There would be other nights to revel in the beauty of this place. Tonight, he had to confront its ugliness.

He almost missed the spur that cut off to the left, up the mountain to the higher villas. He saw it at the last moment, and sand sprayed from beneath his tires as he leaned hard over, almost rolling the bike, until rubber found traction on asphalt. He tucked his knee in and twisted the throttle at the same moment. The motorcycle's engine surged with power, and he hurtled up the spur road.

Minutes later, he slewed to a stop on the coral driveway. Kicking the stand down, he jumped off the bike and ran to the door, pounding insistently until the porch light came on and a disembodied voice emerged from the security intercom mounted in the wall.

"Who is it?"

"Declan Quinn. I need to talk to you, Mr. Morgan."

"It's late," the voice said.

"I don't have much time," Dec said. "It's about...your wife. I think she's in danger."

The door opened a crack, and he saw Gary Morgan's owlish face. "What kind of danger?"

Declan met his eyes. "I think you already know."

Yes, it thought. A body. But first...first, the weak one. After all, secrecy was important. And people who would reveal its secrets were unnecessary problems.

It had found his house days ago. Hovered in the distance, listening to his spineless self-doubts, his endless paralysis of analysis. Now it moved within with cold, hard surety. He was half drunk, sitting in front of that picture box that seemed to fascinate so many of these beings. Well, half drunk or not, he would feel it.

It struck with a suddenness that left the man gasping for air. It could feel his thoughts, the ragged screaming of nerve endings. Ohhhh, the joy of it.

It had known others' suffering before, back when it had been alive, but then it could only watch. It could only see from the outside, see the wide-eyed looks of terror as hot oil or molten lead was poured into ears or mouths, or joints were crushed in hard iron vises. It could only listen to the inhumanly high-pitched screeches. It could only smell the rising odors of urine and feces as bodies lost control. It had experienced all these things. But only from the outside.

Now its thoughts directly tied to the man's; it could experience it from the inside, completely. It could *know* his fear, *feel* his agony, as it slowly twisted apart cell from cell, slowly crushed bone, wrenched a kidney into a pulpy mush, always leaving the nerves themselves alone. It wanted the nerves intact until the last possible instant, to carry the agony to the brain, so the man would feel every rip, every explosion from within himself, feel it all and know that his last thoughts would be consumed with the excruciatingly exquisite manner of his death.

Oh…it was wonderful to share. Better than the time it had boiled that baby in the soup. Better even than the satisfying, wet *thwuck* as the cleaver had sliced into its father's neck.

For it, Steve Chase's death was…orgasmic.

* * *

"I think she's after you," Dec explained.

Wendy sat on the chair, wearing a black satin robe over what looked to be a lace negligee. In another time, in another setting, on another woman, the sight would have sent a delicious tremor through his body. Tonight, here, with this woman, it simply made him feel like an intruder.

"I don't think so," Wendy said softly. "In fact, she may be…afraid of me. She's not omnipotent. She has weaknesses. And she knows I can see them."

"What weaknesses?" Dec asked.

Now Gary spoke. "She was killed, you know. Horribly. She probably deserved worse than she got. But they were…it was as bad as they could make it. Fire. By the time they were done, she was nothing but ash and a few fragments of bone."

"I only dare look into her when I have one of these," Wendy said, holding up a cigarette. "She doesn't seem to want to get too close. Fire and ash. I think that's what she fears."

"She wants a body," Dec said. "I'm certain of it."

Wendy seemed to study him for a moment, then slowly nodded. "Yes, I imagine she does. She wants…"

"What?" Dec asked.

"She wants to fuck again," Wendy said. "Sex and death. Those were her addictions. She can have death now. But she can't have the other. She craves it."

Something was wrong, Dec thought. He'd had all the pieces arranged. Annie would come here. She would want Wendy, the parapsychologist who could touch her mind. It made perfect sense. And yet…Wendy seemed to *know* Annie wouldn't choose her. Much as his theory had seemed airtight, he had to listen. As Loleen had said, he had to listen with his heart.

"Who, then?" he asked.

"I don't know," Wendy said. "It's not like I'm always…attached to her. I had to make it happen. I don't want to go there again."

"What if I said I needed you to?" Dec asked. "What if I told you it might be the only way to stop her?"

Wendy took a drag on her cigarette, then looked down. "I don't know if I can do that again. You have no idea what she's like."

The pain and fear in her eyes were real. Dec knew he shouldn't press her. He had no right. And yet, so many had died. It had to stop somewhere.

"I don't think we have a choice," he said softly.

Wendy looked up at Gary. His eyes were gentle, but his face was firm. "You have to do it."

Her eyes moistened. "I will. For you."

Kato sniffed at the earth, trying to block out the familiar smells of his own markings, of Markie's footsteps, of times he'd rolled in the grass, groaning in the sheer ecstasy of playing with her. Trying to block out the night scents, the salty breeze from the ocean, the lingering remnants of meals cooked in nearby houses, the damp, warm tendrils of herons curled up in sleep. Most nights, when Markie gave him his last nighttime walk, he took his time, drew in the last, rich breaths of his comfortable world. Tonight, he ignored them all.

He was not certain exactly what scent he was looking for. Markie's thoughts had given him only the vaguest idea. Obviously she wasn't sure, either. A box or a sack, it seemed, with shiny metal inside. But he had only the dimmest notion of who might have handled it, what scents it might have gathered over years spent buried in the dirt. All he could do was look for the one scent he knew of. The black, rotting scent of her.

He circled the lawn, then circled it again and again, varying his route, drawing in quick tastes of air, huffing them out, then starting anew. Markie had found a shovel and was leaning on it, watching him, waiting. Unlike most humans, she understood patience. She understood that her world was not the whole world. And that the rest of the world sometimes yielded its secrets and needs reluctantly, a little at a time. He could sense her frustration but, at the same time, her willingness to wait. She was, simply, remarkable. He hoped the man-mate knew that, would see it and appreciate it.

Thoughts of a future with her and the man-mate simmered in the back of his consciousness as he labored on. The man-mate was special, too. He had not touched the man's thoughts yet, not truly, but he saw in the man an openness that hinted at possibilities. And he knew what they had shared that morning, the scent of her pleasure filling the air. They would be a good pack, the three of them. He would protect them, and they would protect each other and him. It could be a happy life, full of warmth and love and genuine connectedness of the sort that humans seemed to find so rarely. Soul-sharing. Yes, it could be a happy life.

He first picked up the scent near the corner of the cement porch on which Markie so often used to sit in the evenings. The faintest whiff. Then again. And more.

His paws went to work with inherited skill, shredding blades of grass, then tufts of sod, and finally reaching cool, damp earth. He sniffed again. *Yes.*

He looked up at Markie. *Here.*

"I've only done it...*ummmm...*"

Wendy's voice trailed off, but Gary picked up her meaning. "She'll need some privacy for this."

"Of course," Dec said.

If he had figured out what she meant, he was kind enough not to let it show. Instead, he simply excused himself and stepped out of the room.

"You'll be fine," Gary said, soothingly. "I'm right here, darling."

She looked up at him as she shed her robe and negligee, then lit a cigarette. He wished he could follow her into this place where she went. Instead, he could only watch as the woman of his dreams, the woman whose love had rekindled a glow he'd thought long lost, stepped into a netherworld to do battle.

She had brought out a kind of strength he had never

imagined he could have. Annie might have been the
first to tap into it, but it was Wendy who had welcomed it, savored it, made him feel safe in asserting
it. With that newfound power, he knew, came responsibility. Responsibility to protect her, physically,
emotionally, spiritually, as they explored this new
way of sharing their lives. And he could not do that
now. He could only watch, wait and hope.

Her eyes grew distant, unfocused, as she sank into
the trance. Then her body let out a fleeting jerk, almost too tiny to notice. She had made contact, momentary, but contact all the same. It was as if she
were searching, probing around in inky blackness,
following a spiritual scent by some means he could
only barely imagine.

Her breasts rose and fell with each breath, her nipples hardening in the cool, air-conditioned room. She
was such a beautiful woman. Her skin was smooth,
even where it dimpled at her thighs with the unavoid-
able legacy of the passing years. Her hair shone in
the dim light. Her sex, now shaved smooth for him,
a dusky pink flower against which the most beautiful
rose paled. She was all he would ever want. All he
could ever imagine wanting. And, he had come to
learn, so much more.

His brow furrowed as she jerked again, then
reached for her pencils and sketchbook. This time her
body did not relax. She had found her prey, and she
was not letting go. He could only hope that the hunter
did not become the hunted. He could never lose her.
To lose her would be to lose everything that made

life worth living. Annie Black must not take her away.

The pencil traced erratically over the paper at first. But then, patterns began to emerge. Those same eyes she had drawn so many times before. Larger, though. The pupils tiny dots. Eyes. Always eyes.

She slashed with the pencil, the tip snapping as it dug into the paper. The tearing sound seemed to fill the room as the pencil slashed again and again at those eyes.

And he knew.

He reached out and touched her.

"Wendy. Darling. Come back to me."

The slashing continued, savage rage wrought on the paper until the eyes were unrecognizable.

"Wendy!" He shook her shoulder. "That's enough!"

She let out a cry and shook, the pain obvious, as she tried to wrench her consciousness free.

Aarrrrgh!

This was not the joyous screams of pleasure-pain they had explored earlier. This was real pain, without any hint of love or tenderness behind it. He had to break through it. He could think of only one way.

He reached for her cigarette, took it from her hand, closed his eyes, shaking with desperation and horror, and pressed the tip to her arm.

"*Wendy!*"

She recoiled, her face snapping around to his, eyes still distant for an instant, before she drew a deep, shuddering breath and collapsed to the floor. In an instant, he was beside her, holding her, stroking her face, murmuring words not even he would remember.

Finally her eyes found his.

"I love you," she whispered.

"I love you, too."

"You have to tell him," she said. "It's her that Annie wants. It's…"

"I know," he said, glancing over at the shredded paper. "I know."

Kato sat at alert, standing guard, as Markie plunged the shovel into the dirt. She could tell by his posture that he knew what was coming. More than that, she could read it in his thoughts.

There was no longer any question of the connection between them. It was there for the asking, freely given, freely shared. The wolf seemed to want that, to need it. And that, she realized, made perfect sense. It was the way of his kind, and he was separated from that. She owed him more than food and warmth and shelter and love. She owed him that connection, that bond that transformed a group into a pack. She owed him family.

"Yes, boy. I know."

His eyes flicked over to her, and, for an instant, the corners of his mouth turned up. A smile. Then his focus returned to the night sky and the darkness they both knew was coming.

Racing against time, she hefted spadeful after spadeful of earth, widening and deepening the hole. She had no idea how far down she would have to go.

Two hundred years of wind and rain had moved a lot of earth around. Not to mention the army bulldozers that had graded out the gridwork of streets in old Martina Town. It could be only a few inches. It could be halfway to China. All she could do was dig and let Kato stand watch.

Gary Morgan's words had hit Dec like a cannonball, plowing a hole through his heart.

Annie wants Markie!

Adrenaline surged through him as he lowered his head, hoping that by doing so he could gain just that fraction more speed that would get him there in time. The moon was dead overhead now but hidden behind clouds. Except for the glow of his headlights, he could just as well have been driving through ink.

Racing to kill the woman he loved.

Hoping that, by killing her, he could save her.

If he had done everything right. If the chemical brew he had concocted would work fast enough. Tetradotoxin normally took effect over a period of hours. He knew he would not have that long. It would have to work within seconds. Otherwise, Annie would have her.

Even if it did work, then came the other nightmare. What if he had given her too much, or the interaction of chemicals did not work as he had imagined? He was no molecular biochemist, no pharmacologist. He was a medical doctor, a trauma surgeon, floundering around in an area of science about which he knew far too little and in which he had to trust far too much.

Even the tiniest mistake would mean a nightmare from which he would never recover.

Markie would be dead.

And he would never, ever forgive himself.

On the horizon, he saw the faint glow of the town lights. Almost there. Almost time. He would have to make a decision. A decision that could very possibly kill the woman he loved and ruin his life forever. He couldn't schedule a consult for a second opinion. This would be his decision. His responsibility.

And her life.

27

~ഏ~ഏ~ഏ~

As Markie's shovel struck metal, the night gasped. It was as if the air had been stolen, stilling the breeze, silencing the night sounds, muffling even the distant beat of the surf.

She froze and glanced toward Kato. He'd risen to his haunches, his ears pricked forward on high alert. His lips fluttered a bit as he silently tasted the breeze.

Trusting him to alert her, she dropped to her knees and began to dig with her hands. Rotting scraps came away, probably ancient leather. Then her hands touched the cold of metal.

Annie's treasure.

She pulled handfuls of it from the earth, dumping it on the grass, amazed that even in moonlight shrouded by clouds, even covered with earth, its sparkle called to her. Gold. Lots and lots of gold coins. Probably worth more now for archaeological value than the weight of the gold itself.

According to the oral histories, the islanders had buried it because they feared its taint. Feared it would draw Annie's evil attention even though she was dead. It had drawn her attention, all right. And Markie was suddenly, perilously, aware that she was holding it in her hands.

As if it burned, she dropped the coins she held onto the growing pile on the grass. It was enough that she had found it. She didn't need to dig it out.

Kato huffed, and his lips drew back, baring his teeth. Markie looked up from her hands, wondering if it was clouds that covered the moon or something more. A whisper of cold teased her neck.

Instinctively she reached for the pouch Jolly had hung around her neck only hours ago. It was gone.

Panic flared in her, then a vague memory of feeling something tug and snap as she had helped lift a two-hundred-pound mastiff into the back of a Jeep.

But her cross was still there. Finding it with her fingers, she gripped it tightly and whispered to the night, "No."

The island wasn't that big, but as Dec barreled toward town and Markie's house, he began to feel it was doubling in size with every mile he rode. Either that or time had slowed to an impossible crawl.

He looked up again at the sky, wondering if those were clouds obscuring the moon or the blackness he had seen behind Markie's house. He accelerated even more, hoping he could keep the damn hog on the upcoming turns. Because he dared not slow down.

Kato's growl deepened. Markie eased away from the hole, away from the pile of gold coins she had unearthed, away from what Annie Black wanted. She thought of trying to run but knew she couldn't outdistance the threat. Visions of Alice's macabre final dance reminded her of the horror she was facing.

''Take it,'' she said to the deepening shadow. The world still seemed too silent, too far away, as if she and Kato were encased in some kind of bubble.

Kato snapped his teeth in warning. His fur stood on end from his nape to his tail. He was crouching now, lowered into position to launch himself in attack.

''Kato, no,'' Markie said, her voice thickened by fear. Her mouth had grown so dry her lips were sticking to her teeth. ''Please, Kato, don't get yourself hurt. Let her have the gold.''

Kato looked at her. His thoughts could have been flashed on a Times Square marquee: *You don't understand.*

She pushed herself back even farther from the treasure. With one graceful move, Kato leapt over the hole and planted himself between it and Markie. He snapped at the air again, once, twice.

Markie wondered if she were losing her mind or seeing things through Kato's eyes. Because she could have sworn the darkness before her was thickening, taking on shape of some kind. And when Kato snapped at it, she could almost see it shudder and regather itself.

She gripped her cross again, praying soundlessly, as Kato nudged her backward with his rear while snapping at the coalescing shadow. It was as if he could force it back with the threat of his teeth but not grab onto it and tear it as he would any other threat.

"Just take your gold and go," Markie said again, crying the words out to the shadow. "I don't want it. I never wanted it!"

Shock shuddered through her as she felt the first terrifying tendrils wrap around her mind.

It didn't want the gold. It wanted *her*.

The lights of Martina Town were now visible. Another mile or so. The road widened finally, heralding the approach to the hospital, government and school complex. *Almost there.*

He clung to the thought, although he wasn't sure what he was heading toward. Killing Markie? Or saving her? He didn't know. The vials and syringes in his pocket seemed to be growing heavier, and his conscience took that moment to start quarreling with him.

He shoved it aside, stepped down on it firmly. This was no time to be questioning his ethics. He had seen what Annie could do to a person if she wanted them dead. If Markie were going to die, his way was one hell of a lot less horrifying.

And perhaps…perhaps…he could save her.

From what, he wasn't sure. Could Annie really fully possess a body and soul? Loleen had hinted at it. Had warned him. Had assured him he would know what he needed to do when the time came.

He hoped the vials in his pocket were the right thing, because he had nothing else. They were it.

The road narrowed as he reached old town. He slowed down because he had to, fighting every impulse to keep speeding. Just a few blocks to Markie's house.

God, he hoped he found her before it was too late.

An oily coldness seemed to be slithering into Markie's head, between her brain cells. With it came a darkening of her vision. The battle had become internal.

Kato turned, biting at the cloud that surrounded her, though all she could see were his golden eyes. She had to fight. But she was scared to fight. If she fought, she might wind up like Alice. At least, if she didn't fight, she might survive to...

To what? Even as the reptilian fingers of darkness clouded her thoughts, some light that was Markie clung to existence. What did she hope she could do if Annie possessed her? Find a cure? Get an exorcism?

Hell, she was hanging on to a blessed crucifix and it wasn't stopping Annie.

The pouch might have stopped her. Filled with the wisdom of old ways that had met and battled such as Annie before, it might have held her at bay.

But the pouch was gone. And Pedro wasn't here to defend her with prayers and holy water.

And Annie's malevolent essence seemed to be sinking into every cell of her body. She wished she could recoil from the horror of it, felt stunned that anything so purely evil could exist. The merest touch was too painful to bear, and it was now filling her everywhere.

Kato whined and backed away. He sensed it and didn't know what to do. He didn't want to hurt Markie. That least of all.

But Markie was becoming the thing he loathed.

He snarled at her, bit at the air around her with frenzy.

Then, suddenly, he froze.

Markie felt the darkness inside her try to force her to reach out and hurt the dog. There was still enough of her left to refuse.

"Go, Kato," she said hoarsely, from that last bit of her that was still herself. "Run."

But he didn't run. Instead, he came closer, his golden eyes boring into her, holding her. She had to cling to those eyes, she realized. Hang on to Kato's presence.

She felt the touch of his warm, loving mind against her curled-up self, felt it as comfort and strength.

He had become her lifeline.

Dec squealed into Markie's driveway with a roar of his engine and a shriek of his tires. He braked hard, switched off his engine and dismounted.

Markie's house was silent. No one came to greet him. Kato's head didn't pop up in a window. For a second he had the panicked feeling that Markie had gone somewhere else and he would never find her.

Then he heard a mournful howl from the back of the house. As clear as if the dog spoke in his head,

Dec knew Kato was summoning the pack. Was summoning him.

They were here.

He pulled the vials out of his pocket, picked the one with the deadly stew of tetradotoxin, and drew a cc into the syringe. He didn't bother recapping the needle. He might need it too fast to fuss with a cap.

Moving with caution now, he walked carefully around the side of the house. Dec's heart beat heavily with anxiety and fear. The last time he'd felt this way had been before his first solo surgery. But then he'd had backup nearby. This time he had no backup at all.

And he might well kill the woman he loved.

Except, he realized as he rounded the corner of the house, she was no longer the woman he loved.

Standing in the middle of the yard, arms thrown wide in celebration and triumph, a stranger looked back at him from Markie's eyes.

And then she started to laugh.

He watched, his skin crawling, realizing he now faced a tactical problem: how to get close enough to administer the injection without alerting the thing that had taken over Markie.

The answer struck him almost as soon as he considered the question. Act like he thought it was still Markie. Annie was famous for her hunger for men. Lovers. Maybe she would let him approach.

"Hi, honey," he said, smiling.

Her head tipped down, and she looked at him.

Kato, however, had other plans. He leapt at her, knocking her to the ground, putting his nose to hers and giving a shrill whine.

To Dec's amazement, even in the darkness, he could see Markie's gaze focus on the wolf. On the wolf's eyes.

"Kato," she whispered.

The wolf licked her chin, his golden eyes never moving from hers. She reached up a hand as if to pet him, but it turned into a claw, grabbing his scruff and trying to push him away. The dog growled and dug all four paws into the earth, refusing to be budged.

Dec hurried forward, hoping he could get control of Markie's arm long enough to give the injection.

But even as he had the thought, her arm fell limp to her side again. Woman and wolf stared at one another, locked in a struggle for life.

Kato, he realized, was hanging on to Markie's soul, refusing to let it fly. How he knew that he couldn't say. But he felt it with every cell of his being.

He dropped to his knees beside Markie, beside the love of his life, whispering, "God help me...I'm sorry...."

He plunged the needle into her arm and rammed down the plunger.

Markie jerked.

Her eyes fluttered, tried to close, but Kato moved, refusing to let anything break eye contact.

"Dec..."

"It's okay, Markie," he said soothingly. "Trust me."

He just wished he could trust himself. But that ugly thing he had seen in her eyes moments ago couldn't be allowed to take her over. Even if it meant her death.

Where he had struggled before, he was now filled with surety.

Without the tetradotoxin, she was dead for all intents and purposes. She would be nothing but a husk filled with the evil of Annie Black. With it…if Annie thought Markie was dead, she would leave. Leave Markie free. If she didn't die.

He prayed as hard as he'd ever prayed in his life.

Then, with a shudder and gasp, Markie grew still. He felt for her pulse. It was gone. He put his ear to her mouth and could hear no breathing.

He waited for a few minutes, then closed Markie's eyes.

Only Kato saw his tears.

The man had killed the woman!

It hunkered in the dead body, rage filling it until it felt it could explode into a million pieces. It had to get out before it died, too. That thought, and that thought alone, gave it control of itself in the midst of fury.

It would kill that man, and then the dog. *Yessss.*

Slowly it began to disentangle itself from the woman's body, plotting its revenge, already imagining how it would crush each and every cell in the man's body. Imagining his pain and terror. Exultation began to fill it, driving away the rage. There would be other bodies. But this kill would be so satisfying.

He had the last of the gold out of the hole. It watched as it began to elevate above the woman's body, resuming its deathless form. It ignored the dog that watched it, knowing it would have time to deal with the animal later.

Now it wanted the man. It could taste his pain and horror already.

The man grabbed the cloth on which Markie had piled Annie's hoard and tied it up into a bag. He was taking it away.

At least, that was what he thought.

It swept toward him on a killer urge. This was going to be so good. It was going to draw out every single second of the man's suffering to the ultimate.

But it couldn't reach him. It was as if an invisible wall surrounded him. A silent howl of rage filled it as it battered against the barrier. A spell. It was a spell. And when the man moved, the barrier moved with him.

Another roar of silent rage filled it, then it followed him. The chance would come. And it was going to be ready to take it.

"Guard her," Dec told Kato. Not that he really believed the dog needed the command.

Then, acutely aware of the coalescing black shadow that followed him, he carried the gold toward his bike. Loleen had at least been clear about what to do with that. One step at a time, he thought. He climbed on the motorcycle, gunned the engine and shot out onto the street. Overhead, the clouds had parted to reveal a harsh, stark full moon. That there was almost no traffic was a blessing. That he had miles to go, with a black cloud hard on his heels, was a curse.

Arabica trees whipped past as he turned off the coast road and surged up the winding macadam trail that led into the coffee plantation. The strong, pleasant fragrance of beans ripe for harvest wafted around him, mixed with the acrid stench of Annie Black, the scent of pure, distilled evil. He now realized why Kato and the other dogs had gone on alert. This close, with Annie in her full rage, the stench was all but overpowering. To a dog, with an olfactory capacity hundreds of times more sensitive than his, her presence must have felt like an assault.

Higher up the mountain he went, the motorcycle's engine screaming in the night, searching out one plantation spur after another, always upward, upward, until there were no more roads at all. His motorcycle was a street bike, and its suspension groaned as he bounced and flew over rills of hardened magma. The jarring impacts left his legs burning. A searing stab in his back told him he'd strained a muscle, at the very least. He put the thought out of his mind, allowing adrenaline to numb the pain.

Higher, higher, until the sharp edge of the mountain almost seemed to disappear before him. He slammed on the brakes and half rolled the bike, knowing he was at the volcano's rim, the scent of sulfur stinging his nostrils.

He grabbed the bag and stepped to the rim, looking back at the onrushing black cloud.

The man had run out of room to run. It had him now. There was nowhere to go. It closed in on the man with a fury that had lain brewing for two centuries. Death had come, and it was death's messenger.

It would get past the barrier, and then…this was going to feel so good….

Dec waited until the cloud was upon him, then turned and threw the bag of gold over the rim, aiming for the faint glow of a small fissure fifty feet below. He prayed that his aim was true.

Noooooooo! The man had thrown its gold over the edge. Killing would be too kind for him. And kill him it would. But first, the gold. The gold that held its very soul. It swooped past the man and chased the bag down.

Dec felt an almost physical blow as the cloud swept over him and down after the plummeting bag. For a moment he thought he'd missed the mark. But gravity had a mind all its own. Retching at the sulfurous cloud, he watched.

The gold was almost within its reach. Just at the end of its grasp. And then it looked beyond the falling bag, into the opening maw of hell itself.

* * *

With a brief, bright glow, bag and shadow passed into fire and ash. His aim had been true. Annie Black was no more. He had won. He and Markie had won. *Markie!*

28

If the ride up the mountain had been frightening, the ride back down was nothing short of sheer terror. Pulled by gravity, spurred by the knowledge that Markie lay dying, Declan abandoned all caution as he shot down. The bike's tires alternately skidded on the smooth lava face and grabbed harshly at roughened edges, leaving him in a constant battle for balance and control.

He didn't see the giant snake of cooled molten rock until the last instant, hardly long enough to brace himself, let alone avoid it. He hit it at an angle, and the front wheel of the motorcycle kicked hard to the left. He felt himself rise with the back of the bike, in eerie slow motion, tumbling in midair, the bike's engine now whining free.

Pure instinct, honed by years of riding, told him to let go, throw his head forward and try to roll as he hit. The maneuver worked, but it could do only so much to lessen the damage of a human body crashing and tumbling across rock. Dec heard the *pop* in his back, beneath the shoulder blade, a split instant before the pain of the fractured rib surged into his consciousness. Air flew from his lungs as the world turned over and over, the moon doing an insane dance in the sky, until finally he came to rest.

He was hurt. That much was obvious. The question was, how much? He lay still and, trying to discipline his thoughts, took inventory. He'd broken a rib, definitely. Each breath felt like a knife in his back. His left ankle throbbed. But when he flexed it, the pain was manageable. A sprain, at worst. The sticky, wet, burning smears on his hands spoke of multiple lacerations. He looked up at the moon, said the names of the days of the week in reverse and held an arm out in front of him. It was as stable as could be expected.

He was hurt. But he could still ride. He had no choice.

He screamed as he hefted the bike upright, the sound echoing off the mountain, booming out into the distance. Biting his lip, he climbed back on the bike and restarted the engine.

Every bump, however tiny, was now an exercise in agony. His body screamed for him to slow down. His heart and mind knew there was no time.

Markie was down there…paralyzed…aware…no doubt terrified…and very possibly…dying.

There was no time to slow down.

So this is death, Markie thought. She could still hear Kato's mournful howls, feel his warm breath and cold nose as he nuzzled her neck. But she couldn't open her eyes to look at him. It was all happening at a distance, as if to someone else's body. The buzz in her head and her inability to move told the real story.

This is what it feels like to be dead.

She realized that she missed the comforting rhythm of her own heartbeat. Odd that she had rarely noticed it when she had been alive. There had been the time when she was sixteen, that first time she'd looked into a boy's eyes from mere inches away as she'd leaned in to kiss him. And there had been the day she'd opened the letter from the veterinary college, wondering if she had been admitted. The times she'd tightened her mouth as she was dressed down by the man she thought she'd loved. And the one sweet time she'd been undressed by a man she truly loved. Yes, there had been a few times when she'd been aware of the beating of her own heart.

But not enough, she realized. Too often she'd ignored that steady, soothing presence. Taken it, and the life it gave, for granted. Its absence was a silence she had never imagined possible.

This is death.

This was not death.

Kato knew it, and tried to communicate it to Markie. Her soul had not taken flight, and while he could tell she no longer breathed, that her lifeblood no longer flowed as it had, he sensed her essence still firmly planted within her shell. Its grip was growing tenuous, though, and he began to fear her soul might yet shake free.

So he reached out to her with his own essence, tried to make her even more aware of him than she had been in the past. He invited the Markie spark inside her to join with his spark and see the world through his eyes.

She would think it was only a nice dream, but it might distract her from her chance to escape her confining shell. It might make her smile, and he might carry her along for a while on the music of the night scents and the aroma of stirring leaves. He knew she didn't perceive those things the way he did. She was crippled. But now, reaching out to her, he set her free in a new way.

Smells were like music, and sounds were like smells, and all of them held a rainbow sparkle of color. Everything carried with it a message.

He shared that with her as he lay beside her, his head on her breast, his fluttering nostrils blowing air into hers.

Keep her here.

That was his imperative.

See? he asked her consciousness. *See how every breath is a new window into an ever-changing world? Over there, by the door, where you cooked the meat you had marinated. Can you still taste it? I can. And here, in the earth. A family lived here once, in the time before time. They ate fish seasoned with sugar*

cane, and its essence is still right here, in this dirt.
Come see my world with me. Be with me. Always.
Please?

Even the slightest bump in the road felt like a jave-
lin driving into Dec's chest, but he knew he could
safely ignore it. His lung wasn't punctured. The rest
was mere pain.

The moon was bright now, as if the last cloud had
blown away. The highway stretched before him like
a silver ribbon, and the air felt lighter than it had in
weeks.

In weeks.

Had Annie's presence been poisoning the entire island that long? And how the devil had Tim and his
cohort managed to rouse her? How had she been wak-
ened all those years ago at the fort?

He hoped that after he reached Markie, he still gave
a damn about those questions.

Kato heard it long before Markie would have. *He*
is coming! Hear the roar? He is coming! Don't give
up!

The world of his senses was strange and confusing
for a human mind, accustomed to organizing the
world in human ways. And yet, it was beautiful. Markie now saw why dogs behaved as they did. It wasn't
simply that every hour of every day was a new adventure. Every *breath* was a new adventure.

If she had neglected the sound of her own heartbeat, how much more had she ignored the rising and
falling of each breath, the taste of the air, the sheer
joy of drawing in air the way a child might wander

through a candy store, senses wide-open and hopeful. Every heartbeat, every breath of her life, had been a miracle waiting to be seen. And she had missed so many of them. So many.

Yes, Kato, that is where I made the Korean spare ribs that I shared with you. And yes, I can still taste them. I remember the look in your eyes when you took that first, tentative taste. Then you looked up at me with that silly, happy wolf grin. That day, in that moment, I felt as if I were truly alive. I felt one with you. And yet...

Yes, Kato answered. *You needed another of your kind with which to share that moment. If I let myself think of such things, I, too, might long for my kind, for forests deep and wonderful, for the hunt, for the kill. But know this, my human mate. I live each breath. Each heartbeat. And each breath is filled with you. Your scent is with me every moment. Your warm touch is never more than a moment away. And in that, in each breath, in each heartbeat, I am content with you.*

A wash of joy flowed over Markie's being. *I will forever bless the day that God brought you to me. There will never be another like you.*

Nor you, Kato replied. *Nor you.*

Declan climbed off the motorcycle and made his way to the back. What little breath he could draw froze in his throat. Markie lay there, still, not even the rise and fall of breath, Kato beside her, his head on her breast, his nose pressed to hers.

He cocked an ear in Dec's direction, but his focus remained on Markie. Yet there was no whimper. No long, painfully empty howl of grief. It was as if they were sleeping together.

Except she wasn't asleep.

He limped to her side and painfully lowered himself to his knees. Kato's eyes turned to him, golden and soft, his black face relaxed.

"I'll try, boy," he said around a gasp. "I'll try."

He drew out the second bottle, the antidote, and a second syringe, knowing this was as dangerous as the shot of tetradotoxin he'd given her earlier. The antidote itself was toxic. And even for those who did survive, brain damage was all too common.

For a moment, he paused. Her life had not been in vain. She had lived, and loved, beautifully. If he let her be, she would pass peacefully into the arms of a God whose existence he no longer doubted. If he gave her the antidote, he might save her life and destroy her mind. Was it for her that he wanted to save her life? Or for himself?

For he knew, with complete certainty, that there would never be another like her. No one else whose merest smile could touch every crevice of his being. No one else he would ever want in his arms, in his loins, in his heart. For his sake, he could try to save her.

But what about her? As he'd told Joe Gardner, it was always about the patient. And though he loved her with all his heart, she was a patient now. A patient whose life he might already have ended. A patient who even now might well be reaching up to the heavens, stepping into the embrace of God. And if ever a human being deserved that embrace, she did. What would she want? What was best for her? To draw her back into his arms or surrender her into God's?

It was Kato who answered for her, turning to nuzzle his hand, the hand holding the syringe, and nudge it toward her arm. *She wants you, man-mate. We want you.*

Drawing as deep a breath as his ribs permitted, he whispered a Hail Mary and pushed the needle into her vein. With slow, steady pressure, he pushed the plunger.

All he could do now was wait.

And hope.

Epilogue

Gary held Wendy in the morning light, the rise and fall of her breasts in somnolent breath a warm pleasure to behold. Life had taken so much. Love had given it back.

He reached out to caress her hair, and she stirred a bit, her lips curling into a faint smile. Warm lips. Lips he could kiss for the rest of eternity and never tire of. Her features, softened in sleep, free of worry, bore the kind of beauty that made poets put pen to page, made singers put voice to word, gave flowers a reason to bloom.

She was all his. And, in the love they had shared last night, the words they had exchanged, the new promises they had made, she was all his.

And he, all hers.

Only they would know the significance of the tiny gold chain she now wore around her neck, or the reason she had let out a tiny gasp of pleasure as he had sealed the clasp with glue. Most people, he knew, would never have or want to have the kind of love, the kind of life they had pledged to each other.

But new days brought new beginnings. It was the love, the life, they both needed. To be whole.

And one.

Her eyelids slowly opened, and her eyes met his.

"Good morning, my darling. I love you."

She smiled. "I love you, too…Master."

Dawn hadn't waited by Tim's bedside, although she had slept—as much as she could—beside Brindle every night. The dog was healing now, stronger, eating, able to walk at least for short distances. Tim had betrayed her love. But Brindle had not. And she would not betray Brindle.

It was Brindle's low growl that had announced the decision. Tim had come to the house after his release, but he got no farther than the front door before Brindle passed judgment. Never again.

And Dawn agreed. Never again.

She had told the police everything, sparing no detail, however damning it might be. To her surprise, her father-in-law had come to sit beside her as she talked. When she wept, he had touched her hand. When she finished, he had looked at the detective. Not a look of authority demanding obeisance, but that of a father-in-law seeking mercy and understanding.

The detective had nodded. She had acted in self-defense. She was free to go home.

And it would be, she had decided, her home. Here,

in the heart of Old Martina Town, near the music of beach bands, the laughter of children. She had declined Abel's offer to come live with him until she found another place. *This* was her place.

And Tim had no place in it.

Brindle's growl, and Dawn's unstinting stare, had said all that needed to be said. With a silent nod, he'd turned and made his way back to the taxi. Charges would be filed, and perhaps had been already, for animal cruelty. As for the deaths…under the law, he was not responsible for what could only be seen as supernatural acts. Though he had set in motion the chain of events, the law could not hold him to account. That would be for another court, in another life, with another Judge.

The memories would never be totally washed away. But neither should she be chained to them. She was alive. And Brindle was alive. And in the mastiff's bottomless brown eyes, she saw hope.

She clipped the leash to her collar and motioned toward the door. "C'mon, girl. Let's take a walk."

Dec knelt beside Markie as Father Pedro recited the prayers of the consecration. The Christmas homily had been full of life and hope and the inherent promise of a God who would come down to earth in the form of a baby. In the consecration, that same God became present in the bread and wine offered for communion. It was, Dec thought, a profoundly intimate experience. Touching God. Tasting God. It was…making love.

And what better person to share that with than the woman who knelt beside him? Markie's recovery had been brief and remarkable. She was not the same woman he had known. No one who had endured what she had could be. Her eyes were more contemplative now. The lilt of her voice still carried music, but it was a richer, fuller music. It was the music of the universe, and beyond.

He reached out and grasped her hand as he listened to the prayers, and looked back at all the years, all the ways he had pretended against what he had always known. God is love. And love is beautiful.

Markie took his hand in hers. The hand that had taken her away from Annie, the hand that had given her over to a new world, the hand that had brought her back so that she could share that new world with him. The air in the church was rich with incense and the faint tangy scent of poinsettias. Here and there, a faint whiff of perfume, probably a Christmas gift opened early. And beneath it all, the impatient shuffling of children anxious to get back home and dive into their presents.

She had no such need. Her present was right here. Kneeling beside her. The man who had taken her life and given it back. And, forever, claimed her heart. Last night, when he had haltingly whispered the words, she had felt a peace unlike any she had ever known.

Yes, Declan Quinn. I will marry you.

Her present was right here, in every heartbeat, in every breath.

Her present was life itself.

Kato waited for them at the window. Watched them park. Watched them walk up to the door. He would not meet them at the door, though. He had other plans. For just as Markie had stepped into his mind, he had stepped into hers. And for the first time, he had understood this day when humans opened gifts, laughed, ate hearty meals of turkey and ham, and basked in the comfort of each other. He had known, and he had known what he needed to do.

Finding it had been easy, now that he knew the scent of gold. Nudging the box off her dresser had been a bit of a challenge, but only a small one. On another day, in other circumstances, she would have been angry with him. But not today. She would understand.

And so he trotted back into her bedroom and waited. Listened to them calling his name. Wished he could laugh in their way. Instead, all he could do was lift the corners of his mouth, let his jaw hang loose, and smile at the thought of the moment that would happen so soon now.

He heard them walking down the hall. Heard them open the door. Listened at the Markie's first gasp as she saw the pile of jewelry on the floor.

Then his tail thumped as she looked down, between his paws, and saw it lying there.

Her mother's wedding ring.

It would fit her, too.

USA TODAY Bestselling Author

CHRISTIANE HEGGAN

She uncovered a deadly conspiracy.
Now she's on the run—and trying to stay alive…

Manhattan photographer Jenna Mayerson is attending her first
exhibit when her ex-husband suddenly shows up, claiming to
need her help. Before she can agree to give it to him, Adam is
found murdered in Central Park.

With the police convinced his death was a random act of violence,
Jenna seeks the help of Adam's former best friend, private
investigator Frank Renaldi. Together, they must stay one step
ahead of a killer who will stop at nothing to get what he wants.

SCENT OF A KILLER

"Heggan dishes up an addictive read; her fans will be
thrilled, and she should collect new followers as well."
—*Publishers Weekly* on *BLIND FAITH*

Available the first week of January 2004 wherever paperbacks are sold!

Power. Passion. Politics.
The unforgettable novel that has it all.

BONNIE HEARN HILL

One minute you think you know
where *Intern* is going…
The next you can't believe what you're reading.

"…more than enough suspense to keep the reader
intrigued…[a] page-turner."
—*Publishers Weekly*

*Available the first week of January 2004
wherever paperbacks are sold!*

MIRA®

RACHEL LEE

66885	JULY THUNDER	___ $6.50 U.S.	___ $7.99 CAN.
66802	A JANUARY CHILL	___ $5.99 U.S.	___ $6.99 CAN.
66658	WITH MALICE	___ $6.50 U.S.	___ $7.99 CAN.
66554	SNOW IN SEPTEMBER	___ $5.99 U.S.	___ $6.99 CAN.
66298	CAUGHT	___ $5.99 U.S.	___ $6.99 CAN.
66173	A FATEFUL CHOICE	___ $5.99 U.S.	___ $6.99 CAN.

(limited quantities available)

TOTAL AMOUNT	$_____
POSTAGE & HANDLING	$_____
($1.00 for one book; 50¢ for each additional)	
APPLICABLE TAXES*	$_____
<u>TOTAL PAYABLE</u>	$_____

(check or money order—please do not send cash)

To order, complete this form and send it, along with a check or money order for the total above, payable to MIRA Books®, to: **In the U.S.:** 3010 Walden Avenue, P.O. Box 9077, Buffalo, NY 14269-9077; **In Canada:** P.O. Box 636, Fort Erie, Ontario L2A 5X3.

Name:_____
Address:_____ City:_____
State/Prov.:_____ Zip/Postal Code:_____
Account Number (if applicable):_____
075 CSAS

*New York residents remit applicable sales taxes.
  Canadian residents remit applicable GST and provincial taxes.

MIRA®

Visit us at www.mirabooks.com

MRL0104BL